P9-DNE-815

THE
SURVIVOR

BOOKS BY IRIS JOHANSEN
(IN ORDER OF PUBLICATION)

For a complete list of books by Iris Johansen, as well as previews of upcoming books and information about the author, visit IrisJohansen.com.

THE
SURVIVOR

IRIS
JOHANSEN

GRAND
CENTRAL

New York   Boston

Grand Central Publishing
Hachette Book Group
1290 Avenue of the Americas, New York, NY 10104
grandcentralpublishing.com
twitter.com/grandcentralpub

First Edition: June 2023

Grand Central Publishing is a division of Hachette Book Group, Inc. The Grand Central Publishing name and logo is a trademark of Hachette Book Group, Inc.

The publisher is not responsible for websites (or their content) that are not owned by the publisher.

The Hachette Speakers Bureau provides a wide range of authors for speaking events. To find out more, go to hachettespeakersbureau.com or email HachetteSpeakers@hbgusa.com.

Grand Central Publishing books may be purchased in bulk for business, educational, or promotional use. For information, please contact your local bookseller or the Hachette Book Group Special Markets Department at special.markets@hbgusa.com.

Library of Congress Control Number: 2023932137

ISBNs: 978-1-5387-2637-2 (hardcover), 978-1-5387-5655-3 (large type), 978-1-5387-2639-6 (Canadian trade), 978-1-5387-2640-2 (ebook)

Printed in the United States of America

LSC-C

Printing 1, 2023

THE
SURVIVOR

PROLOGUE

Close.

Run!

Dear God, they were so close.

Maya could hear Aden Nadim's men yelling, howling like wolves on the hunt, as they broke through the brush behind her. She could see the harsh glare of the flashlights bouncing off the lush green jungle growth. It would only be minutes before that light speared into the ditch where she was hiding. Then they would be all over her, on the attack, clawing to be first to please Nadim.

Time to go aerial.

She rolled out of the ditch into the creek and got to her feet, heading for the trees. She thought she'd seen a stand of spruce in this area. She could hear her boots splashing in the water, but those hyenas behind her would be yelling too loud for them to hear her until she reached the mature trees deeper in the forest.

She hoped.

Then she was there. There was a large spruce to the right of the creek.

Climb!

Fast.

Hurry. Get above the glare of the flashlights and into the dense leaves of the tree.

Nadim's crew were at the ditch now. She could hear Nadim's furious voice urging them on. Telling them to get the bitch or he'd have their dicks.

Then they were past the ditch and right below her.

And she heard Nadim screaming into the darkness: "I know you're out there, you vicious bitch. Do you think you're going to get away? We'll rape you and then cut your heart out. Do you hear me?"

She held her breath. *Go on, you bastards.* She knew she wasn't safe. She didn't think they could see her this high in the foliage, but she couldn't be sure. Or the tree bark could be wet from her body. Or there was always a chance that she'd left streaks of blood on the tree from Nadim's wound. The son of a bitch had bled like a stuck pig.

They were going deeper into the forest!

She let her breath out. She gave them a minute more and

then she started moving through the branches from tree to tree until she could no longer hear them. She was almost back to her camp now. She just might get out of this alive.

This time.

But with Nadim there was always going to be a next time...

CHAPTER

1

Maybe it wasn't true, Maya thought. It could be just a rumor. The Neztart village didn't really have any experience with that bastard Nadim. They'd always been terrified of the stories about him.

Well, so had Maya, because most of the stories weren't rumors, and she had more experience with Nadim than she ever wanted to repeat. Her heart was beating hard at just the thought of him. But she mustn't let Charles Bevan see that fear. She'd never really trusted him. He was too slick and self-serving. She could never tell if he would take advantage of any weakness.

"You're sure it's him?" She kept her tone cool and absolutely calm. "Where did you hear Nadim was anywhere near the island? You can't trust any of the northern villages. He's supposed to still be in India."

"But we both knew he'd be back as soon as he had enough bribes floating out there to buy his way back into the local landowners' good graces." His voice was slightly mocking as he leaned back in her office chair. "You made Nadim very angry when you stuck that dagger into his hand. I'd only just arrived here on the island when I heard the story of how you just strode over to him and stabbed him. I couldn't believe it. If you wanted to get rid of him, you should have gone for the jugular."

"I was angry." She shrugged. "And I'd already had one bad run-in with him. He'd just struck one of my foremen on the head with the butt of his gun. It was a delicate situation. I wanted to punish, not cause the incident to escalate."

"And if you hadn't been surrounded by another ten or twelve more of your men, I'm sure that he would have taken you back to his camp that night for fun, games, and painful interrogation. I guarantee he wouldn't have been nearly as sparing with your blood."

"He didn't have the chance. Besides, I'd already decided I was going to throw him off the island." Her mouth tightened. "And I did."

"Yet bad things could still have happened. That's why I'm here to tell you that you're entirely too gentle for this kind of business. You need to take on a partner." He smiled. "And I happen to be available. Don't you think this is the time?"

"Where did you hear Nadim was on his way?" she repeated.

His smile faded. "I've no objection to bribery, either. And I don't like the idea of Nadim stealing something that I've been wanting to acquire for myself. Nadim's top man, Max Gunter, has been in my pay since the night you kicked Nadim off the island. You'll probably be upset to know Nadim did very well in India. He's got a full crew now and he's ready to go after you and whatever treasure he believes you have tucked away on this island. Plus, he's sure any poaching he does on Palandan will be immensely profitable since you don't allow any hunting on the island or in those mountains that belong to it." He shook his head. "I could be a good partner to you, Maya. We've done business here for the last two years, and you know I've never cheated you. Why not take the next step? I'll protect you and keep Nadim from cutting your throat. In return, naturally, I'll require you to be accommodating enough to consider making the arrangement even closer. I've always had a yen for you when you're not being lethal. You might also furnish me with that prize Nadim thinks you're keeping hidden from him."

She gave him an incredulous look. Then she laughed scornfully. "You don't want much, do you?"

"I want *everything*," Bevan said. "And I'll get it, either from you or from Nadim. It would help if I knew exactly what it was that he was trying to relieve you of, but even Gunter couldn't tell me that. He only said that Nadim told him he'd drain you dry before he killed you. What is it? Jewels? Money? I've been waiting and watching, but you're very clever and I haven't found it for myself yet." He lowered his voice to soft

7

persuasiveness. "But it will come, Maya. You think that all these villagers you have surrounding you here on the island will keep Nadim away? He'll crush them like ants in an ant-hill. I could do it myself. Make the deal with me and I'll find a way to keep you alive."

"I don't think so." Maya shook her head. "I'm not as gentle or tenderhearted as you think, Bevan. And I don't appreci-ate that you've been waiting until you were sure you'd have Nadim as backup before you decided to make your move. Neither you nor Nadim had better threaten or attack any of these villagers, or I'll find a way to punish you." Her lips tight-ened. "It's true I don't like to kill or maim, but I believe I could make an exception in your case." She opened her desk drawer, pulled out her Smith & Wesson, and pointed it at him. "I think you'd better leave now."

His smile faded as he saw the weapon. "You're making a mistake, Maya."

"I've made them before, but I don't think this is one. This feels entirely right. Get out, Bevan. Don't come back."

His face flushed. "Oh, I'll be back. There's no point in get-ting all upset over a disagreement. Let's forget this little discus-sion. You're an exceptional businesswoman, and my produce and construction companies have made you and your villagers a good deal of money in the past couple years. I only want the best for you. I'll give you another chance later to reconsider... an expansion. And I guarantee you'll welcome me. Perhaps on your knees, Maya." He turned on his heels and strode out of the house.

Maya's hand instinctively tightened on the gun. He'd tried to mend fences in those last few minutes, but that initial threat couldn't have been more clear. Then she deliberately relaxed her grip and returned the weapon to the desk drawer. She'd been a little hasty. *Think about it, acknowledge the threat, but don't let it get in the way of keeping Palandan safe.*

"He was angry." Tashi, her housekeeper, came into the office and brought them both a cup of tea. In her full-length silk beige-gold sarong and chic upswept, gray-streaked hair, she was elegant, graceful, but definitely disapproving. "I eaves-dropped, of course, and I think you should have shot him. He showed you no respect."

"And I showed him the same lack of respect." Maya sipped her tea. "It was that kind of conversation." She chuckled. "And you always think I should shoot first, negotiate later."

"It would be safer for you." Tashi sat down in the brocade chair beside the desk. "Jann Lu would have done it. Some-times the old ways are best."

"Jann Lu is dead."

"She would not be dead if she'd shot the last man who tried to kill her," Tashi said. "She was not fast enough, but she never hesitated to go after any enemy. You should learn from her." She gazed at Maya critically. "Bevan frightened you. You hid it from him, but I could tell. You were frightened for us. You should know that we are much better fighters than Bevan or Nadim."

"But they have more lethal weapons." Maya leaned wearily back in her chair. "We're too vulnerable. We have to change and become stronger. We've always been able to take down the Nadims and Bevans of the world, but technology is making it harder. And what about India and China right on our doorstep? Who knows who will be next? It's a different world, and there are too many Nadims ready to leap out and attack. Bevan could be right; it may be time to make a deal."

"No!" Tashi shook her head. "You cannot do that. You *won't* do that. We won't let you."

"You can't stop me." She reached out and affectionately covered Tashi's hand. "And you know that I would never do anything that would bring pain or dishonor to the island, nor to the villagers who have given their lives to protect it. But maybe I can strike a balance. Bevan could be right about making a deal. This might be the time when I can reach out and change our world. Would you trust me?"

Tashi didn't answer immediately. "Perhaps. You're thinking of Riley Smith? I thought you'd given up on that possibility." She didn't wait for an answer. "We'd be willing to let you try. If you're not foolish enough to get yourself killed rather than pull that trigger. That can't happen."

"It won't." Maya was frowning. "But the situation is going to be very sensitive, and I don't know how much time I'll have. Did someone follow Bevan when he left here?"

Tashi nodded. "Dawa. We knew you'd want to keep track of him after he treated you with such disrespect."

"In case you wished to punish him?" Maya asked sarcastically. "At the moment, all I want is to know where he is and who he's meeting with here on the island. It would help if I knew when and where he might also be meeting with Nadim. I believe that will be inevitable."

Tashi nodded. "Then we will find out." She rose to her feet. "Bevan was right: You should have slit Nadim's throat when you had a chance. It would have been much more efficient." She shrugged. "But you have problems making that move. I understand. You are still young. It is good that you at least have a certain intelligence."

"I'm glad you believe I have something going for me," Maya said wryly.

"You've been with us for many years. You have a good heart, and you fight for us. Therefore you belong to us, even if you could be wiser. But you must work on it, Maya." She swept gracefully toward the door but stopped before she reached it. "I almost forgot, thanks to that foolish Bevan. You have to go see Bailey right away. She wants to see you before she goes to sleep. She is worried."

"About what?" Maya sighed. "Or who?"

She shrugged. "I'm not sure. I didn't think it would matter to you. You know she will not sleep until she sees you. She was working on her studies all evening and then decided she had to see you. She was going to come to you. I knew you wouldn't want that tonight."

"No." Maya headed for the door. "And you're right, it wouldn't matter. But I already dropped in to see her this afternoon, and she wasn't worried then. I need to know if I'm going to have a trip or just an update."

"It is Bailey." Tashi was following her out of the main house and down the walk to the arched bridge, past the armed guards. "Either way it will be fine." She watched Maya cross the bridge and head toward the curved door. "And it will be good for you to not have to think about Bevan or Nadim for a little while. Do you want me to wait for you?"

Maya looked over her shoulder. "Why?"

"Because you belong to us, and you're a little sad tonight."

"I won't be sad while I'm with Bailey," she said gently. "But I thank you for the thought."

"You're very welcome," Tashi said as she turned and headed back toward the main house. "If you can, I suggest you let Bailey take you far away for a little while."

"I might do that." Maya opened the door and peeked into Bailey's room. It appeared Tashi had been wrong. Bailey was curled up on the couch with one of her textbooks, but she appeared to have dozed off. Maya could see her tousled mop of golden hair against the embroidered teal cushion. Maya just stood and gazed at her for a long moment. Curled up like this, she looked smaller and younger than her ten years, and yet Maya knew when she woke her blue eyes would be filled with spirit and intelligence and probably the worry Tashi had told her about. Maya suddenly wanted to touch her. She took a step closer . . .

And Bailey instantly opened her eyes, wide awake. "Hi, Mama." She gave a quick yawn and sat up on the couch. "I'm glad you're here. Though it took you a long time."

"But here I am," Maya said. "I came as fast as I could." She sat down and put her arm around Bailey's shoulders. "What are we supposed to be worried about?"

"The baby," Bailey said. "I'm worried about Riva's baby."

"I didn't even know Riva was going to have a baby." She tried to remember exactly which deer Riva was. "Why should you worry about her?"

"Because she's always alone. I didn't know she was going to have a baby, either, but she always kept to herself and away from the rest of the others. Then today I was sitting here and thinking about her, and I suddenly knew why."

"Knew? Are you sure?"

"Of course not," Bailey said. "I don't know much about babies. I've only read about them in some of my books, and I saw one being born on the mountain once. That was cool." She added quickly, "And scary."

"Well, do you think that we have to really worry about Riva? Does she look like that mother who gave birth on the mountain?"

She shook her head. "Skinnier."

"Do you think you might know if Riva was close to that point?"

Bailey shrugged. "Maybe." Then she asked, "You mean the same way I learned about the baby?" She thought about it. "Yeah, it was as if she told me. Maybe she didn't want to be alone any longer."

"So if I send the herdsman, Chima, up to the mountain to keep an eye on Riva, do you think that would be safe for her? You like Chima, don't you?"

She nodded. "And he could tell me if she wasn't feeling well and then I could go?"

"If you feel comfortable with it. I don't want you worried. It's up to you, Bailey."

She was frowning seriously. "That's scary, too. But I don't think Riva would have been able to let me know about the baby if it wasn't natural and right. In my books, it says that animals can know all kinds of things that people don't. They smell better and hear better, and they know when earthquakes are going to happen. It's like magic, isn't it, Mama?"

"I don't believe that's what all your books would tell you." She pressed her lips on the top of Bailey's head. So silky soft, so beloved. "But maybe something a little like it. You can tell me after you read a few more books on the subject. Okay? Now, have you drawn any pictures of Riva? I can't see you sitting here waiting for me and not keeping yourself busy."

Bailey was already giggling and handing her a sheet from her art book. Maya studied the picture of Riva critically. "You have to be smarter than me. I can't tell whether she's going to have a baby or not."

Bailey broke out into laughter. "She knows she is, Mama. And now I do, too. You don't have to know anything. You're just being silly. I'll show you when we go to see her."

"Whew, what a relief." Maya grabbed Bailey and rocked her back and forth. "Good thing I have you around to fill in the blanks. Now just show me what else you've worked on today. After that we'll cuddle a little and I'll hold you until you go to sleep. Then I'll go back to my office and call Chima's dad and tell him to send his son up the mountain tomorrow. Does that work for you?"

———

Maya took a moment to talk to Bailey's nanny after she was sure her daughter was asleep and then left for the main house. Tashi had told her that she should let Bailey take her away for a little while, and that was exactly what had happened. It was amazing how innocence and love could change and balance a world that seemed to hold only darkness. But that time was over, and she had to return to reality and solutions. Tashi might remain optimistic, but Maya could see that the situation on the island had gotten considerably worse over the years. If she couldn't find a way out, then Maya and these villagers might be caught between Nadim and his scum, and that up-and-coming vermin Charles Bevan. She couldn't stand the thought of what that would mean for any of them.

So she mustn't let it happen.

As soon as she entered her office, she slowly picked up her phone. Riley Smith was now at Cambry, Morgan Cade's palatial estate outside London, where the Helen of Troy Museum had been established. She set up the phone for visual, then punched in the number.

Riley Smith answered on the third ring. There was a shocked silence when she saw Maya's face on the screen. "Maya? Are you all right? Why are you calling?"

"I'm fine." How should she start? "You're surprised to hear from me? It's only been five years. I told you that I might call you if I changed my mind about payback. I'm humiliated to admit that the time might have come." She paused. "Do you still want to talk to me?"

"How can you ask?" Riley asked impatiently. "When my father and I would have both died that night on the island if you hadn't saved us? I told you then that I pay my debts."

"But life sometimes changes people. I've been keeping track of you, and you've become the famous archaeologist your father always thought you'd be." She paused. "I heard that he died tragically recently. You know I always respected him, even though I couldn't give him what he wanted."

"He respected you, too," Riley said. "And neither my father nor I really thought that we'd find Helen's tomb on your island. It was too far to the southeast, but we had to explore every possibility. We'd heard the legends and my father followed them, as he had every clue for the past thirty years."

"But according to the media, after his death you did find

proof that Helen of Troy existed. That must have been exciting for you." Maya was silent. "At least for a little while. How long did it last, Riley?"

"What are you trying to say? You don't believe it was enough for me? I was as dedicated to the search as my father, Maya."

"You were fascinated by Helen. You liked the adventure and taking the next step. But I always thought that there would be another step for you. That's why I kept my eye on you after you left Palandan Island." She smiled crookedly. "I was afraid I might someday need someone to take more than one step with me. If I can make it worth their while."

"That sounds like an offer." Riley's eyes narrowed on Maya's face. "And why now?"

"Perhaps because in the time since you left the island, you've become a kind of celebrity. You're quite famous in academic circles these days. I might be able to use it."

"Celebrity?" Riley made a rude sound. "Maybe I've accomplished what I set out to do in finding Helen and bringing her to everyone's attention again. I'm proud of that."

"You've also made contact with Eve Duncan, the foremost forensic sculptor in the world. That could be very valuable. She's done extensive work in the past with historical restoration. She even did the sculpting on your Helen of Troy. You were lucky to get her. She's quite wonderful." She paused. "Don't you think she might be intrigued by the stories that drew you to the island?"

"Perhaps," Riley said slowly. "But she's also a professional who has a career she cares about. Mere curiosity wouldn't tempt her."

"But friendship might, and the media has done a lot of talking about your relationship since you began setting up that London museum."

She stiffened. "I wouldn't impose."

"Your choice. Then should we discuss Morgan Cade? Another very close friend who might prove useful. According to the media, he's half Indiana Jones, half Robin Hood, and he has a special hatred of traffickers of both humans and animals. One of the richest men in the world, winner of a Congressional Medal of Honor, archaeologist, humanitarian, famous environmentalist and animal activist…" She paused. "That latter qualification alone might lure him to the island. And did I mention that almost every news story I've read lately can't resist publishing a photo of you with Cade? Are you still living with him?"

"That's none of your business, Maya. Are you trying to make me angry?"

"No, I'm trying to be honest." She added wearily, "And I'm trying to point out that I might be ruthless enough to attempt getting any help available if I need it. I'm trying to warn you in case you want to tell me to go to hell. I don't want you to do anything against your principles, but I also don't want to put you in danger if I don't have to." She tried to smile. "I won't deny I'm in trouble, but I believe I can still come out on top with a little help from my friends . . . and *your* friends. If it turns out to be just the two of us, we might still make it. After all, you found Helen. I think you might be able to find Silvana. I have my own guards on the island, but I don't want them hurt. You'll remember they helped keep you and your father alive. Now I'm going to hang up and let you think about whether you want to help me. If you're smart, you'll probably turn me down. Regardless, I want your promise not to discuss me or the island with anyone else. Okay?"

"Of course. But I don't really know what's happening with you, dammit."

"Think about it. You're very intelligent. You know I have enemies. You ran into a few of them. The situation with Aden Nadim has just gotten more complicated." She added, "And less safe. I'll call you back in a few days to get your answer. I'll try to go into more details then if you want to hear them." She hesitated before she continued, "But there's one thing you should know. This is going to be the endgame for me, and I have to treat it the way Jann Lu would want it treated. That means that the stakes are sky-high, no holds barred. I'll give you everything you want from me, but I'll take whatever I need to keep the people and things I value safe. I can't promise anything else. Do you understand?"

"Hell, no." Riley was frowning. "How could I? It's bullshit. I don't even know what this Jann Lu has to do with it."

"You will. You'll know everything soon if you want to come back to the island. If you don't, perhaps what you have now is worth forgetting. I won't blame you whichever you decide. Goodbye, Riley."

———

Maya cut the connection. She leaned back in her chair and drew a deep breath. It was done.

Or at least it was started. She had never thought she would retrieve that promise from Riley, but never was a long time. Why else had she kept track of Riley's doings all these years? It was true they had become close during the time Riley and her father had visited the island, but Maya had deliberately broken the contact after she had been able to get them safely away from here. Her own life was too full of threat to let young, enthusiastic Riley Smith with her big dreams and driving ambition remain anywhere near her. It had obviously been the right decision. After Riley left, life had been neither tame nor uneventful. She had suffered loss and danger, but success had also followed her like a bright comet.

And now Maya was going to tap that comet.

She leaned her head against the back of the chair and closed her eyes. She hoped she was doing the right thing. It felt good and moral and ethical, and it was the duty she'd been trained for since childhood. That alone should make it right, shouldn't it?

As long as it didn't cause the deaths of good people before it was over...

THE SURVIVOR

———

"Shit!" Riley slammed down the lid of the computer and stood up from her desk. She went to the bathroom, got a glass of water, and drank it. Then she went out onto the balcony and looked at the grounds. From here she could hear the sounds of the Wildlife Harbor Sanctuary, the private zoo that adjoined Cade's estate and the Helen of Troy Museum: the high scream of the monkeys and occasional bellow of the elephants. Usually she liked the sounds, but at the moment they were getting on her nerves. "Maya, what the hell are you doing to me?" she whispered. She was too on edge to settle so she went back into her bedroom, threw on her jacket, and went outside for a walk. Whatever Maya was doing, Riley could tell that her personality hadn't really changed since she had last seen her on Palandan Island. No, that might not be true: There had been no hint of Maya's usual humor on that call tonight. Only concern and a willingness to use whomever she had to in order to banish whatever problem was plaguing her. Not like Maya at all. Maya had told her before they left the island that neither her father nor Riley owed her anything. Yet tonight she had offered Riley whatever she wanted in return.

And Riley had instantly known what that meant. Both she

and her father had researched the history of the area before they'd gone to investigate the possibility of Helen's tomb being on Palandan Island. Neither of them had thought it likely, but they were intrigued by the stories told by the islanders while they were there. Maya had been amused by her fascination and dropped a few teasing remarks that they had both laughed about.

But Maya would also know that the only gift Riley would be interested in for services rendered would be on Palandan Island.

Riley could still feel the same ripple of excitement she had known five years ago at the thought of exploring the history of Palandan. But then it had been a mere tall tale that had amused and intrigued her. Now it had substance, because Maya always had substance. Everyone on the island took her seriously; indeed, she was regarded with respect that bordered on worship by the islanders. But how could she take anything else from Maya after what she'd already given them? It would be too—

Her phone was ringing. Maya? No, it was Cade calling from that meeting in Rome. He had promised to phone after he got back to the hotel. Ordinarily she would have been more than happy, but not now. Because Maya had mentioned using Cade, and there was no way Riley could permit that to happen. She had only lived with Cade for a few months, but she had seen how often he was targeted by the users of the world. She'd just get him off the phone and perhaps talk to him later. She picked up the call. "Hi, did everything go well? Any major break-throughs on the human rights issues?"

"Perhaps with the Arabs. It's hard to tell. But I'll get through to them eventually."

"I'm sure you will." There was no one more persuasive than Cade, and he always managed to get what he wanted. "So when are you coming home?"

"Three days from now. I wish it was tonight." He paused and added roughly, "What the hell are you doing wandering around the grounds?"

"Taking a walk. What the hell do you think I was doing? And who told you I was wandering? No, don't tell me. It was Jon Kirby. And I'll go for a walk wherever I please. Look, you're the billionaire, not me. I'm getting tired of all this secu-rity crap. Did you just happen to tell him to keep an eye on me? That wasn't cool, Cade."

"Sorry, but you'll learn to live with it. I really wasn't that obvious." He suddenly chuckled. "And I didn't have to tell him anything. He knew he had to keep an eye on the entire property while I was traveling." His voice softened. "And that the most precious item on the property is Riley Smith. The rest of the place isn't worth a damn if *you're* not there."

She could feel herself start to melt. She could almost see him there before her. The blue eyes, the dark hair that felt so good as she ran her fingers through it, the intensity as he moved closer, the curve of his lips as he smiled . . . But she couldn't let him get away that easily. "Not true. What about the elephants?"

"I stand corrected. But that's only because your little brother is besotted with that baby elephant." He added, "And I wouldn't have even mentioned your blasted walk if Kirby hadn't said you looked upset. Are you upset? Should I come home? Say the word."

"And disturb the Arabs? I wouldn't think of it." She added, "I'm not upset. Maybe I'm a little restless since I finished the Helen Museum. Perhaps I'll go visit Eve for a day or two." Those words had appeared out of nowhere. Yet she followed up immediately. "Yes, that might be a good idea. I'll call and see if I'll be welcome."

"You're always welcome with her and Joe Quinn," he said, "but let me call Kirby and arrange security for you."

"You think Joe Quinn can't take care of me? Ace detective? Ex-SEAL? Be for real, Cade." She added, "I'll call you tomorrow when I reach Atlanta."

He sighed. "You're being very difficult."

"You ain't seen nothing yet," she said. "Good night, Cade."

"I love you," he said. "Always."

"Me, too." She added suddenly, "And I don't like it, but I know why you do all that security crap. I'd want to protect you, too, if you didn't have the whole world standing in line to do it. Take care of yourself." She hung up the phone.

Then she stuffed her hands in her jacket pockets and headed back toward the mansion. As she passed the guest house, she gave Kirby a derisive wave before entering the mansion. No more midnight strolls. She had to go to bed and think about what might be coming. It could have been impulse or curiosity that was driving her, but it had been strong enough to make her want to talk to Eve about it. Though she knew there was every chance she wouldn't involve her, it would still be good to have her to talk to after all the work they'd done together. She couldn't imagine anyone who would be more excited or interested than Eve when she told her about what might be waiting for Riley if she decided to go to Palandan Island. The legends alone would intrigue someone with a forensic background like Eve's. It seemed that she wasn't going to be able to resist going to Atlanta and at least talking to Eve...

She was dialing Eve as she climbed the steps to her bedroom. "Hi, mind having company for a few days? I promise not to get in your way. If you're too busy, just say the word."

"I'm always busy, but I can use a break," Eve said. "I'm missing Michael since he went back to school in Scotland, and I need a change of pace. I know I can count on you in that category." She paused. "Everything okay with you? I know it can't be the Helen of Troy Museum. I saw a news show on CNN last week, and the lines waiting to get in were out of sight."

"They still are, and the staff here keeps things running like clockwork. Of course your sculpture of Helen is the star of the exhibit. I go visit it at least once a day and think of the night when you first showed it to me."

"That's very touching, but I can't quite get my mind around

the thought of you as a museum concierge. Much too tame, Riley. I was sure you'd have broken out of there by this time. Where's Cade?"

"Here most of the time. But he's at a human rights conference at the moment. He's great, wonderful, stop looking for problems." She chuckled. "Though I remember that before you left, you said something about wondering how long I'd last."

"That wasn't about Cade," Eve said quietly. "I always realized he was unique. That was about you. You'd spent your entire life on one adventure after another and at last completed the greatest one of all. I had a right to wonder what was next for you."

"Well, right now the only thing on my agenda is coming to see you tomorrow and maybe having a long talk and reminiscing a bit." She added awkwardly, "And perhaps getting your advice about a few other things since you're one of the wisest people I know. My mind seems to be a bit muddled right now, and you might help to clear my thinking." Then she broke out with sudden explosive impatience, "And I just want to *talk* to you, dammit."

Eve chuckled. "And I want to talk to you. You've made it too tempting to resist. What are you up to, Riley?"

"Nothing that will cause you any trouble. I'm the one who has an obligation. I've told you what I need. If you don't want to be involved even that deeply, tell me. I'll understand."

"Let me know when you'll be here," Eve said. "Good night, Riley."

———————

Cade called Kirby back fifteen minutes after he'd ended the call with Riley. "All secure for the night?"

"Absolutely," Kirby said dryly. "Including a rather insulting salute from Riley before she went back into the mansion. I'll probably hear from her tomorrow about my interference."

"I doubt it. She'll be too busy. She said she's going to fly out to see Eve Duncan tomorrow."

"Really? Any reason?"

"She's restless. The Helen of Troy Museum is completed, and I think she's bored. She's used to being on her own since she was a kid trailing after her father in the jungle. She's always been a wild child, and we'll just have to find something to keep her interested." He paused. "But I didn't like it that you said she seemed upset. I'm glad you called me."

"Well, I'm not," he said flatly. "I like Riley and I respect her. I don't want her to think I'm spying on her. I know that you worry about her when you're not around, but I'll learn to deal with it."

"I'm making the attempt," Cade said wryly. "We'll come to terms. But I've never had to handle anyone as stubborn as Riley. I need a little more time to convince her that security isn't all bad."

"Bullshit," Kirby said. "I've seen you browbeat dictators and lecture the pope. I realize she's independent and you don't want to interfere, but either one of your enemies is going to target her, or she's going to end up walking away from you."

"That won't happen," Cade said grimly. "I'll work it out. This isn't easy for her. I grew up with the knowledge that I could be kidnapped or murdered by anyone who hated my grandfather or father. She's not used to being a target, and she's not accustomed to having anyone trailing her. But I have a few candidates in mind she might approve of."

"Yeah, you told me. Wild child. So what do you want to do about this trip?"

"See that she gets on the plane at Heathrow and ask Quinn to meet her at Atlanta Airport. No problem. She's not unreasonable. I'll be back in a few days, and we'll have another talk."

"As long as I don't have to be caught in the middle," Kirby said. "And I'll see about a little temporary security while she's at the Lake Cottage."

"I knew you would," Cade said. "And thanks for keeping an eye on her, Kirby."

"I couldn't do anything else," he said grimly. "I know what you'd do if anything happened to her. It wouldn't be pretty. Fix it, Cade."

"Consider it done." Cade cut the connection.

CHAPTER

2

Y ou're sure you weren't followed?" Nadim asked. "I don't
want to have to up anchor and move my ship because of
your stupidity, Bevan."

"I wasn't followed," Bevan said curtly. Then he pasted a
smile on his face. Always keep the customers happy, even bastards like Nadim. "She tried to send someone after me, but I
gave him the slip right away. And you'll find I'm never stupid
when money is involved. Ask Gunter, he'll tell you how valuable I can be to you. Maya thinks I'm just trying to con her
into signing a partnership. It wouldn't be smart to let her know
about our arrangement."

"We don't have an arrangement yet," Nadim said coldly.
"Gunter told me that you were promising him you could be
useful, that you know all the villages, warehouses, and muni-
tion centers on the island. True?"

"Absolutely. When I first came to Palandan, I told Maya that I wanted to purchase some of the fruit grown on the island, and she had me taken to the groves. I've made several purchases in the last years and developed valuable contacts." He shrugged. "I wasn't allowed to go very far inland, but I'll get there eventually. I can be patient."

"I can't," Nadim said bluntly. "I've never learned. I regard it as weakness anyway."

"Well, that puts me in my place," Bevan said ruefully. "And since you're much more successful than I am, I'd be foolish to argue. But we'll see if you still feel I'm weak when I hand Maya over to you. I understand that you're still a bit irate with the lady." He deliberately gazed down at the ugly scar on Nadim's right hand. "Gunter told me it sometimes bothers you even after all these years. Is it true you've put a price on her head with your men?"

Nadim started to swear, his hand slowly clenching. "You think it's funny? I don't find anything that bitch does amusing. I'm going to find a way to cut her heart out. That's the only reason you're here—to show me what you can do."

"What do you want me to do?" Bevan asked. "Name it. But be prepared to pay the price. I'm not cheap, Nadim."

"You've already started, if you've really been able to find a way to gain access to the interior of the island." He leaned back in his chair. "I want to know *everything* about Palandan. Every possible weakness about the island and the people who live there." He added, "Mainly Maya Fallon and the people who surround her. If you can get me the information I need, you'll find me very generous."

This was obviously the opportunity Bevan had been waiting for. "Then we definitely seem to be on the same page." He reached in his jacket pocket. "I didn't want to come to you with empty hands, so I brought you a gift." He handed him a black remote. "It may be small, but I believe you'll find it provides enormous benefits over time. Earlier this week I planted a bug in Maya's office. You'll be able to tap into every transaction she makes." He smiled as he saw the eagerness with which Nadim was examining the remote. "Ah, I can see you're beginning to appreciate me."

"It's a good start. See if you can follow up."

"Oh, I will. Anything in particular you're interested in?"

Nadim's lips twisted. "Don't play games. You've heard all the rumors about what might and might not be on that island or you wouldn't be standing here. The only thing you should know is that whatever is there belongs to me. Understood?"

"Yes, I only asked so that I could be on the lookout for anything that might please you."

Nadim laughed. "You want to know what would please me? I'll tell you. Keep an eye out for the kid Maya keeps in that house in the village right across the bridge from the main house. She's a pretty little girl about ten or eleven. There appear to be guards on duty at all times in front of the place. I've been wondering why. I'm very curious about her."

Bevan frowned and shook his head. "I've never seen her around. But then I might not notice her. I don't care much for kids."

"You don't? I'm quite fond of them. I have a girl only a little older than her down in my cabin right now. I had Gunter hunt her down in the fields when I realized I was going to need something to amuse me while I was waiting for my opportunity to go after Maya." He smiled maliciously. "I might be willing to share."

Bevan shook his head. Nadim was probably just bullshitting. He couldn't imagine him being generous about anything. All Bevan would need was to have those villagers think he was the one who had snatched one of their children. He knew Maya always kept her villagers armed and ready to engage at the drop of a hat. That wasn't the way he wanted to start out this deal with Nadim. "Like I said, I don't care for kids. But I'll see what I can find out about that girl you mentioned."

"You do that," Nadim said as he got to his feet. "Report back to me as soon as you can. I think Gunter said the kid's name was Bailey…"

———

ATLANTA AIRPORT
3:40 P.M.
NEXT DAY

"Eve!" Riley enveloped Eve in an enthusiastic hug when she saw her waiting at baggage claim. "What are you doing here? Kirby told me Joe was going to pick me up."

"So I'm not good enough for you?" Eve laughed. "After all that drama and your elaborate explanations about all the reasons you wanted to come?"

"Be quiet." Riley made a face. "These days my life seems to be so regimented that I question every change. I'm very happy to see you even when you're yelling at me." She reached down and grabbed her suitcase off the carousel. "Where's Joe?"

"We did a switch." She grinned as they walked toward the exit. "Kirby called Joe this morning and asked him to pick you up and he told him he would. But he didn't mention that he'd have to cancel his reservations to Edinburgh and book a later flight because he'd told me he'd let me work the full day on my current sculpture up to the time he'd drop you off." She made a face. "He said it didn't matter to him, but when he told me, it mattered to me. There wasn't any reason I couldn't stop work early and pick you up so that he'd be able to reach my son's school in time to take him out for dinner before the soccer game."

"Sorry. It appears I'm already causing trouble," Riley said. "You should have told Kirby that Joe was planning on going to Scotland. I could have taken an Uber to the cottage."

She shook her head. "Joe and Cade became good friends while we were on the Helen hunt. He felt duty-bound to make certain you were welcomed properly. It was easier for me to handle it." She was striding to her jeep on the parking deck. "And it was no trouble. Stop apologizing."

Riley shrugged. "Regimentation strikes again." Then she threw back her head and smiled as she got into the passenger seat. "But I'm not going to let it bother me. I'm glad to be here with you. I'll find a way to make it up to you."

"Excellent," Eve said gravely. "I'll have to think about what exorbitant fee I can charge you for the ride."

"I'm being ridiculous?" Riley asked.

"Marginal, considering you're my good friend and I'm usually willing to do much more for a friend." She smiled. "I'm glad you're here. Now lean back and relax and let me tell you how marvelous my son is doing at school and what an amazing boy he is. He's on the soccer team and he's going to try out for the rowing team. Actually, Joe's trip was a little unexpected. But it seems the other students all have their fathers coming up to the school this week to talk to the coach. He wondered if Joe could come, too." She shook her head. "Michael was very polite and said he would understand if it wasn't possible. But he thought Joe might be able to help the coach since he'd been a SEAL. What could Joe say?"

Riley was grinning. "Nothing but yes."

"Right, it's almost impossible to say no to Michael," Eve said. "Now, you just chill and pretend to be enthralled while I tell you why. And you can laugh and be admiring and know that we're not going to discuss anything that will make you tense until we're back at the Lake Cottage and have had dinner and a glass of wine."

Riley moistened her lips. "I'm not exactly tense."

"Close enough." She darted her a glance. "Did I tell you how Michael traveled with Cara when she gave one of her concerts? She said he was a big help, and he could do it again next vacation if I'll let him." She laughed. "I never thought that he had an ambition to be a roadie but it seems to be the thing kids want to try these days..."

———

"More wine?" Eve was already topping off Riley's glass as she put the decanter on the coffee table in front of the porch swing. "I thought maybe we'd have dessert later. Wine is more what you need right now." She leaned back on the swing and gazed at Riley. "Okay, are you comfortable?"

"Of course I'm comfortable." Riley gazed at her with exasperation. "Why wouldn't I be? A gorgeous lake, woods, and wonderful peace. This Lake Cottage of yours is perfect. I don't know why you ever left it to help me find Helen."

"Because you had a dream," Eve said quietly. "And dreams are important." She lifted her glass in a toast. "And your dreams happened to coincide with a dream of my own if you'll remember. Though I do love this place. It's been home for a long time for my family. Home can sometimes be as important as dreams."

"I wouldn't know about that," Riley said. "Since I've spent practically all my life in jungles and deserts and following my father into tombs." She shrugged. "And that wasn't such a bad life. Every place has something going for it if you reach out and look for it."

"I can see how you'd appreciate the nuances." Eve chuckled. "But then didn't you tell me you were taught medicine by an African witch doctor at one time? That was an extreme case of reaching out." Her smile faded. "I do hope your present predicament doesn't involve the witch doctor?"

"Not that I know about," Riley said. "One can never tell with Maya, but that was Africa and I believe my problem may be moving from India to an island in the Himalayan Mountains near Tibet."

"Tibet? That's a surprise. I can see this may get complicated."

"Not for you," Riley said quickly. "I told you I'm the one who has an obligation. I owe Maya, and she wouldn't have called me if there hadn't been trouble. I told her that she can't expect help from anyone but me."

"Maya," Eve repeated. "That seems a good place to begin. Who is Maya and why are you under obligation?"

"Wait a minute." Riley jumped to her feet, ran to the guest room Eve had given her, pulled out her computer, and brought it back out to the porch. "I came prepared. I remember how detail-oriented you are. Her name is Maya Fallon." She brought up the document. "She's twenty-eight years old, speaks fifteen languages, has medical and agricultural training, and is probably the sharpest and best-informed woman I've ever met except you. She's also wonderfully charismatic if she makes the effort and can charm the birds from the trees. That's how she's managed to keep the Chinese and Indian diplomatic wolves from attacking since she inherited Palandan Island from Jann Lu when she was only sixteen."

Eve was studying the photos of the tall, graceful-looking woman wearing boots, jeans, and a loose white shirt. She had brown eyes and a thick, single tawny braid that fell down her back; she was smiling gently at a young, sarong-clad woman. "I can see the charisma," she said absently. "Very warm." She looked up at Riley. "Back up. I'm already a little lost. Island? Jann Lu?"

Riley pointed to a sketch of a large island. "Palandan Island. Southeast Asia. It's enormous and supports several different villages. It's absolutely beautiful with several fruit groves and wonderful flowers and abundant wildlife. It rather reminded me of what Eden must have looked like."

"Wait," Eve said, staring at a map. "This is in the middle of the Himalayas?"

"Yes, believe it or not. It's in the center of a large lake, nestled in the middle of a treacherous cluster of mountains. It's difficult to reach, which is what has kept it protected from invaders for centuries. Its altitude and topography create several weather systems, all within a hundred miles or so. To approach the heart of the island, you move through forty miles of blizzard conditions. Then you reach a temperate zone, where most of the residents live. There you'll actually find jungles."

Eve shook her head. "Amazing."

"There's no place quite like it. It also connects with a mountain range that extends a good distance into the Himalayas. Maya is in control of both the island and mountain range. Jann Lu was the woman who was in charge of the island before Maya. She ran everything for over sixty-two years before she had a fall in the mountains. It wasn't easy for a teenager like Maya to take over, but Jann Lu had prepared her and in no time the villagers looked upon her as leader."

"She was a relative of this Jann Lu?" Eve asked.

Riley shook her head. "Jann Lu was only about four feet tall and was of Eurasian descent. You see what Maya looks like. I guess she appears more Nordic than anything else."

"You didn't ask Maya any questions about that?"

"Not about her heritage. That was discouraged. The people who live on Palandan Island are pretty much multiracial. They've welcomed immigrants over the centuries from practically every country in Asia and Europe." She hesitated. "Though while I was there, I sometimes heard the villagers refer to Maya as the chosen one."

"Weird."

"Yeah, I thought so. For heaven's sake, it's not as if she's the Dalai Lama. But in those Himalayan Mountains, anything can seem spiritual. They're that close to heaven. But then there were all kinds of stories floating around among the villagers on the island and mountains. My father and I just accepted it. When you've spent your life chasing down a fairy tale like Helen of Troy, you get used to giving every story a grain of salt, but you never totally discount them."

"Because they were all part of the dream?" Eve asked.

Riley nodded. "But not my particular dream. We came to Palandan Island because we'd heard some of the stories and thought why not? We'd already been traveling all over the world trying to locate Helen's tomb. But we thought it was a little far-fetched for the cultures of Tibet, India, and China to have any connection to Helen of Troy. It turned out we were right. When we got there, we found that Helen wasn't mentioned, and the legends were about an entirely different woman of power. So we thought we'd spend a week or so and then take off north to Azerbaijan. My father was annoyed and impatient and spent most of the time planning for that next journey." She smiled. "Though I got a bit distracted."

"That's hard to believe considering how single-minded you are."

"It was because I was suddenly dealing with a completely different subject than Helen, the most beautiful woman in the world. Helen had beauty and her own strengths, but she was nothing like Silvana. No comparison."

"Silvana?"

"Most of the stories on the island were about Silvana Marcella, the purchaser and founder of Palandan Island. She lived during the height of the Roman Empire, and the more I heard about her, the more interested I became. Since I had nothing to do at the time, I started collecting the legends about Silvana. It amused Maya, and she even told me a few herself. I tried to interest my father, but by that time he'd become totally obsessed with Helen and was impatient with any other subject." She smiled. "I understood. I only wish he could have seen your sculpture of her before he was killed. He always wanted it to be you who did the forensic work when we finally found Helen. That's why I hunted you down and begged you to come with me when I knew I was close."

"And wouldn't let me say no," Eve said dryly. "That's why I can't see you lolling on that island when you could have left and started north right away."

"We needed to gather supplies," Riley said defensively. "It was going to be a long trip to Azerbaijan."

"And?" Eve probed.

"Palandan was fascinating." Riley added, "And so was Maya Fallon. I'd never met anyone like her. She was treated almost like a queen by those islanders, and yet sometimes she seemed younger than me. I...liked her. I wanted to try to understand her."

"And perhaps you were two young women who'd both had hard lives and yet were different enough that you were curious and wanted to explore each other."

"It could be. And, as I said, the legends also intrigued me." She grimaced as she took a sip of her wine. "Though it turned out that I almost waited too long to leave the island. I thought we were safe. The villagers all seemed friendly, and Maya couldn't have been warmer…after she had our documents thoroughly checked and verified."

"You weren't safe?" Eve frowned. "This must be where the obligation comes in, right after the fact that this Maya might not have let you on the island if you didn't have her version of a visa."

"It wasn't like that. It's a wonderful place. They were kind to us. Since we were going to be on Palandan for such a short time, there was no reason why Maya would believe there was a threat to us."

"But there was?"

"Maya had been having a problem for months with a scumbag, Aden Nadim, who had been poaching and raiding the natives living and working in the mountains. He must have thought our camp on the island was a richer target and decided to change his tactics and attack us. But Maya got word about it and sent some of her men to intercept them. She managed to get us off the island and on our way to Katmandu with enough supplies to get us to Azerbaijan. I didn't find out until later from the Tibetan government that Maya had been with the men she'd sent after Nadim and been wounded. I felt terrible about it. I called her right away and told her that I knew I owed her and asked if there was anything I could do to repay her. She only laughed it off and said we'd been her responsibility since she'd permitted us on the island. She told me she hoped I'd have good luck at finding Helen, and if she changed her mind, she'd let me know." She shrugged. "I hadn't heard anything from her since that day. That was five years ago."

"But evidently she changed her mind?"

"Maya admitted she was having serious problems when she called me last night." She met Eve's eyes. "And I believe she could be ruthless if she thinks it's necessary to protect Palandan Island and the people she cares about. She never tried to hide that from me. But isn't that true of most of us? I know she does have a sense of honor and fairness." She smiled crookedly. "And I think she's about to offer me something she knows I'll want rather than relying on my gratitude. If she does, I'm not certain I could turn her down. It would be—"

"Stop right there," Eve said. "I don't like where this is going. Your Maya may be a little too clever."

"Okay." Riley finished her wine. "I'll drop it. The last thing I want to do is upset you." She set her glass on the coffee table. "After all, this is my problem. Why don't you tell me more about your Michael? He sounds like an incredible boy."

Eve sighed. "There's no way I can jump to Michael now. I've got to know the rest. I've already got a hint of what lure Maya is using. It's the only one that would prove irresistible to you."

"Of course you would guess. You know me too well." She tilted her head. "And it might be just a little intriguing to you, too."

"A little," Eve said reluctantly. "Though I'm not thinking

kindly of Maya Fallon for realizing what bait would attract you."

"Why? There's no way she wouldn't know. Running Palandan is her whole life."

"So she dangled Silvana Marcella," Eve said flatly. "And all those tantalizing tales of ancient glory and mysteries to solve. You might have had a chance if you hadn't only recently discovered your Helen. Now it's too tempting."

"Not entirely." Riley got to her feet and walked to the porch railing and looked out at the darkness of the lake. "I'm not a child chasing the past. I have a debt to pay, and that's important. I'm an archaeologist and, as a professional, it's my job to get answers wherever I find them."

"And it helps that you have a curiosity and thirst for knowledge that's fairly incredible," Eve said with a smile.

Riley chuckled. "That, too."

"Then tell me about Silvana Marcella."

Riley leaned back on the railing. "I'm getting there. But I want you to understand that I expect nothing from you."

"You've made that clear. Talk to me." She was frowning. "The name sounds Italian. Is it?"

She nodded. "Though it's not her real name. She chose it for herself when she left Rome and came to Palandan. Her handler called her Flavia Lucia while she was in the arena. I don't know what name she was born with."

"Handler?"

"The professional gladiator troop manager who bought her

in the slave market and sent her to his training school to learn her trade."

"What?" Eve sat up straighter. "Gladiator? Now, that's interesting. I knew there were women gladiators, but I've never had contact with them yet during my professional career. I did most of my forensic sculpting of that era working at the museums of Herculaneum. I found it more challenging near the volcano eruption than dealing with the remains of gladiators who were trying to chop each other to pieces." Her eyes were suddenly gleaming. "But I admit I've always been curious about the role of women as gladiators."

"I was, too. At the time, I did some in-depth computer research, and Maya knew quite a bit. Though most of the legends and stories were passed down from generation to generation by word of mouth, there were ancient tablets found in the caves in the foothills of the mountains adjoining the island." She added, "But I believe I became more interested in the Silvana who came to the island than the gladiator in the arenas."

"Well, start at the beginning and let me catch up," Eve said as she leaned back. "You said she was bought in the market by this gladiator manager. Why? Male gladiators must have been stronger and more popular than the women."

"Most women. But Antonio Gaius, her handler, took a chance on Silvana. He was ambitious and he was looking for something different to attract the crowds. The Roman soldiers who brought her to market told him how fiercely she'd fought before they'd brought her down. She was only fourteen when she was captured with an Amazon troop of nomads from what's now known as Kazakhstan near the Black Sea. It was well known that her tribe rode and fought just like the men and were particularly skilled in caring for the herds of horses they stole during their raids. She was also an expert archer and had killed enough soldiers that the soldiers thought they'd be able to sell her for a higher price to the arenas than to the whorehouses. Antonio had her schooled for the arenas until she was ready. Then he sent her out with another of his students and told them to succeed or be slaughtered. Silvana wasn't about to let herself be slaughtered. But she didn't speak the language and she didn't know she wasn't supposed to kill the more experienced woman they sent into the arena with her. Silvana disposed of her opponent within the hour after she walked into the arena. But Antonio wasn't pleased; he beat her for destroying one of his valuable assets. He preferred that his gladiators only fight to a draw if possible. That way he could keep all his property intact for future battles. Still, the audience had found Silvana so exciting that he began to present her as a novelty. She never lost a battle. The crowd loved her. Slowly she began to learn how to survive. She never killed again unless ordered. She was given prizes for every battle and Antonio allowed her to keep a portion of it. He was enjoying her success and made her his mistress so that he could show her off. He'd also occasionally give her to one of the important men of Rome after a match as a special treat. They found it arousing to have such a powerful woman helpless and forced to do anything they wished. She submitted to everything, but always kept the gold coins and trinkets they gave her. She begged Antonio to let her buy her freedom with them, but he refused. He preferred the arrangement as it was. He'd become enormously wealthy since he'd bought Silvana, and he realized she'd been a huge part of his success. So she watched and waited and continued to fight...and win. She became fairly rich and famous herself in the next few years, but he still wouldn't release her." She paused. "Then she realized she was ready. She'd prepared everything. They were at Antonio's estate in the country, bribes had been set in place, she'd found the property she wanted to purchase far, far from Rome, where she'd be safe."

"Ah, the plot thickens," Eve murmured. "I can see it coming. Who can blame her? She'd done everything she could to escape him. She'd been raped, and forced to kill, and made a slave."

Riley nodded. "Suddenly one bright, sunny day she freed all the slaves on the estate and gave them money to lose themselves in the countryside. A short time later Antonio was found in the gladiator arena he'd built for private entertainment at the estate. He was wearing gladiator armor and his throat had been cut by a sword lying on the sand beside him. Silvana had disappeared from both the estate and Rome itself. It was probably quite the scandal, and though Antonio wasn't very popular, the Roman authorities still set out to try to find Silvana to set an example. But she was smart, careful, and an expert horsewoman—not to mention she had a decent head start. No matter how long they tried, they couldn't find a trace of her."

"And that's the end of the beginning?" Eve asked. "She evidently went through hell. She went directly to Palandan Island?"

Riley nodded. "According to the legend, she showed up at the island dressed in trousers and a red cloak, riding a magnificent white stallion, with two wagons containing five coffers of treasure and four guardsmen in attendance. It was probably the treasure she'd stolen from Antonio. She also had a herd of fine horses driven by several shepherds. By the next week she had vanished into the forests on the island and her guardsmen had disappeared. After that she was seen only with the local natives who lived on the island. They were in awe of her. They weren't accustomed to seeing a woman more skilled than any man with horses and weapons."

"It must have pleased you to learn that," Eve murmured.

"It did. She must have been much, much better to have them admit it. It was a man's world when she arrived on Palandan Island. Yet she made it her own within the next few years. That's why I kept searching for more stories about her. Maya was curious, too. She was able to tell me what she'd been able to search out over the years she'd been on the island."

"And?"

"I became more interested in the Silvana who came to the

island than what she'd been when she'd fought in Rome. Though she had to battle just as fiercely to keep what was hers."

"Those coffers of treasure you mentioned?"

She nodded. "That was a part of it. Word got around quickly about the riches she'd brought to the island. In the early days, there were always thieves attacking her camps. Later she organized the natives to build her a small city complete with temple in one of the valleys where she could store her treasures. But she still had to worry about the cattle and the herd of horses she'd brought from Rome. As I said, they were magnificent and evidently worth almost as much as her jewels and precious coins. She started to train the villagers as warriors to protect them. Landowners started to come from all over the countryside and as far as India to try to buy them, and the thieves, poachers, and brigands were right behind them. Evidently that pissed off Silvana, because she closed down the island and permitted no one to enter without her permission. She even brought out her own set of laws. Palandan became her own private territory complete with a small army." She smiled. "And that was the way it stayed. She lived to be seventy-eight and had two children by men in the village, but no one challenged her authority. She chose her daughter to succeed her and by the time she died, she'd trained her daughter to do things her way and obey Silvana's laws. It had become tradition."

"Maybe then. Surely not through all those centuries?" Eve said skeptically.

"Sometimes things changed for a while, but they always reverted to Silvana's law eventually."

"And that was why you had to have special permission from Maya Fallon even to visit the island?" Eve shook her head. "Hard to believe."

"It kept the island prosperous and safe, the people happy," Riley said quietly. "That can't be all bad. There's a world of countries out there who have created their own laws and lifestyles. Most of the Silvana laws are reasonable and benefit the islanders. It's not as if anyone is forced to live there. They *like* their island."

"But it didn't appeal to you five years ago," Eve said.

"It appealed to me. How could it not? An Amazon warrior who had fought desperately for her freedom and escaped from danger and slavery in the arena to come to that island and make a new life? It's a wonderful story and if I hadn't had Helen beckoning, I might have wanted to stay and see what I could find. I only knew the legends, but there were so many mysteries that I hadn't even touched. I had no idea where Silvana's tomb was located. For that matter, where was this splendid city and temple she'd had constructed on the island to protect her animals and other property? Was that where Silvana's family chose to place her tomb? Why had she brought that large herd of horses to the island anyway? It must have made the journey from Rome even more difficult when you consider the distance and primitive travel conditions. Did those coffers of jewels still exist or had Silvana's descendants lost them over the centuries?" She stopped and drew a deep breath. "You see, lots of questions. It's my profession to dig into the past and learn what's revealed." She shrugged. "And if those assholes hadn't attacked that night, I might have found out even more, which would have made me that much more eager to explore Palandan. But they did attack, and that sent me back on the track for Helen that I never should have left."

"And left you pondering all those unanswered questions," Eve said softly. "And if your Maya is as clever as you tell me, she'd realize that would drive you crazy. You're very easy to read. I can see it, clear as day. Did she?"

Riley slowly nodded. "She'd know."

"Then you shouldn't play her game." Eve took a sip of her wine. "But it's too late to say that, isn't it? You're already heading in that direction."

"I owe her." Then she added, "And I trust her. We became very good friends in the short time I was on the island. I believe she's honorable. Which is why I've been wondering if I should go back to Palandan and see what's wrong for myself."

"And that's why you came here. You wanted me to give you advice about what you should do? Come on, Riley. You know you're aching to find out all those delicious Silvana answers and help a friend who's in trouble." Her lips tightened. "To hell with that. I've listened and heard what you've said. I believe you're very sharp and wouldn't ordinarily be fooled by anyone, but I don't know anything about this Maya Fallon. And I don't like the idea of risking my friend with a stranger who seems damn questionable. You want advice, here it is. We're going to call Joe and tell him to check with his contacts at Interpol about what the hell is happening at Palandan. Then we'll look the situation over and decide what's best to do."

Riley smiled. "Which I could have bet would be your advice. It's practical and caring and very much Eve." She shook her head. "But I promised Maya when she called me that I'd keep everything regarding Palandan confidential. I'll have to tell her that I discussed it with you—though I don't think she'll mind, since she congratulated me on getting your expert help to do the forensic sculpture on Helen. But she'd definitely consider bringing in Interpol as a breach of trust."

Eve was scowling. "You do realize I'll have to discuss this with Joe anyway?"

She nodded. "But you'll make certain that he knows the rules."

"He's not going to like it."

"Yep, but he'll go along with it if you ask him." She dropped to her knees before where Eve was sitting on the porch swing. "Hey, stop frowning. You did exactly what I wanted and I'm grateful. I was confused and you straightened me out. I admit when I got that call from Maya, it threw me for a loop. You listened to me talk and you asked questions and you made me remember Maya and that night five years ago. Now I only have to make a decision. I'm just sorry if I'm not able to take your advice. I'm not sure I was clear enough about everything I experienced there. Palandan is one of those places that you can't describe, you have to *be* there."

"Oh, you've done a fairly good job of bringing it up close and personal for me," Eve said. "Maybe a little too personal. Since the gladiator fights were popular entertainment that went on for about a thousand years, I'd say it took me back to about the first century B.C. I gather you haven't told Cade about Maya's phone call yet."

She shook her head. "He's been busy saving the world. He's got a lot of other things to worry about. Besides, there may not be anything to tell him." She held up her hand as Eve started to speak. "But naturally, I'll let him know if it becomes necessary. That's only fair."

"When your welfare and safety are on the line, I suspect Cade feels he should always be in the loop. He'd insist on it. Right?"

Riley nodded. "Yes, he can be a bit assertive. But then so can I." She stood up, then reached down for Eve's hand and pulled her to her feet. "You promised me dessert. Could we go inside and have it now?"

Eve thought about it. "I imagine I can let you escape for the time being. I have to call Joe and Michael and tell them good night anyway. Are you going to call Cade?"

Riley shook her head. "I called him when I first got here to tell him I'd arrived. He said to give you his regards."

"And you'd prefer not to have to let him know that I'm not enthralled with the way you're handling this?"

"As I said, no use disturbing him if there's no good reason," Riley repeated.

Eve shrugged. "Then we'll have dessert and casual conversation that has nothing to do with Maya Fallon. After that we'll go to bed and get a good night's sleep." She added, "But I'm not giving up. Tomorrow morning we'll have breakfast and then go out on the boat, and we'll have another talk. Okay?"

Riley chuckled. "What a fantastic strategist. You'll have me trapped, surrounded by water." She added gently, "Of course it's okay. You deserve your turn. But no Interpol."

Eve nodded. "I'm sure we can find alternatives that will please us both." She headed for the front door. "In my work as a forensic sculptor, I usually have to make compromises. I may really have to concentrate on this one..."

———

"Here we go again." Joe swore long and vehemently beneath his breath as he tried to mentally put the scenario together. "I didn't need to hear this when I'm up here in the Highlands thousands of miles away. Should I come home?"

"No, I promised her I wouldn't let you investigate this Nadim she's having difficulties with. I knew that would be your reaction."

"I may do it anyway. I don't want you involved in this."

"Neither does Riley. She couldn't stop saying how much she didn't want that to happen. I believe she honestly only wanted someone to talk to." She tried to make her tone soothing. "And she wasn't certain that anyone else would understand. We became pretty close when we were working on Helen. I can definitely understand. Until that time the only one she could confide in was her father. After he died, all she had left was her passion for Helen and her desire to complete his mission. At the time I had a mission of my own, and we managed to combine the two."

"And almost got killed," he said grimly. "That can't happen again."

"She tells me that it won't. I'll make my pitch tomorrow, and I think she'll be gone either tomorrow evening or the next day."

"Unless she talks you into hopping on a plane with her. I could tell you were intrigued while you were telling me about it." He sighed. "And who could blame you? Your reviews on the work you did on Helen of Troy were out of sight. The idea of searching for the tomb of an Amazon gladiator? The woman herself would be unique enough to draw you toward the job. It's just your cup of tea, dammit."

"Perhaps if I didn't have work to do here. You know I had a reason for going after Helen. It wasn't a whim."

"I'm not saying it was. I'm telling you I'll be glad when Riley gets on a plane and either heads for this island or goes back to Cade."

"I won't. Riley always has reason if she's on edge about any-thing. I don't like not knowing what she's going into."

Joe was silent. "And neither do I," he said reluctantly. "After I get off this call, I'll give Hodlow with Interpol a call and see what I can find out about this Nadim."

"I told Riley you wouldn't do that."

"And tied my hands," he growled. "Don't worry, I won't tell him why I'm checking. Okay?"

"Absolutely okay," Eve said softly. "Now let's forget about Maya and her problem that might become Riley's problem. Tell me about Michael's soccer game. Was he great tonight?"

CHAPTER

3

Y ou really meant it." Riley chuckled as she watched Eve
row the boat across the lake toward the white and blue-
trimmed boathouse. "You fed me breakfast and now you're
heading for that structure that's probably your version of
Guantanamo."

"Not really," Eve said. "It's our boathouse. Last night Joe
told me that Michael is definitely going to try out for the rowing team, and he wants you to bring a couple pieces of exercise equipment when you come back to London. Would you
mind?"

"Not in the least." She leaned back in the boat. "You might
as well let me row. I need the exercise." She took a deep breath.
"But this is okay, too. I love the scent of pines. The fragrance
almost makes me dizzy. It reminds me of the trees that grow on
the mountains that adjoin Palandan Island. There aren't many

pines on the island itself. The trees there are mostly tropical."
She corrected herself. "Except for the black diamond apples.
But they're only available two months a year and are hideously
expensive."

"Black diamond?" Eve shook her head dismissively. "I assure
you I had no intention of reminding you of anything about
that island at the moment. It's too much on your mind as it is.
I'd rather tell you about how much fun Joe and Michael have
here on this boat. They spend most of the summer mornings
at the boathouse sitting on the deck and fishing." After tying
off the rowboat at the pier, she jumped out of the boat. "I'll be
right back as soon as I get the equipment. Then I'll open our
carafe of coffee and we'll sit on the deck in the sunlight and
talk." She grinned as she looked back over her shoulder. "I
might even let you tell me about those black diamond apples."

But Riley knew that Eve hadn't given up and that probably
wouldn't be the main subject of conversation. "I'll come and
help you." She climbed out of the boat and onto the deck. She
slipped on the wet boards and almost fell but caught herself.

Pfft. Something whistled behind her.

Pain.

Her shoulder . . . stinging.

Had she rammed it against the side of the boathouse?

Pfft. Pfft.

No, it was her head that she'd rammed. She was dizzy and
everything was spinning.

And Eve was looking at her in horror . . .

"I'm fine," Riley said. "Must have rammed it when—"

"The hell you did. You're bleeding." Eve tackled Riley and brought her down on the deck. "That was a gunshot. Hang on..." She rolled with her into the water of the lake.

They both came up gasping, and Riley instinctively pushed Eve closer to the deck.

Pfft.

Another shot, also muffled by a silencer.

Striking the water only a foot from Riley's head!

"This way," Eve shouted. She pulled Riley lower in the water. "Underneath!"

Both women ducked under and emerged on the dock's underside, giving them just enough room to breathe.

RAT-AT-AT-AT-AT!

More shots rang out, splintering the wood planks above them.

"Those bullets came from another direction," Eve said. "No silencer."

BLAM! BLAM!

Chunks of decking rained down on them.

"Those shots came from the other side of the lake," Eve said. "I count at least three shooters out there."

"What the hell is happening?" Riley dropped lower into the water as more shots tore into the dock. "We can't stay here."

"I won't argue with that." Eve pointed toward the shore. "There's another boathouse where this dock meets the land. If we can get there, we might be able to force open a trapdoor that will take us inside." She became aware of a roar behind her. She turned and saw a speedboat skipping over the waves.

It was headed their way.

"*Shit*," she said through clenched teeth.

"Wait. It might be okay." Riley pointed toward the boat. Two men took positions on each side, holding automatic rifles aimed at the shore. They fired their guns as the speedboat pulled alongside the deck.

A gray-haired man bent toward them from the wheel where he was standing. "Riley Smith?" he shouted.

The boat's pair of gunmen were still firing more rounds at the shooters on the shore, and she didn't know what to answer. "Yes," she finally said. "Who the hell are you?"

"I'm Pete Loring. Jon Kirby sent me." He held out his hand. "Get on the boat while my men are keeping those assholes busy."

"Get Eve on board," Riley shouted. "I'll be right behind you."

He hesitated. "My report said it was you who was shot." As another bullet splintered the wood next to him, he quickly reached for Eve. "Whatever." He effortlessly pulled Eve out of the water and onto the speedboat. "Let's just get out of here." Then as he dragged Riley aboard, he saw the blood pouring from her wound. "Damn!"

The boat's side mirror exploded from another barrage of gunfire.

"Shit! Keep down!" Loring hit the throttle, and the

speedboat hurtled forward. They tore across the lake toward the eastern shore.

Riley crawled over to where Eve was lying. "Okay? This has to be my fault...Sorry."

"You're the one who got shot," Eve said gruffly. "Stop apologizing. Evidently Cade must have sent the cavalry for you, and I don't mind tagging along. But I need to be somewhere I can look at that wound."

Riley glanced down at her arm. "It's probably all right. I don't think it's bleeding any longer. But I don't know what the hell is happening."

"Neither do I. We'll find out later," Eve said. "I think we're safe now. That's all that's important." But she was turning and tugging at Loring's shirt. "Go somewhere I can patch up Riley right away. Do you hear me?"

"I'm working on it," Loring said curtly. "I've already called an ambulance. As it is, I'm going to catch hell from Kirby for letting her get hurt. That wasn't supposed to happen."

"Tell me about it," Eve said sarcastically. "This is my home. She was my guest. I feel...invaded. And if you don't get her medical attention right away, I'm going to show you how angry I am."

He gave a low whistle. "Yes, ma'am. No problem. I'll take care of it."

Riley almost felt sorry for Loring. Eve could be intimidating, and she was clearly in fine form right now. But Loring would have to take care of himself. Riley was soaking wet, her arm was throbbing, and she was becoming dizzier by the minute. The only thing she was certain about was that she was very, very tired...

———

"It's about time," Eve said when she saw Riley's eyes opening. "You scared me when you passed out. Don't you dare do it again."

"Passed out? I'm fine." She frowned as she looked around and realized she was being transported in an ambulance of some sort. "I was just tired and wanted to close my eyes for a minute."

"Well, that minute stretched into twenty while the EMTs stabilized you and started the IV." She glanced down at the needle in Riley's arm. "They finally decided the reason you were unconscious was a combination of shock from the cold water, blood loss, and possible concussion. Anyway, we're on our way to the hospital ER now. We should be there any minute." She made a face. "Though Loring was probably in worse shape than you were. He panicked and called Kirby."

Riley tensed as she realized what that meant. "Shit! Now *I'm* panicking. Cade. I didn't want to face this right now. What the hell am I supposed to say?"

"Good question," Eve said as she took Riley's hand. "One I don't have an answer for. The little I could get from Loring was that he heads a security unit hired by Kirby to watch over you while you were at my Lake Cottage. They were being cautious about a possible kidnap-to-ransom attempt. He was told there was no definitive threat, just a routine bodyguard detail." Her lips tightened. "But there wasn't anything routine about this attack, so he's gone back to ask Kirby why he steered him wrong. If they were trying to kidnap you, it would have been stupid to shoot you. It wouldn't make sense."

"According to Cade, sometimes kidnappers don't make sense. They're into terror. It could be they wanted to show Cade he was vulnerable. Maybe this time they came too close, and a bullet actually struck me."

"And did they terrorize you?"

"No," Riley said. "I'm mad as hell. I want to go after them. Those damn slimeballs. It just reminded me that Cade has had to go through this kind of thing all his life. Which made me even angrier for his sake."

"Well, spare a little fire and brimstone on behalf of yourself," Eve said. "Loring said there were two snipers out there and his guys managed to take out one of them. Maybe they'll be able to track the other one down. Or perhaps you'll get a little help to—" The phone Loring had lent her to replace their own doused ones was ringing and she checked the ID. "Cade. Let me handle him." She pressed ANSWER and spoke quickly, "Hello, Cade. First, you should know that Riley probably isn't in as bad a shape as you fear. Right now it looks like she has a slight flesh wound and might have a minor concussion. She's mad and confused and a little out of it. I'm here with her and we're on our way to the ER, but I'm not going to let you talk to her until she gets checked out. You might call Loring, who probably knows more than either of us about what happened, so you'll have something to tell her when she's ready to talk to you. She needs answers."

"She'll get them," Cade said grimly. "Right now I don't know what the hell is happening, but I'm heading for the airport. By the time I get to her, I'll know what kind of screwup happened out at your place. Can she hear me?"

"Yes," Eve said. "She's right here."

"Listen, Riley," Cade said. "You're safe. No one is going to touch you. We'll figure this out and I'll make it right. I promise you."

Riley reached out and snatched the phone from Eve. "For pity's sake, Cade, it's not as if this is your fault. There are assholes out there. Stop being such a damn martyr. We'll fix it together."

Cade was silent for an instant. "Eve must be right, you're not nearly as bad off as I was afraid you'd be." He added hoarsely, "Now rest and don't worry and do what those doctors tell you. I'm on my way. I'll see you soon." He cut the connection.

———

RILEY'S HOSPITAL ROOM
SHARPSTOWN HOSPITAL
NEXT DAY

The minute Cade got off the elevator Eve could see the sparks flying. It was no surprise considering his military background and the fact that he'd spent the last dozen years going after both human and animal traffickers around the world. Yet the emotional intensity enveloping him was almost tangible. Eve instinctively jumped up from the hall bench as he approached. "Riley's napping. She didn't sleep last night, and the nurse gave her something to relax her."

"I know. I talked to the doctor in his office before I came up." He stopped in front of her. "Stop looking so defensive. I'm not going to go in and wake her. I just want to be here when she opens her eyes. I couldn't just sit down there with that doctor. He was being too damn soothing and superior."

"He *is* superior," Eve said mildly. "And you know it. You're the one who got Loring to hire a specialist to take care of her last night."

"It wasn't that I didn't trust you. I had to be sure," Cade said. "I wasn't here with her."

"I'm not complaining. Though Riley did quite a bit herself. She doesn't like hospitals."

"I had to be sure," he repeated. Then he spat out, "I was a fucking five thousand six hundred and sixty-five miles away from her and I felt helpless."

"You knew the precise distance?"

"You bet I did. I was aware of every single mile while I was flying that Gulfstream."

"And probably bitterly resentful and pissed off that I was here, and you weren't."

"No, do you think I'm an idiot? I was really grateful to you, Eve." He smiled crookedly. "And maybe a *little* pissed off. I'm not always reasonable, as you know."

"You're used to getting what you want. But you usually handle it well."

"Not when it concerns Riley."

"I've noticed that exception to the rule," she said. "I've been grateful for it. All that power can be intimidating. Since she's my friend, I need something to keep you in line." She smiled. "But there are times all your money and influence come in handy. I'm sure you weren't just sitting in that cockpit counting those miles. What did Loring learn that you found interesting?"

"That they weren't able to keep that wounded sniper alive for questioning, but they're checking DNA. We should be getting a report on him soon."

"But at first Loring thought that it might be a kidnapping plot for ransom. It's what you think, too?"

"Not necessarily. Too many loose ends," Cade said. "I never jump to conclusions. On the way over here I called practically everyone I know to probe for information." His lips thinned. "I wanted to make certain that when I go hunting, I blow the right son of a bitch to kingdom come."

"Good heavens, yes, you wouldn't want to make a mistake." Her tone was faintly mocking. "It might hurt your reputation."

"I could survive it." His gaze searched her face. "You look tired. You went through this hell with her, and I haven't even thanked you. I know you did the best you could for her."

"Why should you thank me? I didn't do it for you. I know everyone, including Riley, thinks the sun rises and sets on you. But Riley is my friend, and I was scared to death when this happened to her. You never realize how much you care about a person until you almost lose them."

"No, you don't," he said hoarsely. "Point taken. But you've been under a lot of stress. Will you go home and get some rest and trust me to take care of Riley? I promise I won't leave her."

"That goes without saying." Eve hesitated. Then she shrugged. "I suppose I could use a little rest. When she wakes, ask her to give me a call?"

He nodded. "Whatever you say." He headed for the door of Riley's room. "And if I hear anything more, I'll let you know." He stopped and looked back over his shoulder. "You've been terrific. I really am grateful, Eve."

She gave him a faint smile. "I know you are. And you're not too bad, either. I even told Riley that you're unique enough to keep around."

He started to open the door. "Gee, thanks."

She had a sudden thought. "You said you phoned practically everyone you knew for information. Who did you call?"

"Loring, Kirby, Interpol, Scotland Yard, John MacDuff, CIA, FBI, Atlanta PD." He met her eyes. "Besides Detective Joe Quinn. Should I go on?"

Eve drew a deep breath. "No, that's quite enough. I'll talk to you later, Cade."

He nodded. "I'm sure you will."

The door closed behind him.

———————

Cade dropped down in the chair beside Riley's bed and just leaned back and looked at her. She was still deeply asleep, and she was paler than usual. He was used to her being tanned, glowing, and full of laughter and vitality. He knew she was going to be fine, but that fragility still scared the shit out of him.

Ignore it.

But he couldn't do it. The pain and fear were too fresh.

He reached out and took her hand. He lifted it and pressed his lips to the palm. Her hand felt small and fragile, too.

"Hey, this isn't going to work," he whispered. "Do you hear me? I can't take it. It can never happen again, Riley…"

———————

Cade was there.

She could *feel* him, Riley thought dazedly. She could always feel him when he was close to her these days. It was as if he was a part of her. The scent, the warmth, the magnetism. But she wanted to *see* him.

After a struggle, she managed to open her eyes. There he was, but he looked too grim. "Hi," she said huskily, then tried to clear her throat. "I'm sorry I broke up your meeting with the Arabs. It really wasn't my fault."

"Not funny." His hand tightened on hers. "And I'm not entirely sure about the truth of that, either. But we'll explore it later. How do you feel?"

"Still a little sleepy. I told them I didn't want a sedative. I was fine. It was natural that I hadn't slept well. I was a little on edge. You would have been, too."

"Who, me?" He shook his head. "This would have been just a walk in the park. Though I admit that I felt it my duty to look into the logistics of what happened. Once that was taken care of, I just settled back and relaxed."

"Liar." She grimaced. "I can feel your tension. You don't take downtime until you wrap up a problem completely. Since I imagine you were on a plane, and Eve told me that one of the snipers was dead and the other one had escaped, you wouldn't have been able to do much of anything. Frustrating?"

"Extremely. But you should have more faith in me. There are always ways to get around difficulties if you're motivated." He smiled. "And believe me, I'm motivated."

She could see it in his expression. The knife-hard edge was more clearly defined than she'd ever seen it. "I don't remember much of it, but Eve said that Loring's team seemed very efficient and did their job. You shouldn't blame them."

"I've had similar reports, and he's off the hook as far as I'm concerned." He paused. "Except that he should have known those snipers were on the property sooner."

"I'm just glad he and his men were there to save the day when they did." Riley ruefully shook her head. "I realize I've given you a hard time about all the security you've been throwing at me lately. I can't promise that it will stop entirely. But I'll chalk this episode up as a lesson learned."

"That's valuable in itself, but it might not be enough." His smile suddenly held a hint of recklessness. "I've learned a few lessons myself from this experience. I've decided that I won't be able to risk losing you again. I might have to take steps."

"Steps," she repeated warily. "I don't like the sound of that, Cade."

"Neither do I. So we'd better make adjustments to mitigate the results." He suddenly leaned forward, and his smile lit his face with warmth. "It's going to be okay, Riley. I'm not going to do anything you wouldn't like. I just have to be certain that we don't go through this again. I promise I'll get it all to work."

She frowned. "Get what to work? Stop patting me on the head, Cade. You're confusing me. I'm not sure what you mean, but it sounds like a project for both of us."

"And it will be, I swear. We'll discuss it later. In the meantime, why don't we get you out of here? Eve was telling me that you couldn't wait to get out of this hospital."

That brought her wide awake. "*Yes.*" She sat up in bed and was suddenly grinning. "Why am I worrying about your

Arabs? Or all that weird 'steps' business? Eve said it was probably your fault that the specialist you brought in wouldn't let her take me back to the Lake Cottage. I really feel entirely fine, Cade."

"You don't look entirely fine. But you're on your way." He bent over and gave her a quick, hard kiss. "I'll go get the nurse to help you dress. I need to make a few calls and then I'll whisk you out of here."

"For Pete's sake, I don't need help dressing, Cade."

"It will be quicker." He smiled. "Just being obliging." He left the room.

No, he was being Cade at his most controlling, she thought as she saw the nurse coming into her room a couple of minutes later. Just accept it now and deal with it after she was out of the hospital, and he had no reason to be this upset. They just needed to talk this out.

It wasn't until she saw Pete Loring drive up in the hospital driveway in a Mercedes limousine that she began to have serious doubts again.

"Hi, it's good to see you looking so well." Loring had instantly exited the car and was now helping her out of the wheelchair into the backseat. "For a little while I was worried. The last thing I wanted was to get on Cade's bad side." He grimaced. "I've heard it can be fatal."

"Only if you deserve it. What are you doing here, Loring?"

"Obeying orders. I'm supposed to drive the two of you to Eve Duncan's Lake Cottage. Then my guys will make certain nothing happens to you until Cade gets you on that plane heading back to London. Okay?"

"Yes, okay?" Cade asked as he slid into the seat next to her and motioned for Loring to start the car. "The cottage is just a short drive. We have a few things to do and discuss, and I thought you'd like to see Eve before you left Atlanta. Was I wrong?"

"No, of course not." She was frowning. "But I would have liked to have set up any visit myself. We've been through a hell of a lot and I'm very grateful to her."

"So am I," he said quietly. "But you'll forgive me if I'm eager to express my gratitude in the quickest and safest way possible. You scared the hell out of me."

"And I'm sorry, but it's not as if I did anything to cause it."

"No. But I'd like to do a little more investigating about the circumstances so that it won't happen again. That's fair, isn't it?"

She nodded. "Circumstances? What circumstances? All we did was go to the boathouse."

"Like I said, a little more investigation. I had Loring send me a few photos while I was on the plane." As they got off the freeway on the exit for the Lake Cottage, he added, "The cottage is a few miles down the road. But Loring said the boathouse is the first turn. Let's take a look at it first."

"Whatever. I don't know why we should—"

And then she saw the boathouse. No longer the neatly painted white and blue-trimmed little building. It was burnt and blackened, the windows broken, the deck left with huge gaping holes.

"What happened?" she whispered.

"Loring said that they weren't only firing bullets," Cade said. "When they thought they'd missed both of you, they shot a couple rockets at the boathouse. Loring was lucky to have managed to get you out of the water and away from the deck before the rockets hit."

"I didn't know." Riley felt sick. "All that damage..."

"You were pretty well out of it when I got you out of the lake," Loring said from the driver's seat. "And we just wanted to get you to the hospital. It was clear the bastards were aiming at you."

"But Eve didn't tell me." She was looking back at the ruined boathouse. "Not a word. Why didn't she tell me?"

"You know why," Cade said.

Yes, Riley knew why. They were now pulling up in front of the cottage. She threw open the rear door and was running up the stairs to the sunporch where Eve was waiting. She ran into her arms and gave her a tremendous hug. "You didn't tell me about what they did to the boathouse," she said hoarsely. "It's ugly now. It was so neat and pretty and you had so many memories of Michael and Joe and—"

"Hush," Eve said. "It's only a place. The memories will never go away. We'll make new ones when we rebuild it." She looked over Riley's shoulder at Cade. "Did you have to show it to her?"

He nodded. "I thought it best. There were reasons." He smiled. "One of them was to show her what a good friend you are. But that wasn't all. About an hour after you left me with Riley, I got the ID and report on the sniper who was killed doing the shooting here."

"And?"

"Kamil Zukov. Not a member of any of the local criminal gangs operating out of this state or anywhere else in the U.S.," Cade said. "Born in Moscow but worked in Central Africa when he first started his ugly career. Later he ran with a gang of poachers and artifact thieves who operated out of India and Tibet." His face tensed. "Zukov was very dirty and sometimes worked with another sniper named Paul Lagman. Lately they've both been in India taking orders from a poacher who's been killing animals to sell their body parts for medical research."

Riley tensed, and she suddenly couldn't breathe. "Who?" She took a step toward Cade, her gaze on his face. "What was his name?"

"Does it matter?" Cade nodded slowly, his eyes narrowing. "Yes, I believe it does." He enunciated very precisely. "Aden Nadim."

"Shit." She moistened her lips. "Yes, it matters."

"I thought it might." His lips twisted. "Though I hoped you hadn't left me in the dark to that extent. But it seems you did."

Her eyes widened as she looked at him. "You thought it—" She broke off. "You knew about Nadim?"

"I didn't have a name until I received it from Interpol," he said curtly. "But I knew enough to suspect that the attack here had nothing to do with kidnappers or ransom and everything to do with the fact that your loyalty to Maya Fallon could be a danger in itself. I just had to have it confirmed."

"Why didn't you tell me?" She shook her head in bewilderment. "It seems you weren't the only one in the dark."

"I'm telling you now," Cade said. "And I judged it wouldn't have been the best time to have this discussion the minute you woke in the hospital. The last thing I wanted was for you to feel as if I was attacking you, too. I brought you to Eve where you'd feel you had support."

"How did you find out that—"

"Joe," Eve interrupted. "It had to be Joe who told him everything you'd told me. It's not as if Cade was trying to deceive me. I asked him who he'd questioned when he was on the hunt for answers, and one of the names he gave me was Joe's. We both knew what that meant." She glanced at Cade. "And the minute he said it, I knew that he'd probably gotten anything he wanted to know from Joe. Joe wouldn't see why he shouldn't tell Cade anything he asked when you'd been attacked and he was desperate for answers. He would have felt obligated to help him."

"And I would have felt the same if the positions had been reversed," Cade said. "The minute there was a danger to Riley, there was no way I was going to be shut out." He looked Riley in the eye and repeated, "No way."

"You sound as if you're accusing me," Riley said. "We didn't know that attack was ordered by Nadim. Even Loring thought it was probably a threat from one of your enemies, or a ransom attempt. I hadn't even agreed to help Maya. I had no idea what she was actually asking me to do or what was involved."

"But you were intrigued enough to try to find out," Eve said flatly. "Duty or curiosity, it was drawing you."

"Yes, it was," Riley said. "Though it wasn't a done deal. But I owed Maya help if I could give it, and that meant at least listening to her proposition. That was what I was going to tell you yesterday when they blew up the boathouse." She felt the anger returning as she remembered the sight of that wreckage. "Bastard. Nadim evidently didn't want Maya to get help from anyone. How the hell did they know she'd even contacted me?"

"We need to know the answer to that question," Cade said. "As well as a multitude of others. Your friend Maya Fallon has been a little too vague for my liking. She makes a call and reminds you of how grateful you should be to her and says she needs you, but no details. That's not the way I operate. We're going to know every player and every liability facing us."

"Facing me," she corrected. "I don't want you involved, Cade."

"Obviously," he said. "But I'm already involved. They tried to take something of the utmost value from me. I don't permit that. I also need to remove Zukov's partner from the planet in the most painful way possible." He held up his hand as she started to speak. "We'll discuss the rest after we clarify the final stakes with Maya Fallon." He glanced at Eve. "Could we use your home as a temporary safe house for the next day or two? I think Riley would prefer to be with you until things are more settled. I promise there won't be any more damage. I've already arranged to have Loring's men guard the property."

Eve gave him a speculative glance. "You appear to have everything under control." She paused. "How under control? Why do you need a safe house? Why not return to London?"

He smiled. "Because as I've said, we need a meeting of minds, and I don't want any of those minds scattered over the hemispheres. This is as good a place as any for us to gather. I've already arranged to bring the most important person of our group here. I just had to get your permission."

"The most important person," Riley repeated. "What are you up to, Cade?" Then she snapped her fingers. "Maya? Of course you'd want Maya front and center. But did Joe tell you how important Maya is to those villagers? She won't come when you whistle."

"I'd never be that rude," Cade said. "I just called her from my Gulfstream after I talked to Joe. I asked her if she'd come and visit you since you were wounded and in the hospital. She appeared not to know anything about it and was quite upset. She said she'd try to make arrangements."

"Guilt trip?" Riley asked.

"I didn't really care at the time. I'm still a bit suspicious. I care even less now. We need answers." He added grimly, "And before she leaves here, we'll have them."

"This is *my* business, Cade," Riley said. "And if I'm considered a target, what kind of bounty would Nadim put on Maya? She pulled some strings and got him exiled to India after he attacked our camp on the island."

"I'll keep her safe," Cade said. "And I'll get her back to her island. But not until we get those answers. She's already cost you too much already." He held her gaze. "Payback is all very well, but you realize in this case I'm making sense."

She didn't want to admit it. But how could she deny it when she'd intended to get the answers herself before committing? She slowly nodded. "But Maya has to be safe." She turned to Eve. "Unless you have an objection. You've already had those assholes destroy part of your home. Maya might be an even greater temptation for Nadim."

"I'll trust Cade," Eve said. "I'm very pissed off about my boathouse, and even more so about what they did to you. I want to see them hurt." She shrugged. "And I want answers, too." She turned and headed for the front door. "But right now I have to call Joe and keep him from leaving Michael and getting on the first flight home. I was going to call him when I first got here, but then I decided that I'd wait until I could talk to you and Riley. Michael needs Joe right now, and you'd better make certain that we don't, Cade."

"First priority," Cade said lightly. "And I'll call him myself

78

after you hang up. Not that he won't respect your input much more than mine. But it will give him someone to blame when he can't do what he wants to do."

"There's never blame where we're concerned," Eve said. "When every moment is precious, you learn never to waste one of them."

Cade turned to Riley when Eve disappeared into the house. "Very healthy philosophy. I wonder how long it took to reach that particular state of nirvana. We don't seem to have climbed the first rung of the ladder yet. Did I detect an edge of resentment just now?"

"Perhaps. You have a habit of taking over, and I find that upsetting. Dammit, you lead a fuller and more complex life than anyone I've ever met, and I never question your choices. No matter where you go, what you do." She added, "I accept them, and I expect the same of you. Maybe it would have been more polite to share that phone call I received from Maya, but you were too busy, and I didn't see why I shouldn't handle it the way I've handled everything else in my life."

"Very practical. Ordinarily I could see your viewpoint perfectly. Particularly since I'm familiar with the nomad existence you led with your father, who let you almost raise yourself as you traveled all over the world. But I find I'm having difficulty with the concept after I saw you in the hospital today. I think perhaps we might have to change it. Suppose we talk about it and explore as we go along."

She frowned. "If you like. But it sounds a little cold-blooded."

He chuckled. "That will never be one of our problems. The words I was having trouble with were 'polite' and 'too busy.'"

"But it was true."

"Was it?"

She made a dismissive gesture. "What we have to be concerned with is when Maya is going to get here. Did she give you any idea?"

"I didn't leave the departure time entirely up to her. I sent Kirby to fly down to Palandan Island and pick her up. I thought it safer to slip her discreetly away from there if we can manage it. I did promise you that. He should arrive at the island in another hour and thirty minutes. He'll let us know when they have an ETA here."

"Or when Maya decides to come," she said dryly. "I told you that she writes her own rules."

"You did. Which both intrigues and disturbs me. I can't wait to see what Kirby has to report about her." He turned and headed for the stairs. "But rules can be adjusted. I'd better get busy and see what I can do to make this entire area welcoming and safe for her. I'll see you later, Riley."

PALANDAN ISLAND

"We have to get out of here, Ms. Fallon," Kirby said impatiently as he strode into Maya's office, where the blasted woman was on another phone call. "I have my orders, and Cade isn't the most patient man even when he's not dealing with a bastard like Nadim. I'll give you another ten minutes."

"You don't understand," Maya said coolly. "I don't obey your orders. You'll give me as long as I need to get my people safely away." She ended the call she was on and turned to Tashi. "I've given the guards and the workers in the groves their orders. I want you to leave the main house and go deep into the island. I've already said goodbye to Bailey. Take her to the mountain and keep her there until I get back. If there's any sign of Nadim, send her to the temple under guard."

"You've told me that before," Tashi said. "Do you think I'm deaf or just a fool?"

"Neither." Maya wearily shook her head. "Perhaps I'm afraid *I'm* the fool for being drawn away from here. It may be for nothing."

"It won't be," Tashi said. "You will speak, and he will listen. Riley would not have chosen anyone so stupid as to ignore you. And I don't like you worrying about such nonsense."

"Then of course I won't." She smiled faintly. "Since I'm sure you will handle everything splendidly. I will call you when I reach Atlanta. Goodbye, my friend."

"Farewell." Tashi inclined her head. "All will go well, and I promise nothing will happen to the child." She swept out of the room.

Maya turned immediately to Kirby. "And now we'll leave. I've done what I can here. It might be enough since I was able to find you a safe landing field away from the coast." She got to her feet. "Get me out of here quickly, Kirby. I don't want Nadim to know I'm gone. I've arranged a diversion if he finds out, but I don't want to use it."

"Then you should have put on a little more speed," he said flatly. "You've kept me waiting over two hours."

"It was the best I could manage. You can't imagine how complicated it was to coordinate. But you will, because it's a long flight and I'll explain it to you. In return, I'd appreciate it if you tell me what I need to know about Cade so I make no mistakes with him. I think underneath that gruffness you must be an intelligent man or Cade wouldn't have sent you. Therefore, it's important we learn to know and cooperate with each other."

"It's only important that I get you safely to Atlanta. You can be assured I'll do that."

She shook her head. "You'll change your mind. I think it's necessary we be good friends." As she headed for the door, she glanced over her shoulder and her face lit with possibly the most beautiful and charismatic smile Kirby had ever seen. "Now, don't you think you should stop complaining and do what you came here to do?"

CHAPTER
4

Riley and Cade were having coffee on the sunporch the next day when he received a call from Kirby. "We're approaching Nassau and I have to stop for fuel," Kirby told him. "After takeoff I'm estimating arrival in Atlanta in about two hours. Will it be safe for Maya?"

"No problem. Loring's crew are proving very efficient. I'm trusting Riley and Eve Duncan with them."

"Well, you won't have to include Maya in any calculations for long," Kirby said flatly. "She's already told me she can't waste more than twenty-four hours checking on Riley before she starts back for her island."

"I'm sorry she regards it as a waste of her time," Cade said caustically. "Particularly since Riley would never have been injured if Maya Fallon hadn't contacted her. Too bad. I won't let you take her back until we're finished with her."

"I'm not sure that will make much difference," Kirby said quietly. "Though it may delay her a little. She'll find a way to do what she wants to do." He paused. "And I could tell she realized she put Riley at risk or she would never have left Palandan Island. It was a big deal to her and those people on the island when she decided she had to come."

"Really?" Cade said. "That wasn't the impression you gave me when you called me before you left the island. You were more than a little annoyed with her."

"I wasn't getting my way," he said. "And Maya was acting like a general commanding her troops when I wanted to get out of there." He suddenly chuckled. "And I didn't like being ignored. No one gave a damn what I said as long as Maya was busy issuing orders to everyone on the island. But she was much easier to deal with when she changed her persona from Mr. Hyde to Dr. Jekyll when we boarded the plane. She told me that it would be better if we were good friends, then set out to prove it to me."

"And did she do it?"

He didn't answer for an instant. "Yeah, I think she did. She's exceptionally complicated. I found her to be sharp, able to make decisions in a heartbeat, able to handle those villagers faultlessly. Yet she changed in the blink of an eye when she decided that we had to become buddies. She was amusing, inquisitive, and totally charismatic. By the time we were halfway here, she had me."

"You?" Cade echoed skeptically. "That's hard to believe."

"Why? I may be a cynic, but I recognize honesty when I see it. She's . . . genuine. I couldn't help but like her."

"Riley agrees with you," Cade said mockingly as he met Riley's gaze across the porch. "But you'll pardon me if I judge for myself. I don't like the fact that Maya obviously wanted to use her."

"If she did, she wouldn't have tried to trick her into it. Everything would have been clean and aboveboard." Kirby chuckled again. "But while you're being suspicious, you might as well include yourself in the equation. I told you that Maya was inquisitive. Quite a few of her questions were about you."

"And you obliged her?"

"I didn't see why not. The questions were bold and principally aimed at getting to know how you think and react. I decided that we all need a little help analyzing you now and then. It will be interesting seeing if she manages to manipulate you."

"Are you taking bets?"

"I'm thinking about it," Kirby said. "I'll make up my mind before I get to Atlanta. I'll switch to a helicopter once I land at the airport and I'll see you at that Lake Cottage in a few hours, Cade." He cut the connection.

Cade turned to Riley. "You heard him. Another few hours."

She nodded. "And he was right about Maya. If she was trying to use me, she'd make sure to do it in a way that wouldn't hurt me."

"She's already hurt you," Cade said curtly. "And I'll tell her that when she gets here."

She shook her head. "She saved both my father's and my life. She's come halfway around the world to see me, and I don't want you to do that. You'll be charming and courteous, and we'll listen to what she says . . . and maybe try to help her."

He didn't speak for a moment. "We'll listen to her."

She made a face. "You're impossible. It's not like you to be so hardheaded. Even Kirby could see that Maya is exceptional."

"Which only means that she could be more dangerous than I thought. Kirby isn't easily fooled, and a woman that persuasive might be an expert con artist."

"Cade."

"Okay." He suddenly smiled and then was across the porch and taking her in his arms. "I'll try not to be rude to her." He kissed her. "I can't promise I'll be warm and welcoming. I'm still mad as hell that she was the reason you ended up in that hospital." He kissed her again. "And I don't like the fact that we're stuck here waiting for her and constantly surrounded. I'm always trying to forget that I haven't been able to make love to you for nearly a week."

And that had been far too long, she agreed. He felt so hard and good against her. She pressed closer to him. She could feel her body readying. "Your fault," she whispered. "You're the one who's always off saving the world. Want to go for a walk in the woods? We still have a few hours before you have to face being warm and welcoming. I'm beginning to feel very warm and welcoming myself at the moment."

He sighed. "No, I've made sure the sentries know everything that goes on in those woods. I don't want any of them to know you *that* well." His lips brushed the hollow of her throat. "I'll find a place." He pushed her away. "Soon."

Not soon enough for her, she thought. But then the sex had been this intense with them since the very first time. She took a deep breath and moved over to the front door. "Then I'd better go interrupt Eve's work and tell her that Maya is going to be here soon. She might want to discuss it." She winked at him over her shoulder. "And I find I'm suddenly in need of a distraction."

Riley and Cade were waiting at the helicopter pad in the woods when the chopper landed several hours later. Maya jumped out and strode toward them, smiling tentatively at Riley. "I'd like to give you a hug, but I figure since I evidently screwed up, I should restrain myself and all overtures should come from you. You look well, better than I deserve." She turned to Cade. "You must be Cade. You frightened me when you told me she was in the hospital. I think you probably meant to do it because you were angry with me. After I hung up, I called and checked her condition with the hospital. I was relieved that the wounds were minor, and she wasn't lying at death's door."

"But could have been much worse," Cade said coolly. "Yet you still came. Did you have a reason?"

She smiled faintly. "I always have a reason. She was hurt because I wasn't careful enough. That was enough of a reason this time." She looked at Riley. "And I was desperate enough to want to finish what I started with you, even though I'd obviously irritated Cade. But in the past you usually walked your own path, and I thought you still might." She shrugged. "It was worth a shot. Should I get back on the helicopter?"

Riley was gazing at her searchingly. "Desperate. How desperate?"

"I told you, it's the endgame." She added, "But I don't cheat, and you'll all get your share if you help me. I thought long and hard before I decided to call you, Riley." She smiled crookedly. "Though I had a hunch about you even back when we first met. But after you left the island, I watched and waited to see what you were going to do with all that enthusiasm and talent. You were amazing, and it seemed as if you were meant to help me." She glanced at Cade. "Even when you chose the most difficult people, I realized I could work with them."

Cade made a rude sound. "You're not really telling us anything. *Talk* to us."

"She's trying," Riley said as her gaze raked Maya's expression. "And she's the same person I knew five years ago. I think she does feel desperate." She frowned at Maya. "But he's right,

you're not being clear, and Cade always needs everything crystal clear." She took a step forward and embraced her. "There's
no reason to feel desperate. See, I'm making the first move. We
just need to straighten everything out."

"Oh, shit," Cade said.

And Maya started to laugh. "I don't blame you, Cade. She's
just as affectionate and curious and impulsive as she always
was." She returned Riley's embrace. "I promise I'll make
everything crystal clear. But I assume we're on our way for me
to meet Eve Duncan, so shouldn't I wait until you can all hurl
questions at me?"

"Excellent idea," Cade growled as he turned back and called
to Kirby, who was still at the helicopter. "Go find Loring and
get something to eat. I don't know how long we'll be up at the
cottage before this is over."

"Hmm…" Kirby was grinning. "Maybe I should have set
up that bet."

"Nah," Cade said as he started toward the cottage. "Because
in the end, Riley is holding all the cards."

"I wouldn't be too sure," Maya murmured as she fell into
step with Cade. "I don't know the stakes, but you might all
be able to win if we play it right. For instance, we can't omit
sweeping up anyone we even suspect of working with Nadim."

"Is this a teaser?" Cade asked.

"No. I'm trying to hold off until we get to the cottage. But I
will tell you that Nadim isn't the only bad guy in the mix. The
reason he knew I'd contacted Riley was that Charles Bevan

must have bugged my office and sold the info to Nadim. He might have even made a deal with him. But Nadim has been bracing himself to attack the island, and he probably wouldn't have wanted Bevan's interference unless Bevan proved valuable to him. The bug could have been the opening negotiation. As soon as Nadim knew Riley's destination, all he had to do was send a couple of his snipers here in time for her arrival at the Lake Cottage."

"You're certain?" Cade asked.

"Close enough. After you told me about the attack on Riley, I searched my office. I found the bug and got rid of it. The only person who had been in my office anywhere near that time was Bevan." She added, "I wouldn't play ball with him, so he went to Nadim. He also probably knows more than I'd like about the island. We can't trust him."

" 'We'? I have no idea yet if we're going to be involved in your schemes."

"You'll probably be working against Nadim regardless. You won't like the way he operates."

"How do you know?"

"Nadim is involved in a number of ugly criminal activities, but one of his most profitable is poaching. He'd have to know you're famous for hunting down men of his profession and putting them permanently out of business. One of the reasons that he was so upset that I was calling on Riley for help had to be that your relationship with her is all over the media. He wouldn't have wanted you to stick your nose in his business."

"And you're saying it's my fault he went after Riley?"

"No, I'm saying it's entirely my fault, but you should know that Nadim will always be a threat to you now. He failed and he'll hate it. You should be ready for him. Though he doesn't operate anywhere near the places you usually target. Call Kirby and tell him to look him up for you. Try India."

His brows rose. "Are you giving me instructions?"

"I'm trying to keep you alive. I don't think Riley would forgive me if I didn't." They had reached the cottage and Maya was looking up at the staircase. "I'm a little nervous. I've heard a lot about her."

"Do you need her to like you?"

Maya lifted her chin. "I don't need anyone to like me." Then she added, "But I respect her, and it would be nice." She quickened her pace and caught up with Riley. "Will you introduce me, Riley? I saw a photo of the sculpture of Helen she did for you. Wonderful..."

———

"It appears Maya has a crush on our Eve," Cade said to Riley as he watched Maya helping Eve place cups and saucers on a tray at the bar. "At least she's not telling her what to do as she did me."

"Did she really?" She looked at him skeptically. "No one orders you around. You probably misunderstood."

"I believe I got all the nuances," he said dryly. "She's

obviously accustomed to being in charge. But she did make it clear that she didn't think I was at fault for almost getting you killed. She took sole responsibility."

"Because you had nothing to do with it." Her eyes widened. "Neither did she. It was Nadim and those snipers. Of course she wouldn't blame you."

"No?" His lips twisted sardonically. "I found it very logical since it was my first thought when I found out what had happened to you."

She frowned. "Then you're an idiot. You didn't even know why I was going to see Eve."

"But maybe if you'd felt you could tell me, I would have been able to stop it."

"I told you why I didn't tell you."

"I was busy?" He shook his head. "Doesn't hold water."

"Yes, it does." She was genuinely upset. "It's not as if I wasn't going to tell you. We need to talk about this."

"And we will." His gaze was on Eve, who was carrying the tea tray into the living room. "As soon as I finish deciding why I felt that Maya might have been wrong. Right now, we have a few more decisions to make." He was moving across the room and taking the tray from Eve. "Sit down and make yourself comfortable," he told her. "Tea can wait. We've all imposed enough on you. We're here for a purpose and not a social occasion." He turned to Maya. "And you're that purpose, Maya. You've caused us a great deal of trouble, and Riley could have been killed. I believe it's time that you tell us why we shouldn't return the favor."

"You'll have to do what you think best," Maya said quietly. "But I doubt if you'll try to punish me when you realize I'm only offering you a proposition and not trying to harm you." She glanced at Riley. "You felt you had a debt to me, and I used that to get your attention. I had no intention when I helped you of ever doing that." She shrugged. "But times change and so does the world. I'd gotten information that Nadim was closing in on me, and I had to find a way of fighting him."

"You saved us," Riley said. "Of course that got my attention. But I would have tried to help you anyway." She frowned, puzzled. "What proposition?"

"I have to rid Palandan Island of Nadim once and for all. He's much more powerful than he used to be. After I pulled strings to get him tossed out of the area, he moved to India and took up arms dealing as well as poaching. He's got contacts now, and enough money to bribe officials to turn a blind eye if he decided to start raiding the island again." Her lips tightened grimly. "And he will do it, it's only a matter of time. He hates me. He's only been waiting for his chance to go after me."

"Why?"

She didn't speak for a moment. "We had an encounter." She shrugged. "I'd already made him angry by scooping up Riley and her father and getting them off the island. He thought he'd punish me by capturing and holding hostage Dalar, one of my foremen who worked in the orchards. It could have meant a death sentence for Dalar if Nadim had thought it would irritate me. I took several sentries and went after him to Nadim's camp. Nadim has no respect for women and thought it was funny. He offered to play cards for Dalar's life. Then he tried to cheat me. I didn't like that." She smiled. "So I stabbed his hand with my dagger and pinned it to the table. Then I ran like hell while my sentries grabbed Dalar and took off in the opposite direction. Nadim and some of his thugs followed me, but they were slowed down because they had to try to get the knife out of Nadim's hand first." She added reminiscently, "He was screaming quite a bit."

"I can imagine," Cade said. "And I can also see why he might dislike you. You're lucky to be alive."

"I had to free my foreman. They'd already started to torture him. I had a plan. All I had to do was distract Nadim."

Riley was shaking her head. "By using yourself as bait. Cade's right, it's no wonder he's hell-bent to attack the island."

"I admit I'm a featured attraction," Maya said, "but I'm not the sole reason Nadim is ravenous to go after Palandan. You're not the only one who was fascinated by all the legends, Riley. There have been islanders who have moved away, and the legends moved with them. Nadim has heard all the tales of the temple with chests overflowing with gold and jewels, the tomb of Silvana Marcella hidden somewhere in the mountains." She paused and then glanced deliberately at Cade, "And the one about the strange one-horned creatures that may be extinct everywhere else on earth."

Cade stiffened. "Was that last remark aimed at me?"

"It could be," Maya said.

"A one-horned animal, extinct everywhere but Palandan Island?" Cade asked mockingly. "You're reaching, Maya. Are you actually trying to convince me that there might be unicorns strolling around the island?"

"Unicorns? Of course not. Though it is one of the legends, and it's also a reason Nadim might want to raid the island. No one knows better than you how poachers value the body parts of wild animals to sell to clients for medicinal reasons. I've read that you've targeted them in the past."

"Was it interesting reading?" he asked. "Now I wonder why you chose me to study."

"I was looking for anyone who would be against Nadim," she said flatly. "And you were an unexpected bonanza that I found when I decided to ask Riley for help. You have a worldwide reputation for being a warrior like Silvana. Plus the fact that you're a billionaire many times over wouldn't hurt. You've both guessed I intended to use you if I had to. Though I didn't believe I'd be able to do it. Yes, I knew you and Riley were an item, but I realized my chance of getting her to persuade you to help was probably zero. Particularly after my carelessness had almost gotten her killed. However, that wouldn't have stopped me from paying you a visit and asking you to stop that bastard from killing any of the people or animals on the island."

"I would have helped you myself," Riley said soberly. "But I would never have used Cade."

"And I would have used anyone I had to," Maya said. "Because I have to save Palandan Island one way or the other. Even if I have to tear it apart to do it." Her lips twisted. "As I believe I'm going to have to."

"Why?"

"There are too many legends, too many Nadims ready to pounce, too many reasons why someone would want to dip their hands into mysteries that have lain dormant for thousands of years. It's my duty to be the caretaker, but I'm bound to lose something by trying to hold on to everything. It's much better that I give a portion to people I trust who will have the means and dedication to care for it." She tried to smile. "So here's the proposition. Help me get rid of Nadim and his scum and make the island as safe as possible. In return, I'll help you find Silvana's tomb and set up a memorial like the one you did for Helen that's taken the public by storm. It might be even more successful since it will have the uniqueness of being the tomb of a woman gladiator. I'll also give you half the jewelry in those chests. The other half will go into trust to maintain the island and the people who live there."

"Very generous," Cade said. "Anything else?"

"You're thinking about those single-horned animals?"

She smiled. "But I've never said that they actually exist. Just another legend..."

Eve suddenly spoke. "As far as we know, neither did Silvana or those fabulous chests of jewels." Her eyes narrowed on Maya's face. "Yet you have no hesitation in offering those."

Maya chuckled. "Perhaps those particular treasures have been sighted in the past? Much easier to identify than a creature that might prove to be extinct." She was still grinning as she added, "But I'll add that to the proposition if we happen to stumble on any while you're there."

Eve shook her head. "Not me. Though I admit I was fascinated by hearing about your Silvana. I was originally brought into this because Riley wanted to use me as a sounding board while she made up her mind. I'm still only striving to clarify it for her."

"I'm sorry to hear that," Maya said. "I would have liked you to see my island." She smiled. "And I would have liked my island to see you." She turned back to Riley. "So there it is. I've probably failed to impress Cade. I always knew it was a crapshoot. But do you want to hunt for Silvana's tomb with me? You wanted to five years ago. I could see you thought it would be a great adventure. Since then you've found your Helen and let everyone in the world see what you can do. Don't you want to do it again?" Her eyes were suddenly shining with intensity. "Now I'm even throwing in a few more legends and treasures for you to explore. Come along and I promise you a journey we'll never forget. Don't you want to—" She stopped and then shook her head ruefully. "But you have another life now. I'd try to keep you safe, but it would be a risk. You should tell me to go to hell."

"You're giving me all the pluses and minuses you can think of," Riley said in exasperation. "I'd appreciate it if you'd stop telling me what to do. I'll make up my own mind. Five years ago I might have been wobbling back and forth and you thought you might have to make up my mind for me, but even then, I made the right—" She had a sudden thought. "You're very clever. The attack that night *was* genuine, wasn't it? Nadim was going after us?"

Maya laughed. "I promise, you would've been dead before morning if I hadn't gotten you out that night. But that's no reason why you should go back into the frying pan because I ask you. I'll find another way to save Palandan Island."

"But you said you were desperate," Riley reminded her.

"Maybe I was lying to you," Maya said. "You were just saying how clever I am and wondering if I'd fooled you."

"And you said I hadn't, and I believed you." She added firmly, "I still believe you."

Maya turned to Eve. "I'll leave it up to you. Do what she asked you to do. Make her see things clearly. Because I'm capable of trying to sway her in my direction, and I'm very good at it." She turned and headed for the door. "I'm going for a walk by the lake so I won't be tempted." She glanced over her shoulder at Cade. "I'm done here. I'll be ready to leave with Kirby within the hour."

"But Kirby has already had a long flight. He might not be ready to leave yet," Cade said. "We'll have to discuss it."

She nodded. "Whatever you say. But I need to be back on the island by tomorrow. See to it." Then she was out the door and going down the stairs.

"She may need an attitude adjustment," Cade murmured as he turned to Eve. "She seems to respect you. Perhaps you'd be the one qualified to take care of that problem."

"Too late," Eve said. "I could have told you that when she was telling us about sticking the dagger through that asshole's hand. Besides, I still have to finish training Michael and Joe. I don't have time to trek after Maya to her island." She glanced at Riley and added, "And I believe you've been thinking very clearly indeed lately. Don't expect any lectures from me." She was pouring the tea. "But you might need to go out on the porch and have a discussion or two with Cade..."

"I'm not ready to discuss anything to do with that damn island at the moment, Cade," Riley said as soon as they reached the porch. "I was furious with Maya, but I felt like running after her and comforting her. She was up against all of us in that room today. And probably felt as if the entire world was against her." She went over to the railing and looked out at the lake. "Maybe it has been for most of her life. She never talks about her past. All I know is that she has that whole island depending on her."

"She's tough," Cade said. "And I'll bet she doesn't want anyone feeling sorry for her. She'd probably spit in their eye."

"Maybe. I don't blame her. I'd feel the same way."

"I know you would," he said quietly. "You're a lot like her. I can see why you bonded while you were on that island. It wasn't only the fact that you felt you owed her a debt. You're tough, too. And you've been chasing ancient history with your father since you were a little kid. Naturally, the Silvana legend would intrigue you, and Maya must have seemed part of it."

"Yes, she did. Perhaps because my father and I had been trying so hard to find Helen, and sometimes I doubted if we ever would. But we were there on that island where Silvana had fled from Rome, and I listened to her legend, and I thought perhaps…" She broke off and shook her head as she turned back to face him. "Silvana was so brave fighting all those battles both in the arena and against the men who had made a slave of her. I wanted to be part of honoring her and showing the world what she'd created for herself in spite of all they'd done to her." She shrugged. "And I think Maya felt the same way though she laughed at me as if I were one of the village children. But that didn't stop her from telling me all the legends. I think she enjoyed them as much as I did."

"And when she called on you to help, it caused you to remember more than the fact that she'd helped save your neck," he said. "It confused you enough that you decided to come down here and talk to Eve." He paused. "And completely ignored the fact that I might be interested in hearing about Nadim and even Silvana." He snapped his fingers. "Oh, that's right, I was busy."

"You *were* busy." Her hands closed into fists. "And I would have told you eventually. I just had a decision to make."

"Eventually," he repeated. "But that sniper obviously interfered. What a shame." His hands were suddenly grasping her shoulders, his eyes glittering. "Dammit to *hell*. You know how I grew up being fought over by my parents because of my grandfather's billions. I swore I'd never be torn like that again. And when I found you, I knew it was the real thing and thought I'd gotten lucky. What have I done to you that you think I wouldn't want to share everything? I *love* you. I thought we had a relationship."

"We do." She moistened her lips. "I do love you. But feeling like this about anyone is new to me. We just came together all of a sudden, and it was as great and exciting as the crash of cymbals. We were involved with the search for Helen, and the sex was fantastic and so were you. But we haven't been together more than a few months. I told you, I'm accustomed to running my own life and making my own decisions." She had to make him understand. "Look, it's not easy living with a muckety-muck billionaire who has lunch with presidents and conferences with Arab princes. My experience is limited to

African witch doctors, Egyptologists, and tomb raiders—who are much more interesting, but it's sometimes hard to strike a balance. It's better to just keep the groups separate."

"Not if it also keeps me separate." His hands dropped from her shoulders. He drawled, " 'Muckety-muck,' Riley?"

He wasn't angry any longer, she realized with relief. He was back in control and sounded almost amused. "It seemed an accurate indication of the differences between us."

"You'd already indicated that without using that extremely unpleasant word."

"It wasn't really an insult. 'Muckety-muck' only means 'important.' "

"With strong hints of arrogance," he said. "When have I ever dared to be arrogant with you?"

She made a face at him. "You'd dare anything, but you've never tried to do that." She hesitated. "You can be a little overpowering sometimes. It gets in my way. I was just defending myself. Do you understand?"

"I'm beginning to understand what you were doing, though I don't know why." He reached out and gently brushed her hair away from her face. "But I'm starting to make guesses and I believe we have to nip this in the bud. You're right, we haven't known each other very long, and you're not feeling you know me well enough to trust me."

"I *do* trust you."

"Not enough or I would have been the first one you turned

to in any situation. We've got to change that." He brushed a kiss on her forehead. "Because I found out when I was on my way to the hospital that it might not have been long enough for you, but it was for me. I know the real thing when I see it." He turned away from her. "But I've got to have it all."

She went still. "Does that mean that you think we're not right for each other?"

"No, it means we have to make a correction so that there's never going to be any doubt who you'd turn to in any difficult situation." He was heading for the stairs. "And I can think of one opportunity that will give us an excellent way to explore who and what we are together. Care to come along?"

"Where are you—" But he was already down the stairs and heading toward the lake. Then Riley realized where he was going and ran after him.

He'd almost reached Maya, and she turned and looked at him inquiringly. "You decided that Kirby and I should leave right away?"

"No, there might be preparations to make. It depends on how you answer me," Cade said. "You might get what you want." He turned to gesture to Riley, who had just caught up with him. "You're very persuasive, and you started a long time ago with Riley. Even if she turned you down now, I'm not at all certain that she might not be tempted to follow you later."

"Do you want to make certain?" Maya asked sardonically. "Let me help. I've been feeling guilty since I asked her to come." She turned to Riley. "I was playing dirty. Throwing one last pitch in a game I'd lost. There's no way I'd take you with me if I went hunting for Silvana."

"And I'm not a chess piece for either of you to move around," Riley said. "Do you think I didn't guess that might only be a strategy? Ordinarily you're very honest, but you wanted to convince us, and you were desperate. Even then, you were trying to talk me out of it."

"I didn't try that hard," Maya said. "I had to get out of there or I might have gone the other way." She glanced at Cade. "Is that what you wanted? And how does that give me a possibility of getting what I want? Was it a trick?"

"No trick. I knew Riley was too clever not to see through that carrot you were dangling. That wasn't the question I wanted you to answer. Your proposition was very intriguing and meant to appeal to both Riley and me in our separate ways. You obviously wanted to draw me into this conflict you're going to have with Nadim. You were frank enough about that."

"Frank enough to ignore the fact that Riley would never consent to involving you willingly," Maya said. "But I still had to try because you were essential. I knew that the instant I finished researching you. You have the money, influence, and team to take Nadim down. You also have a hatred of poachers and a record of eliminating any that you run across."

"And you realized you might have at least a chance of being able to get to Cade through me," Riley said bitterly.

"I had no choice," Maya said. "He was perfect, and I had to save the island."

"I *hate* it, but I can see your logic. A good many people in the world have the same opinion of Cade and want to use him. But it makes me want to slug you." She turned to Cade and asked curtly, "What do you want to ask her?"

He took a step closer to Maya. "If we take your proposition, I'll only accept it if I'm in charge. Kirby says you like power and use it well, but I won't be a second in command. Yes or no?"

Maya hesitated. "I knew this was coming. As long as you consult with me... You know nothing about the island. The villagers may not take your orders."

"Is that a yes?"

"As long as you don't turn into an asshole. Then I might have to make an adjustment."

Cade chuckled. "A lethal one?"

She smiled. "But only if you're an asshole."

Riley looked from one to the other. "You're actually going to go through with it, Cade? There's no way on earth I'd ask you to do this."

"I know you won't," he said. "But it's not only that opportunity I spoke about. I want to get a look at those one-horned creatures she mentioned."

"Which might not exist," Maya said. "I didn't say they weren't the stuff of legends."

"You dangled them in front of me," Cade said. "I'm betting

that there might be some authentic 'stuff' in that legend that you're not ready to reveal yet."

"Why would I do that?"

"Perhaps to hold something in abeyance as a special incentive? It would be very smart."

"Well, since you're going to be there, you'll be able to see if I'm that intelligent." She drew a deep breath. "It's going to happen? You're both actually going with me to the island? When?"

"I'll tell Kirby to order supplies, weapons, and ammunition to take with us on the Gulfstream. If we can get it right away, we'll be out of here by tomorrow."

"That may not be soon enough," Maya said. "Can't Kirby take me back today?"

"It's only one day," Cade said.

"But she has responsibilities," Riley said quickly. "People count on her. Can't we take her out in the Gulfstream tonight and have Kirby bring the team and weapons tomorrow?"

"You're that eager to leave?" Cade asked.

"If we're going to do it, let's do it," Riley said. "It's possible, isn't it?"

"Anything is possible," Cade said as he reached for his phone. "I'll tell Kirby to call the airport and get the Gulfstream ready to go."

"Thank you, Riley," Maya said quietly as Cade started speaking to Kirby.

"It's Cade who's doing it," Riley said coldly. "I only

remembered how much those islanders seemed to need you."
She started back toward the cottage. "And don't think that
I'm not still upset with you. I hate being used, and you were
very...calculating."

"Yes, I am," Maya said soberly. "When I have to be, and I
thought I did. I hated doing it. I genuinely like you, Riley. I'd
say I was sorry, but I know that's not enough. I promise I'll
make it up to you."

"Yes, you will," Riley said firmly. "Because we're going
hunting for Silvana's tomb and we're going to find it. That was
part of that fancy proposition you tried to dazzle us with, and
I'm going to make you pay up. I'll help you all I can to get rid
of Nadim, but you're going to make sure Cade is safe and this
job is worthwhile for him."

Maya smothered a smile. "Yes, ma'am."

Riley ignored the mockery. "I'm glad we understand each
other."

"We'll understand each other better when I find a way to
make all this up to you. Then we'll be able to be friends again."

Riley shook her head. "I don't know if that's possible."

"I do." Maya's smile suddenly flashed bright. "Just wait and
see."

———

"You'll be leaving tonight?" Eve repeated as she watched Cade
going down to talk to the sentries.

Riley nodded. "As soon as Cade makes final preparations. We'll be out of here."

Eve frowned. "You're sure that's what you want, Riley? Somehow, I wasn't sure this was the way things would turn out. I thought Cade was going to throw in a roadblock."

"Things became a little complicated," Riley said. "I assure you, I wasn't the one forcing him to go." She glanced at Maya. "Neither was she, though she dangled a few choice prizes to lure him. But none of that matters. We'll make it work. I'll see that Cade gets whatever he wants and comes out of this alive." She met Maya's eyes. "And I'll get what I want, dammit."

"Yes, you will," Maya said. "We'll start working on it as soon as we get back to the island. I look forward to it."

Eve suddenly chuckled. "That all sounds entertaining. I'll be disappointed not to be able to see it."

Maya turned to face her. "I won't ask you to come. I've already put too many in danger today."

"And I didn't say I wanted to go with you," Eve said. "I'm just a bit wistful about Silvana. My work is here. I've not only got my forensic sculpting to do, I'm going to start overseeing the rebuilding of that boathouse." She crossed to Riley and gave her a hug. "I'm glad you'll get your answers, after all," she whispered. "I hope you get a few more than you'll find with Silvana. Keep everyone safe."

"You keep safe," Riley said. "And you will. Cade is sending his own crew to the island tomorrow. He's leaving an entire troop of Loring's men here after we leave. I'll call and let you know what's happening on the island." She kissed her cheek. "Thank you for putting up with me."

"My pleasure," Eve said. "No one can say you don't make life interesting." She turned away. "Now let's make a thermos of coffee and pack your bag." She looked over her shoulder at Maya and smiled. "You're very intriguing. If you don't turn out to be troublesome, I could get to like you. Be sure you stay alive so that I get the opportunity."

CHAPTER

5

ON BOARD THE PLANE

FOURTEEN HOURS LATER

Okay, I'm officially bored." Maya dropped down in the seat next to Riley. "I have to tell you, my trip to Eve's with Kirby was much more entertaining. That plane might not have been as fast or palatial as this beauty, but at least someone was talking to me. I realize communication goes two ways. But I left you alone for two excellent reasons. First, I thought that time would help you to cool down a little, because I knew you were angry I'd somehow managed to talk Cade into coming. Second, I wanted to give you and Cade a chance to ignore me and repair whatever damage I'd done by showing up in your life at all." She grimaced. "I believe I struck out in both cases. Right?"

"Yes and no," Riley said as she closed her computer. "I'm more disappointed than angry with you about your interference in my life. You were smart to let me get over that first reaction. But don't compliment yourself that you talked Cade into anything. He always has his own reasons and plans for any action. It wasn't your persuasion; it was only that you happened to be there when it all came together for him."

She chuckled. "You'll remember I threw in a 'somehow' in that sentence. I definitely wasn't patting myself on the back. But you have to admit I was right about my screwing up the chemistry between you and Cade." Her smile faded. "I don't think he's left the cockpit more than a couple times in all these hours."

"He had Kirby up in that cockpit with him helping to fly the plane. He also had plans to make with him so that we'd be ready when we landed," Riley said. "Now are you finished with your guilt trip?"

"No," she said definitely. "But I can't expect you to admit anything to me. After all, I'm not Eve. I just want you to know that I'm here for you." She paused. "And I'll be as open as I can with both you and Cade from now on. Which is difficult for me since that's not how I've lived my life. But I'm grateful to you, and it's time I showed it."

Riley smiled. "I won't turn that offer down. I've been feeling as if I was lost in a maze since you called me the other night." She tilted her head. "Come to think of it, you've left quite a bit to my imagination since I first met you five years ago. Just enough to tease and tantalize, but not enough to satisfy."

"I'm turning over a new leaf," Maya said. "You'll see. I promise."

"Prove it," Riley challenged softly. "I'll start you off easy. Fill in a few of the blanks. Tell me why you became caretaker when you were only sixteen."

Maya looked a little taken aback. "That may take a while," she said warily. "You might need the background."

"Then you'd better start now. We should be landing fairly soon, but I have time for a little background. Start with 'caretaker.' Since everyone kowtows to you, I assumed that it was just another name for the boss or person in charge. Does it have any less obvious meanings?"

"Not really. The title goes back to Silvana. Because she bought the island and worked all her life to improve it for everyone, the villagers began to call her 'the one who cares for us.' Then after Silvana's daughter took over the reins, the villagers kept on referring to her in the same vein. She was known as the caretaker. Or honorable caretaker. Or the leader who cares. Or half a dozen other titles depending on which area of the island folks lived in." She shrugged. "I guess caretaker was simple, so it stuck. Whenever there was a new leader chosen, they were known as the caretaker."

"And how is the new one chosen?" Riley asked. "I gather no one votes at the polls?"

She shook her head. "That's not efficient. The new caretaker is chosen by the one in charge. It's their duty to make the choice in order that they can groom them to perfection. That way they won't make mistakes and cause trouble and worry to the islanders."

"Perfection," Riley repeated. "That isn't easy. Particularly when the one they choose is only sixteen. I don't think I like that system."

"Neither did I," Maya said. "I was scared to death. But there wasn't usually any problem. Jann Lu should have chosen someone much sooner, but she said no one seemed right to her. Most of the caretakers had their heirs chosen and trained decades before they had to take charge."

"But you appear to have done all right," Riley said. "Scared or not."

"Sometimes I have doubts. It's a big responsibility. Particularly now. But most of the villagers think I'm doing a good job." She gazed at her inquiringly. "And that's how I became caretaker. Satisfied?"

"Not entirely. But I'll let the rest go for now. I have only one more question. Have there been any male caretakers?"

Maya smiled. "You're thinking because Silvana was an Amazon and had a rough time with Antonio and those other Roman bastards, she might have made some kind of edict against male leaders?" She shook her head. "I believe there were four or five men chosen through the centuries. But even then, two of them selected female caretakers when it came time to choose a successor. Women definitely dominated in Silvana's world."

"Good. I'm glad they did. But I'm also happy they didn't cheat to get there. It seems as if Silvana had a hell of a lot of dirty tricks played on her during her lifetime, but she didn't let it twist her."

"I'll second that," Maya said. "Perhaps it's a good sign we might be able to agree on other things on the island?"

"It's possible," Riley said. "Though I haven't pushed you yet on that point you skipped over—why she chose *you* particularly to become caretaker."

Maya's smile ebbed. "And are you going to do it?"

Riley studied her expression. "No, I don't think so. I'll save that for later." She opened her computer. "I want to be ready before we land. I think I'd be better served with having you pull up my map of the island and start filling me in on points of interest that you believe we should know about. As I remember, when my father and I were here together all those years ago, we weren't permitted to go anywhere on the island except a few of the apple groves and the villages near them that were close to the southern seaport. Everything else about the island was off limits."

"Were you frightened and scared of the villagers?" Maya was smiling. "Did you find those areas where we took you to be cold and ugly?"

"Everything was absolutely beautiful, and the villagers couldn't have been warmer or more hospitable. I wanted to see more."

"Your father didn't complain. He was just a little impatient.

After he visited a few of the villages and found no artifacts that would indicate anything to do with Troy, all he wanted to do was start preparing to go north. We tried to make you both comfortable while you were with us."

"I don't think that there was any doubt of that," Riley said. "I told Eve that it reminded me of Eden. The warmth, the beauty—you even provided the biblical apples when we visited the groves and had us try those rare diamond apples you grow on the island. The only thing lacking was the freedom to explore. It didn't bother my father, but I'd already started to hear the Silvana legends and I was really curious. You even encouraged it. You told me a few yourself."

She nodded. "And I really shouldn't have. The only reason I allowed you to come was that I liked the idea of having a noted archaeologist like your father visit the island. We don't encourage visitors, but I thought if he came and was disappointed, it might ward off any other treasure hunters wanting to try their luck. The main objective was to have you come, spend a little time, and then send you on your way. But I liked you, and I was enjoying having you know about my island. I suppose I was a little lonely. I have a lot of responsibilities and sometimes it was hard to relax. I didn't think it would hurt to keep you around a little longer." She made a face. "I didn't count on having to deal with Nadim. I thought he was safely out of the picture. But the greedy bastard decided that hitting your camp might be worth coming out of the mountains. I had to get you out of there fast."

"And you were wounded."

"I deserved it for indulging myself. I should have kept to the plan." She looked down at the map on Riley's computer and drew an X on the southern end of the island. "This is the main seaport where you and your father arrived. That should be familiar to you. That's where I met you at the central residence and had a guide take you down by the apple groves to set up your camp." She pointed to the area on the far west of the island. "This is the path that leads from the island up to the lower foothills of the mountains. You start out in the orchards of the island that are mild as Eden. It takes about half a day to get to those foothills, and it gets cooler by the hour. Even though you haven't reached the actual mountains of the Himalayas yet, the temperature plunges to almost freezing after sundown." She marked three other places at the north and extreme east sides of the island. "These are possible bays where Nadim could access the island." She put another larger X deep in the north-central area of the map. "And this is the temple." She leaned back in her seat gazing at Riley, waiting for the reaction.

Riley wasn't going to give it to her. "That was too easy. That can't be where the treasure is."

Maya chuckled. "I didn't say it was. But there are treasures and then there are treasures. It all depends on what you're looking for. But it's certainly the place Silvana intended for her treasure. Perhaps she was also planning for her tomb to be there, too."

"You've been there before," Riley said. "The temple's no secret to you."

"No, as caretaker I have constant access, but the villagers regard it as a sacred place, and no one is allowed there but the sentries who guard it. And Nadim would be very happy to know where the temple is located. I'm sure he's hunting for it even as we speak." She handed Riley's computer back to her. "And I think that's all I'm willing to reveal at the moment. I do have to retain a few secrets so that you won't undervalue me. I've given you a hint or two, but you'd need me to find any of those places for you." She inclined her head. "I'm at your disposal at any time."

"I'll tell Cade."

"I knew you would. I thought you'd need a key to start the search so that we'll know we're all on the same page. Is there anything else I can do?"

"No." She hesitated. "The map is actually quite a bit."

"I couldn't expect you to go in blind. We made a deal." She added quietly, "I'll make it as easy as possible for all of us to get through it." She got to her feet. "And now I'll move back across the aisle. You can call Cade back here and talk about it if you like. I'll be out of your way but available for questions."

"I can wait," Riley said. "We'll be landing soon, and he'll be able to concentrate. There's no hurry."

"Whatever," Maya said. "These days I find myself not wanting to wait for anything." She headed across the aisle. "I'm always afraid I'll fall behind and never get caught up."

Riley felt a chill go through her. Her own life lately had seemed to be balanced on seconds, not minutes. How did she know how much time she had? She reached for her phone and dialed Cade. When he answered she said, "Maya just filled in a map of the island for me. Would you like to come back and take a look at it?"

"I'll be right there," he said curtly. "I was coming anyway. A radio message just came in for Maya from her housekeeper. She couldn't reach her by phone, there was too much interference. She said it was an emergency." He hung up and the next moment the cockpit door opened and he was striding down the aisle. He stopped beside Maya's seat. "Tashi, your housekeeper called. She said to give you a message that there was a fire at Mabato village and they'd sent help. She said there were signs it was probably Nadim."

"Shit." Maya jumped to her feet. "I need to talk to her. Can you get me through to her?"

He shook his head. "I've got Kirby trying. But there's too much interference. We'll be on the ground before we can reach her," he said. "She said they'd sent help. As soon as we land, we'll be on our way, too. Where the hell is Mabato?"

"It's on the northern coast." Her voice was panicked. "She didn't say anything about Bailey? Did she have Bailey?"

"I gave you her entire message," Cade said. "Who's Bailey?"

"My daughter. Tashi was looking after her." Her hands were clenched into fists at her sides. "Get this damn plane on the ground. I have to find out what's happening down there."

119

"We'll be down in five to seven minutes," Cade said as he turned on his heel. "Riley, take care of her." The cockpit door slammed behind him.

"How in the hell am I supposed to know how to take care of you?" Riley said as she jumped up and came to stand beside Maya. "This is big stuff, and I didn't even know you had a daughter." She took both her hands and looked her in the eye. "And we both know you're tough enough to tackle this on your own. All I can say is, I'll be here with you until we get it straightened out. Cade is a great fixer and I'm not so bad. You're not alone, Maya."

She nodded jerkily as she sat down in her seat. "Then sit down and fasten your seat belt. I don't want you to break anything." Her voice was shaking. "I'm going to need all the help I can get once we land, and I see what I'm facing."

"Right." Riley sat down and reached for her belt. "Since you ask so nicely. But I meant what I said, Maya."

"I know you did," Maya said hoarsely, gazing straight ahead. "And we'll get through it..."

They landed six minutes later, and as soon as the wheels stopped turning Maya was on her feet and headed for the exit. Riley was right behind her.

"Hold it." Cade pushed in front and was unfastening the

door. "Kirby is running a visual scan of the airport. We don't want any unpleasant surprises. Go to the cockpit and see if you recognize anyone on the runway."

Maya asked no questions. She was already running toward the cockpit. She was back seconds later. "Open it. It's Tashi with Dalben, the captain of the local sentries."

Cade already had the door open, and Maya ran down the steps to Tashi. Riley followed, but Maya had already reached Tashi and was gazing frantically into the housekeeper's face. "Bailey?"

"Safe," Tashi said instantly. "Did I not tell you that I wouldn't let anything happen to her? When I heard there was trouble on the coast, I took her to the temple. Even if she was a target, no one could get past the sentries there."

"Thank God." Maya drew a deep breath. "Was she frightened?"

Tashi shook her head. "Only for you. This is Bailey. Though she didn't want to leave the mountain."

"She never does. But I can't deal with her right now." Maya gestured to Riley and then to Cade, who was coming down the steps with Kirby. "I've brought help. Tashi, Rolf Dalben. You remember Riley, and you met Kirby. This is Morgan Cade."

Tashi nodded. "I told you that you would get him to listen." Her lips twisted. "And just in time for Nadim to send them a greeting."

"I have to get to Mabato." Maya turned to the uniformed

sentry. "What's happening there, Dalben? Something about a fire? Is it the entire village?"

"We don't think so. Just one area according to the report we got from the village chief. But they can't get near it to put it out. Nadim set loose a team of his snipers to attack the village and they've been picking off anyone who shows themselves. The captain of the local island guard said that the snipers are calling out your name and using it to mock the villagers." He pointed to the faint wisp of smoke rising to the north. "They seem to be using that fire they set as a lure." He added grimly, "We've got a body count of twenty-two already."

"Snipers again, Nadim must like them." Cade's gaze was fastened on the smoke as he came to stand beside them. "Typical poaching trick used to bring down animals." His lips tightened. "Only these aren't animals." He turned to Dalben. "I'll need a jeep and someone who can guide me to where they lit that damn fire." He looked over his shoulder at Kirby. "Get weapons from the plane."

"I'm on it." He was running back toward the steps.

Maya shook her head. "My job, Cade. You don't even have a team on the island yet. They won't be here until tomorrow."

"Your people don't appear to be doing so well at the moment, Maya. I don't like snipers and I'm hoping one of them might be that other asshole who was shooting at Riley at Eve's." He looked her in the eye. "I gave an order, and your sentry here hasn't moved a muscle. We have an agreement, Maya."

She hesitated and then said to Dalben. "It's okay. Get him anything he wants...quickly."

Dalben turned and reached for his phone as he headed at a run for the vehicles parked on the side of the runway.

"This isn't the time for you to do this, Cade." Maya swung back to face him. "You should wait until I can—" She stopped when she saw his expression. "I'm going with you. You won't need a guide. I know every inch of this island."

"You might be useful, but I could regret it. I'll still accept it." He glanced at Riley. "Because I know I can't keep Riley away from that village when she might be able to help them. The first time I met her, she was in a first-aid tent bandaging a little kid while she was giving me hell. She's been standing there and listening, and I've been watching the impatience growing." He tilted his head at Riley. "Right?"

She nodded. "As long as you're going to go see if you can get your head blown off by those snipers, I thought you might need medical attention." She added, "And from what Dalben said, some of the islanders already need help...if they're still alive."

Dalben brought the jeep to a screeching halt a few yards away, and Maya headed for it. She tapped him on the shoulder. "Out!" When he quickly jumped out, she slipped into the driver's seat. "Let's get out of here, Cade."

Kirby was back with two automatic rifles and gave one to Cade. "Shotgun?"

"No, I'll ride shotgun," Cade said as he got in the passenger seat. "You get in back with Riley and guard the rear."

Tashi took a step closer to the jeep and put a hand on Maya's shoulder as she was about to leave. "I will go back to the temple and tell Bailey you are coming to her soon. You've done well so far. Don't disappoint me by letting one of those snipers kill you. Let this Cade take care of them. He seems to have the right idea about attending to business."

"Like Jann Lu?" Maya asked dryly. "I admit while I was worrying about Bailey before we landed, I was thinking that Jann Lu's methods weren't entirely unacceptable." She shrugged. "Though I'll have to think about it."

"When you come to that point, you don't think, you just act." Tashi stepped back. "But you won't have to search your soul while I watch over the child. Go and do what must be done..."

"How far is it to Mabato?" Cade asked as Maya drove out of the runway area and onto a rough stone road through the jungle. "I don't like the amount of time we've already had to spend just getting on the road."

"Neither do I," Maya said. "And it's at least another forty minutes. I want to contact Jelsko, the village chief, and get all the info I can before we try to go after the snipers. I have to go around the back of the village the long way so we won't be noticed. It's driving me crazy." Her hands clenched on the steering wheel as she gazed out the windshield. "Because I'm thinking that Nadim is probably looking up at that wisp of smoke and enjoying what his men are doing to those people. I want it to stop."

"It hasn't begun yet," Cade said quietly. "And you stay at the village until Kirby and I scope out the area for any possible prisoners and decide where to position ourselves to take out as many of the snipers as possible."

She shook her head. "I'll have to see how many of the soldiers we sent are still able to help you. I might have to lead—"

"You stay at the village," Cade interrupted. "Or I go back and get on that plane and that's the end of our deal."

"Listen to him, Maya." Riley leaned forward from the backseat. "He knows what he's doing. I've seen him in action. Do you think I'd let him go if he didn't? Look, this is what I was afraid of when you decided that you had to involve Cade. But you wouldn't have it any other way. So shut up and let him do what he does best. Get the hell out of his way."

Maya stared at her for a moment. Then she looked straight ahead. "We'll have to see what the situation is at Mabato."

———

The situation at Mabato was hideous, Maya thought as she drove toward the back of the village. Bodies everywhere, weeping women and children. The island guard was nowhere in sight. Where the hell were they? She saw Jelsko, the chief, kneeling beside a young man dressed in guard fatigues. She stopped the jeep, then jumped out and ran to fall to her knees beside him. "Jelsko. What's happening?" She looked down at the soldier. "Can I help him? Let me get—" Then she stopped as she saw what two bullets had done to the young man's head.

"No one can help him." Jelsko lifted his eyes and she saw the pain and tears in them. "It is my son, Calar. He was so proud when he was old enough to join the island guard. Even as a child he wanted to be a soldier and help people." His voice broke. "He was only twenty, Maya. Why two bullets? One would have done. The second must have just been for their pleasure."

She put her arms around him. "I share your sorrow. How can I help?"

"You cannot help my son." He pushed her away. "But you are here. Maybe that will make them stop. Those beasts kept calling out and asking where you were and why you didn't help us. Are you not the caretaker?"

"We will help you." Cade and Riley were suddenly beside them. "You don't know me, Jelsko," Cade said, "but Maya will tell you that I'm a friend. Will you permit us to take your son inside your home while you tell us what we need to know? And Riley has medical skills that will heal your friends and neighbors."

"Heal?" Jelsko repeated, looking down at his son. "Will we ever heal?"

"I know it doesn't seem that way." Riley's hand tightened on her medical bag. "But we can only do what we can. I noticed a young woman over there by the fountain tending a soldier who might need help. I'll go over there and see after we get you and your son settled."

"Tell me how many of the island guard are left," Maya said. "I need numbers, old friend."

"They sent a unit of thirty-six when I called after the attack. There were nine of us who had already been killed by the snipers by the time they got here. They fought them off the village and then followed them into the forest. I was so proud of my son. He was like a lion."

"I'm sure he was," Maya said gently. "Perhaps that was why there were two bullets. They thought one would never put the lion down."

"I didn't think of that," he said. "It might be true." His face twisted. "But when they followed the guard into the forest, it was a trap. The snipers had double their number waiting in the trees and they started cutting them down. The guard fought well, but it was useless, there were too many. Eleven finally fell back to the village to protect us. I thought my son might be among them." He shook his head. "But he was one of those cut down in the forest. After dark I went after him and brought him back. I've been sitting here with him." He was rocking back and forth. "I was listening to their mocking and watching the fire they set in the trees. They seemed to be tending that fire as if it was a burial flame."

"How many of the guards are left?" she asked again.

"Only eleven or twelve. But it seems to be enough to keep the snipers from attacking the village. They appear to want to wait until it's easier to gather us up and finish us."

"You said they were calling for me," Maya said. "Did they do that very often?"

"I don't know. It seemed as if they did."

She looked at the wispy smoke floating up over the trees. "I can understand calling it out once, but why repeat it?"

"Because you're the caretaker," Jelsko said wearily. "Why else? They knew you had to come to help us."

"I'm just wondering." She got to her feet. "Now we'll take your son inside if you don't mind. He shouldn't be lying out here."

"We'll do it." Kirby knelt beside the boy's body. "Cade?"

Together they carefully lifted Calar's body and carried it into Jelsko's hut.

Riley and Maya watched until they disappeared inside. Then Riley turned toward the wounded man by the fountain. "I've got to go see what I can do for that soldier. Do you want to come and help?"

Maya shook her head. "Perhaps later. I want to go over to the edge of the village and take a closer look at that fire. Something Jelsko mentioned caught my attention." She held up her hand as Riley started to protest. "I'm not going any farther than the edge of the village. This has nothing to do with my argument with Cade." She turned and headed toward the stone wall that encircled the village.

———

"You know that one of those snipers could have you in his sights right this minute?" Cade said as he joined Maya twenty minutes later. "Riley didn't like you this close to the forest. You shouldn't worry her."

"And having Riley not worry is paramount?" She turned to face him. "But the wall was so high where I was standing that a sniper would have had to be almost standing on his head to have a good shot at me. I'm not stupid, Cade."

"But if you'd moved two feet either way you would have been vulnerable."

"I had no intention of moving. I could see what I wanted from here."

"And what did you want to see?"

"I wasn't sure. But it had something to do with that fire they built in the forest. It obviously wasn't intended to start a destructive forest fire because it was small and well contained. Yet it's not a campfire to keep those bastards warm. From here it appears to look almost like a tent enclosure, but no one is going inside except to keep the fire burning. Why did they build the damn thing?"

"You tell me."

"I have no idea except that I believe it has something to do with me. Jelsko said they kept mentioning my name. They did terrible damage that first night, but now they seem to be sitting around and waiting for something. Why haven't they attacked again?"

"It's your puzzle, solve it."

"I think I will." Her eyes narrowed intently. "You stay right here and keep your eyes sharp and that rifle ready."

Cade stiffened warily. "What the hell are you going to do?"

"I'm going to move that two feet to the right." She was turning to face the forest and looking straight in the direction of the fire. "That should do it..."

"Shit!" He pushed her to the ground and lifted his rifle.

The bullet from the trees crashed into the stone wall next to her!

She rolled back to her former position beneath the protection of the taller wall as Cade returned the gunfire. She heard a scream from the direction of the forest.

"Satisfied?" Cade asked her.

"Not yet. But now I'm certain they got a good look at me. If I'm one of the targets of this attack, they know I'm here."

"And you could have gotten yourself killed," he said roughly.

She shook her head. "You promised Riley that wouldn't happen, and you had to keep your word."

"It would help if you gave me a little assistance." His gaze was raking the area where the snipers were clustered near the fire. "They're not rushing us. They appear to be carrying that sniper I shot deeper into the forest. Still, they might come back once it gets dark."

"Or they might not," Maya said quietly. "They missed their chance at me. Maybe they're going on to phase two."

"Phase two? Would you care to elaborate?"

She shook her head. She was trying not to shudder as she looked at that fire. She didn't want to talk about it. She could hardly force herself to think about it. "All this killing may only be the opening gambit." She didn't take her gaze from that twisting curl of smoke over the fire. "Are you as good as I've heard you are? I think you must be or Riley would not have such faith in you."

"I'm very good," Cade said. "So is Kirby. What do you have in mind?"

"You wanted to go out and locate those snipers and perhaps get rid of any strategic command posts you find. I'm not going to argue with you about it now. Wait until dark and then grab a few of the island guards and go do it, but first I want you to take a look at that sentry post near the fire. I want you to tell me why they built that fire. I have to know."

"You're not going with us?" Cade asked flatly.

"No, I'm not. I'll rely on you." She smiled sardonically. "See how much I trust you? I think you'll know if I should show myself again to those bastards."

"That will be a definite negative."

"We'll have to see." She turned and headed back toward the

center of the village. "In the meantime, I'm going to go help Riley with the wounded and try to find a few of Jelsko's relatives to stay with him."

And make an effort to block this growing sense of sickening dread as she waited for darkness to fall.

———

Cade showed up at the makeshift first-aid hut that Riley and Maya had set up close to sunset that night. Riley had just finished bandaging the throat of a young island officer when she saw him standing in the doorway watching her.

She carefully hid the relief she felt at the sight of him. "How nice of you to drop in," she said. "After what Maya told me about releasing you to go after those snipers, I thought you'd be on your way."

He shook his head. "Not without telling you. It's been fairly chaotic since we landed, but that would never be an option as far as I'm concerned. You might take it as an example of how I want you to behave. That would drive me crazy." He crossed the tent and cupped her face in his hands. "You realize this isn't the way I wanted this to work? So far, the only thing I've been able to do is try to keep Maya from getting into trouble."

"I don't know what you mean. She's been doing a great job," Riley said defensively. "She's been helping me, checking on the villagers, and talking on the phone to get more guards sent here. They should be here by midnight." She gazed into his eyes and tried to ignore the heat that was beginning to build at his touch. "You could wait for them and not go out there after those snipers with a crew the size of a postage stamp."

"A small crew is sometimes better." He kissed her, hard. Then he let her go. "And I'm curious to see what Maya calls phase two."

"Phase two?"

"Maya didn't mention it to you? Maybe that was only meant for me. Never mind. She was a bit erratic today."

"Can you blame her? All I noticed was that she was on edge," Riley said. "But then these are her people."

"Including her daughter? You never mentioned she had a child."

"I didn't know about her. I still don't, we were too busy for personal conversation." She added quietly, "But after today neither of us can doubt that she has big-time trouble on this island."

"I haven't doubted that since I got that call that you were in the hospital," he said grimly. "That brought it all home to me with a vengeance." He turned and headed for the door. "I'll call you when I'm through out there tonight."

She couldn't let him just walk out of here. "No need. It's not as if I won't be waiting for you when you get back to the village."

He grinned at her over his shoulder. "Waiting for me," he repeated. "I like the sound of that. Kind of homey. But this isn't like Cambry House, is it?"

"It doesn't have to be."

He tilted his head. "Because you never felt as if it was really yours? I always meant you to know that what was mine was yours. It seems I failed there, too."

She didn't want him to feel that way when he'd never been anything but generous to her. She found the words tumbling out. "It didn't matter. It was just a place. I liked it because you were there. I've never felt anything about a place like Eve does about the Lake Cottage. But that was because of her memories. I've never been in any place long enough to have a lasting memory."

He was suddenly smiling. "It's not only places that furnish memories. I think we've created a few together that had nothing to do with brick and mortar. We've just got to combine and embroider a little more." He winked. "See you later, Riley." Then he was gone.

And Riley was left to look after him and try not to think about what he was going to face within the next minutes. It was all very well to tell Maya how good he was and that she shouldn't worry about him doing what he said he could do. It was different having to stay here and watch him walk out that door.

Then why do it? she thought recklessly. She was done here; why not go find Maya and wait with her until Cade came back? She left the first-aid room and caught sight of Maya across the square, standing gazing at the glow of the fire in the forest. She started across the village to join her.

———

"Why is it so quiet out there?" Maya murmured. "We've only heard four shots since they went into the forest. That was thirty minutes ago. What's happening?"

"As long as those four shots didn't go into Cade or Kirby, I don't give a damn." Riley's voice was shaking. "And I'm not sure they didn't. Why the hell couldn't he have waited until midnight when they'd have backup?" Her eyes were straining as they focused on the flames. "I haven't even seen any of those bastards who were guarding that blasted fire since I came to stand beside you. Though I thought I caught a glimpse of someone on the far side of the fire five minutes ago." She shrugged. "But then he was gone. It might have been a shadow or my imagination."

"Or it might not." Maya grabbed her arm. "Because I just caught sight of Kirby." She pointed to a shadowy figure emerging from the smoke. "Though there's no sight of Cade yet. But don't start worrying again. Kirby doesn't look as if he's on edge."

But Kirby was definitely alert and carrying his rifle with care and purpose Riley noticed. The next instant Cade was beside him and then they were both running toward the wall.

Riley was on her feet as they slid behind the wall. "What's happening? Why didn't we hear any guns?"

"Because there wasn't anyone to fire them," Cade said.

"Kirby and I were very slick about slipping behind enemy lines, and we were about to start picking off the snipers." His lips twisted. "But we couldn't find any. What a conundrum."

"What are you talking about?" Maya asked hoarsely.

"I think you might have an idea," Cade said. "Nadim's snipers had flown the coop. They must have slipped away earlier in the evening and taken off for their designated pickup place."

"Why?" Riley asked blankly.

"My guess is, their job was done," Cade said. "Just to be sure, we did a thorough look around the area. It was entirely clean of all the vermin who had been tormenting the village. I set a few of the island guards to reconnoiter, but I don't expect to find anyone else."

"It's too soon," Riley said. "Why would they leave almost as soon as we got here?"

"Yes, why?" Cade turned back to Maya. "Would you like to hazard a guess?"

"No, I'd like to have an answer." She moistened her lips. "Did you do as I asked you?"

He nodded. "Would I disappoint you?" He held out his hand to her. "Back out. I don't want to do this. *You* won't want to do this."

"But I have to do it. You're just making it harder."

He muttered a curse. "Then are you ready to come with me?"

She took his hand and let him pull her to her feet. "Not ready, but I have to do it. I'll be right back, Riley."

Riley shook her head as she examined Maya's pale face. "I don't think so. I don't like the way you look. What's happening here?"

"Maya just wants a closer look at the bonfire those snipers built for us," Cade said through clenched teeth. "I promised I'd show it to her. Of course, she could back out. She won't do it."

"Then I'll go with her," Riley said.

"No, you won't," Cade said sharply. "You stay here."

"To hell with it." Maya shook her head and started across the field. "They wanted me to see it. I'll see it."

Cade caught up with her in six steps. He muttered a curse. "Why don't you give it up? I think you know what's there. I'll tell you about it."

"Then he'd win. He wants to hurt me. I have to show him he can't do it. But I've got to see it." She was looking at the glow of the fire as she grew nearer and nearer. "They must have put fresh wood on the flames before they left or it would have gone out by now," she said dully. She could feel the heat now, the scent of the wood and something else . . .

Keep going.

Don't let him hurt you.

She was next to the tentlike enclosure now. Her hand was shaking as she pushed aside the cloth to go inside.

The heat blasted her face as she entered.

Dear God.

The fire was in the center of the room. But to the left of the fire was a pallet on which lay the corpse of a young girl, maybe eleven or twelve. She was naked, her eyes were wide open, her hands tied above her head. Her expression reflected a terrible horror.

Maya couldn't stop staring for an instant. But then she couldn't stand it any longer and turned her eyes away.

And that was when she saw the red streamer fastened across the tent with a single name dancing in the heat of the blaze.

Bailey.

It was too much. She staggered to the opening of the tent and threw up again and again.

Then she was aware of Riley beside her, holding her steady as her stomach was wrenched by spasms. "Cade! What the hell did you do?" Riley was gazing around the tent with the same horror Maya had felt. "Why did you let her come here?"

"I couldn't stop her," he said roughly. "I should have known you'd run after us. I didn't want you to see this."

"Why?" Riley repeated.

"She said she had to come," Cade said. "You heard her. She wouldn't be told no. She would have come by herself if I hadn't brought her."

"You shouldn't have paid any attention to her." She was wiping Maya's face with a handkerchief. "Come on, we're getting out of here."

"No," Maya said hoarsely. She took a deep breath and then turned and went back to the naked girl on the pallet. "We can't leave her here. Look at her face." She gently closed the girl's eyes. "She must have already gone through hell and now Nadim is using her as part of this hideous charade. I won't *have* it." She turned to Cade. "Take down this tent and wrap her in it. Have her taken back to the village. We'll find her parents and give her a decent burial."

He nodded. "That's exactly what I would have done if you hadn't insisted on seeing Nadim's ugly scenario."

"No choice. I had to do it. I knew it had to be something horrible like this. I couldn't let him force me to hide my eyes and pretend I didn't see it. I can't let him take anything away from me or anyone on the island. I can't let him beat us." She swayed and closed her eyes for a moment. "But dear God in heaven, what he's done already."

"Can we go now?" Riley slipped her arm around Maya's waist and was helping her from the tent. "We'll do anything you want after we get you out of here. I think you've had enough for one day, Maya."

"I'm sure Nadim thought so, too," Maya said as they started to cross the field toward the village. Her voice was still shaking. "He must have taken a long time setting up that horror for me. His instructions to that sniper team must have been very explicit."

"Don't think about it." Riley kept her grip strong around her, giving her whatever support she could in a world where she must be feeling bereft of all humanity and solace. "I know it's hard but try not to let that bastard do this to you."

Maya looked at her wonderingly. "How can I help it? You saw what they did to her."

Riley didn't know what to say. All she could do was tighten her grasp and look behind her at that column of smoke spitting up from that damn tent. She couldn't see Cade. He must still be in the tent, taking care of getting that poor child away from that hellish cocoon where they'd placed her. But Kirby was only a few paces behind them following them back to the village. As he saw her glancing back, he put his hand on his rifle and nodded. Cade must have sent him to guard them in case Nadim had planned some other beastly addition to this hideous night. Riley nodded back at Kirby and increased her pace until they reached the stone wall.

Then she turned to Maya and said gently, "I believe we'll go to the first-aid room so that you can have privacy. I'll see if there's anyone else I can help."

Maya looked at her dazedly and then shook her head as if to clear it. "No." She sat down beside the wall. "I'll stay here until they bring that child to the village. She's the one who should have privacy. They can take her to the first-aid room while we try to find out who she is."

"I can do that for you," Riley said.

"Yes, you could. But it's my job, and they'll talk to me." She looked her in the eye. "Don't argue with me right now. It's difficult for me to think. There's one other thing I have to do before I concentrate on helping that child." She took her phone out of her pocket and punched in the number. "I have to call Tashi…" Two rings and Tashi answered. She cut her off before she could speak. "I can't talk right now. I just have to ask you a few questions. Are you at the temple?"

"Yes, I told you that I would be."

"Is Bailey still safe?"

"Of course."

"There's no 'of course' about it. Double the guards. Nadim knows about Bailey."

Tashi didn't speak for a moment. "You're sure?"

Maya closed her eyes for an instant as she remembered those obscenely dancing letters reflected in the flames. "Absolutely. I'll join you as soon as I can."

She ended the call and looked at Riley. "I can go on now." She got to her feet. "We have to find out who the girl is. She can't be from this village, or we would have heard about a missing child after we arrived here. We can't ask Jelsko for help. He's had enough death to deal with today. We'll go around the village and talk to the women. The villages talk to each other on the phone, and mothers always talk about their children." She had to stop for a moment as she remembered her first glimpse of that poor girl. "And she was probably eleven or twelve but that's close enough in age to be considered a child by family members. Someone had to be worrying about her."

"Perhaps we should split up and each take a share of the huts near the chief's house," Riley said. "If you won't let me do it by myself. I shouldn't have any trouble communicating. I remember that most of the villagers on the island speak English as a second language."

Maya nodded. "That might save time." She headed for the center of the village. "I want this over as soon as possible for these people so the healing can begin. The people in this village were probably innocent victims of Nadim. They had nothing of value that he would want. The attack came out of nowhere and seemed aimed at killing and sending a message."

"To you?"

She nodded. "I told you that he hated me."

"You told Cade you wanted him to show you what was in that tent where they were tending that fire. How did you know?"

"I didn't. It was guesswork." She swallowed hard. "I certainly never expected to have Nadim use an innocent child to hurt me. That was the height of depravity. One of the first things Tashi said when she met us at the plane was that those bastards had mentioned me when they attacked during the night. When we got to the village, the chief said the same thing. Why would they be so persistent about taunting me unless they had orders?" Her lips tightened grimly. "And that fire and tent were made a focal point, and there had to be a reason. When I showed myself so they could recognize me, after that one shot, they didn't attack. Not necessary. They knew that they'd drawn me, and their job was done. Nadim probably didn't mind that they hadn't killed me. He's probably looking forward to doing that himself."

Riley gave a low whistle. "You're right, he must hate you."

"I told you that the night I called you." She shrugged. "It's the endgame, Riley. But he's upped the ante and I'll have to go after him right away. I can't risk him getting any closer to Bailey."

"Bailey," Riley repeated. "I was surprised when you mentioned her before. When I researched you and the island on the way here, I didn't see anything about a daughter."

"No one knew about Bailey if they didn't have to. There were reasons why it was best no one connect her with me. I had to keep her safe. But that devil evidently managed to track her down." She changed the subject. "You take these four houses in the row. I'll take the ones across the street. I'll meet you back at the first-aid hut when we've finished." She was crossing to the other side of the street as she spoke. "Be careful, Riley. After what we saw in that tent, I wouldn't put it past Nadim to have left another hideous booby trap to surprise us..."

CHAPTER

6

NADIM'S LAUNCH

AN HOUR AND FIFTEEN MINUTES LATER

B evan turned and strode down the deck toward Gunter. "I caught sight of the snipers heading for the other launch. Did they report in to Nadim yet?"

"Why don't you ask me?" Nadim asked sarcastically as he came up from belowdecks. "And the answer is yes. It all went beautifully, just as I planned. I knew it would, once I was able to zero in on Maya's weaknesses."

"I don't mean to correct you," Bevan said. "But I'm the one who was able to find out about Maya's daughter and sent that info to you. Don't you think I deserve credit?"

"No. It would have been worthless if I hadn't arranged to use the girl I'd been toying with to give Maya a foreshadow of what was to come. My men said Maya was in a panic while she was running around the village. I would have loved to have seen her face when she finally saw what I had waiting for her in the tent." He added grudgingly, "Though perhaps you do deserve a bonus for getting me the info about where that maid was taking the kid when she left that house in the city."

"How generous," Bevan said ironically. "I only hope to continue to please you. But locating that temple may be worth a lot more than a bonus considering what we may find there other than the kid. You've heard the rumors about the treasure. I'm your best chance at finding that temple. I've spent two years paying off my men whenever they've brought me any information about it."

Nadim reached out and grabbed his arm. "You *know* where it is?"

"I know where it *might* be." He shook off his grip. "It's evidently difficult to access, and I'll need a little more time to learn how. But I've recently been able to hire one of the pickers in the groves who was formerly with the temple guards."

"I want his name," Nadim said harshly. "Are you playing with me, Bevan?"

"I wouldn't be such a fool," Bevan said. "But if I gave you his name, you'd no longer need me. Let me do the prep work and then I'll turn him over to you...for a very moderate fee." He wasn't getting through; he'd better sweeten the pot quickly. "I'll make certain you get Maya and any troublesome friends she may have brought to plague you."

That did it. Bevan could see Nadim's tension ease. "You'd better be superior to the sniper who took a shot at her at that village," Nadim growled. "He was a total asshole."

"But you wouldn't have wanted him to kill her," Bevan said. "My way is going to be much more satisfying for you. The daughter and then Maya. I can hardly wait to see it." He turned and headed for his speedboat. "I'll be in touch. You won't be disappointed in me..."

"Wait just a minute," Nadim called.

Shit. Bevan turned to face him. "Another problem?"

"Since you've been bragging about all your contacts, maybe you can help me with something else. I've been having trouble with breaking into that damn mountain stronghold that Maya has guarded like Fort Knox. We haven't been able to get near it. Maybe that's where the coffers are located and not the temple."

"It's possible." Bevan tried not to show his annoyance. "I'll work on it. I do have a few men I've sent up there to look around. They haven't been able to get very far, but a little applied pressure can work miracles."

"That's what I've found, too." Nadim's smile was totally malicious. "So get me a complete report on what I can expect to find up there." He met his eyes. "And I want it right away, Bevan. That little game I played today wasn't nearly enough. I'm hungry for more. I want to see Maya and all those friends she brought to help her start to bleed..."

———

FIRST-AID HUT

MABATO VILLAGE

When Riley came back into the first-aid hut over two hours later, the area had been cleaned and cleared of the bandages that had remained after she'd finished with her last patient. There was now a long rectangular table in the middle of the room on which the young girl lay on a stretcher covered in a white sheet, another white sheet over her naked body. Riley stopped and then forced herself to stand beside the stretcher and look down at the girl's face. "Hello," she whispered. "If you're somewhere out there, all this must seem strange and bewildering to you. But there's no one here who wants to hurt you; that's all in the past. I know you wouldn't want your parents to know about all that pain you went through so, if you don't mind, we're going to wash you and wrap you in a pretty blanket. It will make them feel a little better. I'm sure that's what you'd want. Okay?"

"I'm sure that's what she'd want, too," Cade said gently from the doorway. He came forward to stand beside Riley. "But you don't have to do this. I could get a couple of the island guards to do it."

"Don't be silly. I want to do it. I think she'd want me to do it. It's not as if I haven't spent years in the tombs of Egyptian rulers who have been dead a thousand years longer than Siena."

"My apologies," Cade said. "By all means, continue." He nodded at the thick, colorfully striped woven blanket she was carrying. "You seem to already have a plan in mind. Siena? You found out who she was?"

She nodded. "Siena Fazkar. It took a little while. But one of the villagers remembered that a few days ago, one of the women who worked in the orchards was calling around to other villages and asking if they knew anything about her daughter Siena. She had stayed home from school to help with the harvest and hadn't come home that night. I ran and got Maya and she called the orchard and talked to the mother. The girl was still missing, and they'd been searching frantically everywhere for her. Maya had her text a photo of the girl." She looked down at the face of the girl on the stretcher. "She looked very happy in that photo, but there wasn't any doubt. Maya had to tell her mother she wasn't going to find her little girl."

"Why isn't it Maya in here getting her ready for her parents?"

"Because I told her to go get the parents and bring them here. The orchards are almost as far as the airport. They wouldn't have been in any shape to drive after she told them about Siena." Her lips tightened. "Though she didn't tell them in what kind of shape we'd found her. That's why I came in here right away—to do a little damage control."

"I'm surprised Maya didn't want to do it herself."

Riley shook her head. "She's the caretaker, and she's good at it. She knew what her job was in this nightmare."

"Then will you let me help you?"

She shook her head. "I know what my job is, too. I'll call in a few neighbors to give me a hand. I want it done quickly, before her parents show up. Go find something else to do. I'm sure that won't be difficult. Have you been able track those snipers?"

"To an inlet where they were picked up," Cade said. "But I'm not worried. It's only a matter of time. You can't believe how motivated I am."

Yes, she could. She'd seldom seen him more lethal than he'd been since that moment standing over Siena's body. "You have to consider this could all have been an elaborate trap aimed at Maya."

"That's obvious. But it doesn't change the fact that some assholes are meant to die, and in this case I cheerfully volunteer to take care of it." He paused. "It's clear that Nadim has something more sinister in mind for Maya, however. He gave those shooters permission to take her down if the opportunity permitted itself. But that wasn't the prime objective. Otherwise, they wouldn't have withdrawn so quickly after I took out the sniper who missed that shot at Maya. Nadim wants to make her death a production to soothe his wounded ego and show everyone around him that no one can treat him the way she did." A muscle jerked in his cheek as he looked down at Siena. "He wanted her to see this poor kid and associate what he'd done to her with Maya's own child. But anyone can see it's only the beginning."

"Maya knows that," Riley said. "She had it figured out before she made you take her to that tent. She's always said it was the endgame. Now she knows she has to end it quickly. After we finish here, she's going to go to the temple to see her daughter, but then Nadim is next on her agenda. She as much as told me that she had no other option."

"Which puts me squarely behind the eight ball," Cade said bitterly. "I promised you I'd take care of her, and that nothing would happen to her. But I saw how she operates today. There's no way she's going to sit around and let me go after Nadim on my own. She's going to hunt him down herself."

"She has reason," Riley said. "Who could blame her?"

"*I* could," he said harshly. "Because she's not only risking her own life. Today you followed her into that forest, and you had no idea what you were getting into. You just knew that you had to help your friend. And I can see it happening again and again. I couldn't stop her, and I'm not going to be able to stop you unless I can figure out a way to keep her safe."

"It's not as if either one of us is totally dependent on you, Cade," she said quietly. "We've both learned to take care of ourselves almost from the cradle. I'll be grateful for anything you can do for Maya, but I wasn't being foolish when I ran after her. I was armed, and it was clear you thought the situation was safe for Maya. Why wouldn't it be safe for me? I wasn't worried about the physical ramifications, but anyone could see how emotionally fragile she was when she went with you." She lifted her chin. "And I was right to follow her. You weren't handling it at all well, Cade. She was *hurting*."

"Are you done?"

"For the time being." She began to unknot the ties binding the blanket. "You can tell the women waiting outside to come in to help now. I've got to hurry to get Siena ready to see her parents. I want them to think that she looks like the angels wrapped her in their colorful cloaks to keep out all pain and cold."

"I'm sure that you'll succeed," he said gently. "I'm glad you're going to allow me to do something." He was heading for the door. "You'll pardon me if I get to work on a few ideas of my own. You're not seeing my personal stake in the situation at all..."

It was almost three in the morning when Cade, Riley, and Maya finally stood in the village square watching as Kirby backed one of the island guard trucks out of the local garage. Then he helped Siena's parents load the stretcher in the back, and they climbed in beside their daughter. Even in that brief moment of separation, Riley noticed that Siena's mother kept a tight grip on the blanket in which Riley had wrapped her daughter. It was as if she couldn't bear not having that contact. It had been a long and achingly sad several hours for Siena's parents after they had seen their daughter tonight. But all through that time the other villagers and even Jelsko had put aside their own personal sadness for the harm done to them and their own village to come by and give a few words of comfort. Riley had tried to be as kind and helpful as possible during that period, but they had only wanted to cling to Maya.

She was the rock that was keeping them afloat tonight, and Riley couldn't have admired her more. She gave them comfort but also the strength to fight through this agony. Riley knew she must be as exhausted as Riley felt, but she never let them see it. Now it was ending, and Maya embraced Siena's parents and jumped out of the truck to the ground. Kirby glanced at Maya as he got into the driver's seat. "I'll get them safely back to their own village, but are you sure you won't give me directions how to get to my next stop? I know you said the location of the temple was confidential, but it would save me a hell of a lot of bother."

Maya smiled. "But then I'd have to kill you. Just come back here and we'll get you to the temple. It's not as if it's a place you can get with a GPS setting. Just take care of seeing that those three heartbroken people you're caring for are settled in their home and then drive the truck back here to Jelsko's village."

"Whatever you say." Kirby turned to Cade. "I texted Anders about the crew coming in later today and told them to arrange for repairs on this village as you ordered. And I'm trying to locate Finn Kagan. Who knows where he is right now." He pressed his foot on the accelerator. "I'll contact you as soon as I have Siena's parents safe. It may take longer for Anders and Kagan."

"Make Kagan a priority," Cade said. "I need him."

"So do half the nations in the world at one time or another. Like I said, I'm working on it." He lifted his hand. "But you may have to go after him yourself."

"Then I will."

Cade watched him drive out of the village before he held open the rear door of the jeep for Riley, then turned to Maya. "I assume you're not going to let me drive us to this temple?"

Maya shook her head. "Even if it wasn't forbidden to reveal the directions to the temple to anyone, you'd only get lost."

Riley gazed at her curiously. "Yet you gave me the general location as deep in the north-central area when you were drawing my map."

Maya shrugged. "It was necessary. I had to break through that wall you both were building against me. It was a way to demonstrate that you could trust me. So I told you enough to keep you happy."

"Was it the truth?"

Maya smiled. "Yes, but I also told you that you'd need me to find it. That was also true." She paused. "Even if you tried to dazzle me with space-age technology. That's usually the first key treasure hunters use to break through barriers." She got into the driver's seat. "Sit back and relax. Sleep if you can. The route is practically all jungle, but we'll have to walk the last few miles."

Cade grinned as he got in the backseat. "I have a very good memory and extensive tracking experience in the jungle. I'll see if I can memorize the way back."

"Do that." Maya glanced at Riley. "You, too?"

She shook her head wearily. "I'm not in the mood for challenges right now. I'm still sick from the sight of what Nadim did to Siena. I just want to shut my eyes and forget it for a little while until we can make him pay." She closed her eyes. "I'll worry about space-age tech and jungle instincts later, Cade. I've watched how those villagers feel about Maya all day and I've decided I trust her. You'll have to make your own decisions. But right now I prefer to just trust her to get us to the damn place."

"No problem." He kissed her cheek and then leaned back in his seat. "Try to take a nap, love. It's been one hell of a day. I believe Maya and I both want it to go away for you for a little while…"

She didn't open her eyes, but she had to ask a question. "Who's Finn Kagan? I don't believe I've ever heard you talk about him."

"An old friend from my service days. He taught me quite a bit before he got bored with me and wandered away."

"Bored with you?" she repeated drowsily. "He must have been crazy. I probably wouldn't like him."

"I think you would. But he's not to everyone's taste."

"Crazy…"

A few minutes later he realized that she was asleep. He pulled her closer against his shoulder.

"What do you want with Kagan?" Maya was looking at Cade in the rearview mirror.

He lifted his gaze to the mirror. "You've heard of him?"

"Of course, but I'm not surprised that Riley hasn't. She's done a great amount of trekking through the jungle, but Kagan is a mountain man. He's done a lot of climbing around here. He's climbed Everest eight times. I've heard he's fantastic." She paused and asked again, "What do you want with him?"

"I think he might be useful." He changed the subject. "But I don't believe he'll be going back to Everest. It was beginning to bore him the last time I talked to him. He was spending a lot of time at K2."

"The most dangerous climb in the world," she murmured. "And you're not going to tell me what you want with Kagan, are you?"

"Probably not immediately. I'll have to think about it. But you shouldn't jump to conclusions about Riley. She was the one who decided that Helen's tomb was probably in the mountains because of the preservation factor. She practically handed me the sarcophagus on a silver platter."

"I wasn't denigrating Riley. I realize how smart she is. No one could appreciate her more than I do."

"Yes, they could." He brushed the top of Riley's head with his lips. "I do." He lifted his eyes again. "That's why I'm being very cautious with you. Riley's all heart and dives in without thinking as long as she trusts someone. I have to do a little investigating to make sure no one is going to play her."

"It wouldn't be me."

"If it is, you won't be around long." He added softly, "And you'd regret it. I hope I won't have to make that kind of judgment. I prefer to keep to our arrangement. But you still haven't let us know enough about you yet."

"That will come. I've always found it's best to learn about people through experience. You'll learn a lot at the temple." She added, "I do realize it's not fair that I know more about you, but that was necessary. I had to do extensive research when I thought I might use you to help save the island. I already knew everything I had to know about Riley."

"Don't be too sure. I've been finding out all kinds of things I didn't know about Riley recently. She's a constant mystery to be solved." He grinned. "If she lets you."

"Thanks for the tip." She shrugged. "But I imagine you might have more problems than I would. I've been taught to negotiate rather than dominate."

"Hmm…" He tilted his head thoughtfully. "Is that why you stabbed Nadim and caused all this uproar?"

"That was an exception to prove the rule."

"If you say so."

"I do say so."

"Then I wouldn't think about arguing, given your faultless negotiating skill." He leaned back in the seat. "I'd rather concentrate on remembering every twist and turn we've been making on the way to your temple."

"And you think you've done it so far?"

"Yes, though I expect it will get more difficult."

"You have no idea. We have guards at the temple who have worked there for years, but they have to be led out by special escorts or they become hopelessly lost. Would you care to make a wager?"

"No, because that would mean I'd have to offer proof, and I prefer to avoid letting you know that I've succeeded. That might become dangerous."

"And it might also mean you've failed and don't want to admit it."

He nodded. "That could happen, too. Another reason not to give you proof either way." He was silent for a moment. "I have a question. If what you've said about those special escorts is true, you have to be one in order to take us to the temple. How do those escorts learn the way? How many of them are there?"

She chuckled. "Wait until you get to the temple and count them...if what I've said is true."

———————

They arrived at the point where they were to leave the jeep two hours later. Riley was wide awake again and gazing outside the vehicle shaking her head. "This is incredible. I've never seen such deep foliage or complicated trails, it's almost... smothering. So much dazzling greenery." She turned to Maya. "How far away are we from this temple?"

"Only a few miles. But you'll have to stick close or you'll lose me on the trail. You wouldn't want to do that."

"No, I wouldn't." Riley made a face. She glanced at Cade. "Unless you think you've got all the trails in these entire woods memorized?"

"I believe we should rely on Maya for the time being. It will be interesting to see her woodland technique."

"Yeah, sure." Maya laughed. "Then keep up." She started down the trail. "And watch close. In about a hundred yards you won't see the trail any longer. I'll be your only point of contact."

Riley instinctively increased her pace.

Then she felt Cade take her hand. "Don't rush. That warning was really for me. There's no way she'd ever really lose you. She just wanted to point out how helpless I could be."

"And are you?"

He shook his head. "I'm like Maya. I'd never lose you."

"I don't believe I like the idea of being caught in the middle of this game the two of you are playing."

"You should. It shows how special you are."

"I already know that." She pulled her hand away. "No more games. Or I'm on my own."

He held up both his hands. "I surrender."

She nodded. "Wise move. Now can you get me back to Maya?"

He took her hand again. "This is a bad move if we can't trust her."

"Then make certain we can. How far ahead is she?"

"Three left turns and one to the right." He was moving quickly. "She's slowing down because she thought she might have lost you. She should be right ahead..." He turned the corner. "And there she is. Hello, Maya."

She smiled. "Hello, Cade. You're even better than I thought. But you blew it toward the end."

"No, I didn't. Riley didn't like our game and she decided to stop it in its tracks. She wasn't amused. I told you not to underestimate her."

"How close are we to the temple, Maya?" Riley asked.

"It's just ahead. There's a cave in about another hundred feet, and once you enter it, it quickly becomes completely dark. But soon there will be lanterns that will light your way until you reach the street."

"Street?" Riley asked. "Not temple?"

Maya grimaced. "For heaven's sake, it was originally built by Silvana. She'd been in Rome too long not to have accepted their luxuries and civilized architecture. Of course there are cobbled streets and fine torches and museums, all to display the glory of Silvana Marcella."

"I thought it was originally built to shelter the animals."

"And it did shelter them in the beginning, but she had another purpose as the island grew more prosperous. She concentrated on breeding the horses she'd brought from Rome and kept only them in the temple stable and valley area. The cattle she distributed among the villages. The temple itself was used as a residence and guardhouse to protect Silvana. There's a compound of soldiers always on duty here to maintain security. She was always wary about the possibility that she could be dragged back to Rome and executed."

"I take it there was never an arena built for gladiator battles in her domain?" Cade asked.

Maya shook her head. "No way. She had been a slave too long and hated it with a passion by the time she ran away. She'd had to kill friends in the arena if the crowds turned thumbs-up, which was the signal for death. Look, she was a warrior and stayed that way for the rest of her life. But she was many other things as well, like any soldier could be. She made this island what it is, and she's still protecting it through laws and traditions."

"And the caretakers," Riley said quietly. "I saw a little of that tonight."

Maya waved her hand dismissively. "That was tradition, too. I was just doing my job."

"There appears to be quite a bit of heart connected to that job." Riley was silent for an instant. "I know we're here to make sure your Bailey is safe. But is there another reason? Are we going to find the sarcophagus and jewels here, too? You're not being very open with us, yet you expect everything. Do you even know the location of the sarcophagus?"

"I might," Maya said. "But that's one of my wild cards. I'd be foolish to reveal everything to you when everyone on this island is depending on me. I've given you my promise that you won't be cheated if you help me, but I have to be very sure of you. When I am, I'll be the one who gives you the details." She emphasized. "*All* the details. Be a little patient."

"We will," Riley said. "But I'm not like you and Cade with your games. I believe we've already shown you that we're committed. We won't be patient for long."

"Good enough," Maya said. "I couldn't expect more from—"

Riley suddenly grabbed Cade's arm. "It's getting lighter in here. It looks like—"

Then they were standing looking out at the cobbled streets, with beautifully shaped lamps hanging from the curved metal stands. The tall, two-story buildings had stained-glass windows that looked more like precious gems in the lamplight. "Beautiful..." Riley murmured. "Silvana?"

"We're talking about centuries," Maya said. "But there were many artists who offered their talents to make it this wonderful." Her gaze was searching the crowded streets. "It was always considered an honor to work on the temple. It took total dedication due to the security restrictions, but when it was finished, it was—" She broke off as she saw what she'd been searching for. "Bailey!" She flew out of the cave and across the street toward a child, dressed in jeans and a turtleneck, coming out of one of the buildings. Then she was on her knees and Bailey was in her arms. "Hey, what are you doing out here alone? Where's Tashi?"

"Being dragged behind her," Tashi said dryly as she came out the door. "She caught a glimpse of you out the window while she was with her art teacher and ran out of there. I, of course, have to accept the blame for her bad behavior."

"No, you don't," Bailey was grinning at her. "You know you never do anything wrong. How many times have you told me that?"

"Because it's true," Tashi said. "And you have to realize that perfection is possible so you can model yourself on me." Her eyes were twinkling. "And not your mother, who has many flaws. One of which is not to warn me that she'd arrived."

"No, she doesn't." Bailey was back in Maya's arms again. "Everyone knows that she always has a reason. Tell her, Mama."

"No reason." She was gesturing to Cade and Riley. "I should have told her I was here. But I was excited because I've brought you two new friends to meet." She took Riley's hand and brought her closer. "This is Riley Smith. I knew her a long time ago. She's very smart and she knows all about queens like Silvana. She even found one of her own and her name is Helen. Maybe she'll tell you her story if you ask her nicely."

Bailey took Riley's hand. "How do you do?" she said politely. "I'm very glad to meet you." Then the formality was gone as her face lit with excitement. "And that's the truth. I *like* to meet new people. I don't get to meet very many because I have lessons and I have to learn to be as smart as my mama."

"You're already way past that, Bailey," Maya said. "Though I do have a fair quantity of practical knowledge that I can still teach you."

Bailey shook her head. "You're wonderful." She looked at Riley. "Isn't she?"

"I think perhaps she is." Riley turned to Cade. "And this is another friend who will agree. His name is Morgan Cade, and he came here to help your mama straighten out a few things. He's very good at fixing things that go wrong."

Cade shook Bailey's hand. "I'm delighted to meet you. But she obviously didn't do anything wrong with you. Maybe we can just enjoy being together."

"Maybe," she answered absently, her gaze searching his face. "You *fix* things?" She nodded as she continued to look at him. "I think...you can. Is it okay if I ask you to do it sometime?"

He chuckled. "Oh, the pressure." He squeezed her hand. "I'll be glad to help you out anytime I can."

"Thank you," she whispered as she turned back to her mother. "I like them so much. Can we keep them here?"

"You'll have to ask them." She gave her a hug. "But they seem to want to be friends and you have a good chance."

Tashi took Bailey's hand. "Why don't we go up to the kitchen and see if we can bribe them with a fine meal. I've always found that works well."

"Mama?" Bailey looked at her mother. "Is it okay?"

She nodded. "Though you might tell her that bribery isn't legal, Tashi."

"People who are perfect don't have to worry about that," Tashi said. "I'll explain that the bribery is purely mine."

Bailey was giggling as she ran back into the house with Tashi.

"She's perfectly beautiful," Riley said, looking after her. "Polite and a real charmer. You told me she was ten?"

"Almost eleven," Maya said. "And I don't have anything much to do with her good manners. Tashi and her nanny, Lisan, do most of the teaching and correcting. I selfishly save most of my time with her for pure enjoyment. She doesn't need much correcting. She's a sensitive kid and doesn't want to rock the boat if she doesn't have to." She smiled. "And she's extraordinarily intelligent. She picks up languages incredibly well, she has an amazing skill when she's dealing with animals, and you should see her artwork. She's pure magic."

"And you're not the least bit prejudiced," Cade said gently. "Though it's clear you have reason. I can see why you were frightened when you saw Siena in that setup in the tent."

"Upset?" She shook her head. "I was terrified. It was my worst nightmare."

"I can understand it." Riley's gaze rose to the second floor of the house where Bailey had disappeared. "The threat was aimed directly at your little girl. Has it happened before?"

Maya shook her head. "I was able to keep Nadim from knowing about her before. I realized that she would always be a threat to me and, therefore, to herself. It was easy enough to arrange to keep her in separate quarters under guard. Everyone loved her and she loved everyone. I usually got to see her at least once a day. I arranged to do things with her that would keep me a part of her life." She paused. "But I'm betting it was

Bevan who found out about Bailey and told Nadim about the rumors that she was my daughter." She closed her eyes and shivered. "And Nadim thought of that foul way to punish me by doing that monstrous thing to poor Siena. Now I have to keep Bailey safe until I can get rid of him." Her eyes flicked open. "And I'll do it. But it might take a little while since he's become more powerful now. I'll probably need your crew who are coming in later today."

"They're not on loan to you," he said. "But I'll arrange to have them available when we'll need them."

"Good enough," Maya said. "Shall I have them brought here?"

"To protect Bailey?" he asked. "Now that I've met her, I can see that there's no way we could ever let anything happen to her. I realize she should be first on your list, but I also have my own priorities. I'll have to take a little time and see what I can do to make it a complete sweep."

She nodded curtly. "Whatever. Just not much time, or I'll have to do it myself." She turned to Riley. "While Tashi and Bailey are making lunch, do you want me to take you around to the Silvana Museum exhibits? I know you'll want to see them. You were always curious about Silvana when you first came here."

"And you were annoyingly closemouthed whenever I asked you too many questions."

"I told you that it would be a new story," Maya said. "We made a deal. I still can't tell you about anything that's confidential, but I'll let you know about Silvana's life as we knew it. Some of it wasn't even about Silvana's life but about the life and culture of the Amazons who raised her."

"I'll take it." Riley's eyes were suddenly shining. "As long as you throw in a little Silvana now and then." She turned to Cade. "Coming?"

He shook his head. "I'll join you for lunch, but I think I'd like Maya to order one of her officers to show me around the compound and introduce me to her men. Okay?"

Maya nodded as she raised her hand and motioned for an officer. "If you like, but you have an archaeology degree among all your other decorations. Wouldn't you prefer to see Silvana's domain?"

"Not at the moment. Right now I'm more interested in the modern world than the ancient. I want to know everything I can that will make me able to function with your cozy little militia."

"They won't tell you anything that's confidential, either." She gestured to an officer dressed in fatigues. "Captain Alex Galdar, this is Morgan Cade. Show him around the compound." Then she turned back to Riley and gestured across the cobbled street. "The museum is right over there. It's always best to hit the Greek vases first. You'll be amazed at what they tell you."

Riley could see what she meant as they strolled through the wonderfully constructed glass cases that contained the Greek vases, each a work of art. Most were obviously very old and told their own stories—stories were of the glory and superb ingenuity of the Amazon women who had gone before Silvana.

"I had no idea so many Greek artists had portrayed the Amazons on their vases," Riley murmured as she bent to examine a woman mounted on a horse drawing aim with her bow. "You said over a thousand?"

"Probably more than that," Maya said. "Actually, the Greeks didn't like the idea of barbarian women being drawn on their vases. They disapproved of their clothing and weapons and I'm sure they didn't commission as many as with more conventional subjects." Maya grinned. "But the artists were enthralled with the way they looked and kept on painting them. They found the close-fitting trousers they'd created to be very sensuous. And the vision of them on the back of a horse was challenging and exciting."

"They created trousers?" Then Riley remembered something. "That's right, you said Silvana showed up on the island wearing trousers and riding a white horse."

"Which was very unconventional. The Romans didn't like them. The Greeks particularly wouldn't have approved. They liked both their men and women to dress in layers. Also, the men didn't wear undergarments and if women rode horses, they would expose themselves. Another excellent reason for them to invent the use of trousers. Not only that but the barbarian women and men wore the same garb. They also fought and worked at the same tasks. In the Greeks' eyes that meant they were attempting equality. Heaven forbid that would ever come to pass." She shrugged. "But the artists found the way the Amazon women dressed to be exciting. They found everything about them exciting. The way they moved, the way they interacted with their horses and other animals. Look at that vase with the warrior with the eagle on her shoulder. It's no wonder the Romans found Silvana so interesting."

"You said that the Greeks didn't like their weapons, either?"

"They found them unusual, but they became accustomed to them. The Greeks said the Amazons were the first to use iron weapons." She pointed out a battle-ax, then went down the line to indicate a bow, a quiver full of arrows, knives, spears. "They preferred light weapons whenever possible. Even their armor was as light as they could make it while still maintaining strength. It was simpler since they used horses whenever they could as part of their weaponry. The Amazon women were magnificent horsewomen, and they took wonderful care of all their animals. By the time an Amazon reached the age of four, she was responsible for the care of her own pony or horse and also helped with the care of the herds. If the child appeared to have a special medical or training talent, she was given extra rations and respect from the elders. If she showed a remarkable empathy with the animals, she was considered exceptional." She led Riley down another aisle. "Here's the chest armor used by the gladiators in the arenas, together with the leg braces. You'll see they've never been used. I heard that Silvana never looked at them again after she had them put in these special cases."

"She was fortunate she never had to," Riley said.

"No one could call her fortunate. But she survived those arenas. And she lived through a very bad time." She paused. "And she gave all these island people a chance to have a better life. I admire her for that."

"So do I," Riley said. "These villagers on the island are hardworking and extremely well educated. Thanks for showing me a little of what Silvana went through out on those steppes."

"It was probably one of the best times of her life. I wouldn't mind living on the back of a horse riding through the wilderness with my sisters." She grinned and turned away. "But maybe that's another lifetime. Now we'd better go have lunch with Bailey, so Tashi won't yell at us."

———

"You're back!" Bailey ran to meet them at the door when Maya and Riley walked into the suite fifteen minutes later. Her face was flushed with pleasure as she reached out to hold Riley's hand. "We've just finished making the stew and while it cooks, Tashi said I could do a sketch of you, if you don't mind?" She turned to Maya. "Would it be okay? I don't think they're going to stay long. I'd like to have something to remember them by."

"It's entirely up to Riley," Maya said. "It would make Bailey happy if you wouldn't mind sparing ten minutes or so. She's very quick."

Riley shrugged. "If you like. It really doesn't matter."

"Sit down. I'll get you a cup of coffee." Maya disappeared into the kitchen.

Riley smiled at Bailey. "Though I don't know why you think we won't be staying long. Your mother just showed me some wonderful Greek vases with beautiful ladies riding fantastic horses. This entire place is very interesting." She was looking around the apartment, which was charmingly decorated in a colorful Asian/modern fusion. She gestured to some sketches on the wall. "Did you do all these? They're very good. I'd be happy to join them." She watched Bailey take out her sketchbook, sit down on the floor with legs crossed, and begin to sketch. "But I'm sorry that I don't have a horse to ride like that lady on the vase."

"That doesn't matter," she said absently. "I can draw a horse anytime. All I have to do is go down to the stable. But people are almost always different and special once you see inside them. I don't think Mama would have brought you if you weren't special." She was drawing swiftly. "I think maybe you're like Mr. Cade who knows how to fix things."

"Where did you get that idea?" Riley asked. "Cade and I are very different."

"You can't fix things?"

She thought about it. "Well, I've been trained to heal sick people. I guess you could say that's a form of fixing things."

"Sure it is." Bailey looked up with a brilliant smile. "Fixing is fixing. I knew Mama wouldn't bring you unless you could help."

"Stop chattering and finish your sketch, Bailey." Maya was back with a cup of coffee. "You and Tashi promised to feed us lunch." She handed the cup and saucer to Riley. "Sorry to waste your time. I guess you've discovered Bailey can be very driven when it comes to any idea she gets into her head."

"She doesn't mind," Bailey said. "Did you know she heals people sometimes?"

"Yes, I've seen her do it very recently," Maya said. "But she's not here to do that. We have other, more important things that need doing. Have you finished the sketch?"

"Yes." Bailey got to her feet. "Thank you for allowing me to sketch you, Riley. If it's all right with you, I will hang it on the wall. Anytime you come back you'll see it and know I've been thinking about you."

"What a lovely thought," Riley said. "And I hope we can come back to see you many, many times."

"Me, too." Bailey smiled and turned to leave. "Now I'll go help Tashi. Thank you again for my sketch, Riley." She ran out of the room.

Riley frowned. "You didn't have to be stern with her, Maya. She wasn't being pushy."

"No, she was just being Bailey, and that means appealing

and persuasive and thoroughly adorable. It also means she could charm the birds from their perches. It's hard to say no to her."

"She didn't ask me for anything but the sketch."

"Yet." She made a dismissive gesture. "And I'm not saying she'll demand anything else. It's only that when she sees something wrong that has to be fixed, she works until it's done. I just know how difficult it is to say no to her."

"I can see that. Who would want to?" Riley frowned. "Why are you making such a big thing about this?"

"Because that absolutely sweet child who could break your heart is also the most stubborn individual on the planet. When she focuses, she never loses control, and once her decision is made, it never wavers. Your only way out is to distract her."

Riley gazed at her in disbelief. "You're joking."

She shook her head. "Do I look like I'm joking?" She made a face. "Look, I hoped I wouldn't have to go into this with you or Cade but that's not going to happen. Cade intrigued her and then you mentioned your medical background. Bailey's been worrying lately about the animals on the property. She thinks she might need help."

"Then get her help. Is it the horses? You mentioned that you have a fine stable here. I'm certain you must have equally fine vets to take care of them. Cade and I would be glad to help out, but I'm sure you wouldn't consider us qualified to care for your valuable animals."

"It's not what I consider, it's what Bailey thinks," Maya said flatly. "And she appears to have taken a shine to you." She shrugged. "I'll try to find a way to ease you away from what might be an awkward situation for you. But it would help if you didn't encourage her."

"I'll do my best, but as you say, she's very appealing. I refuse to be rude to her, Maya."

"Did I ask that?" Maya grimaced. "I'm completely nuts about Bailey. I realize that she poses a number of problems for me right now, but there's nothing I wouldn't do to make her happy. All I want you to do is not to give in to everything she asks...even if she makes it sound reasonable."

"Why don't you just hire her a great vet and put her worries about the animals to rest?"

"Believe me, that wouldn't solve the problem."

Riley frowned, puzzled. "Why not?"

Maya took another look at her expression and then gave up the fight. She waved her hand in a gesture of surrender. "Because Bailey would probably know more than your super-duper vet and not listen to his advice."

"What?"

Maya sighed. "I told you she was very smart."

"You didn't tell me she was *that* smart."

"Now I'm telling you. She scores off the charts whenever they test her. She just doesn't let it get in her way," Maya said. "But sometimes it does get in the way of the people around her."

"Like you?"

"Absolutely not. I know how lucky I am just to have her on this earth. She would never get in my way."

"You said she was stubborn."

"When she thinks she's right. And she almost always thinks she's right when it comes to the animals." She shook her head. "Most of the time it's true. She has an instinct. From the time she was three years old she seemed to know what they were feeling, what they needed, when no one else did."

"Three," Riley murmured thoughtfully. Then she suddenly grinned. "That's a little young even by Amazon standards. Didn't you tell me that women of the clan had to know how to take care of their horses by the time they were four?"

"And Bailey's abilities could have nothing to do with the fact that she was Silvana's descendant," Maya said immediately. "It could be purely coincidental."

Riley chuckled. "But can you tell me that you haven't thought of the possibility that she might be a throwback to our Silvana? You know your daughter and you've studied Silvana; haven't you imagined you've seen a sign or two?"

"She's her own person," Maya said firmly. "I won't believe anything else."

"But so was Silvana," Riley said. "Wouldn't that make them even more alike?" She held up her hand as Maya started to protest. "Just questioning. Actually, I think you'd be a fantastic person to carry on the Silvana heritage."

"I don't," Maya said. "And I wouldn't want Bailey saddled with it, either. I want her to be free."

"Not if she's as special as you say," Riley said quietly. "Eve's son Michael is very special, and she agonizes the same way you do about Bailey. I'm certain she'd like him to be free, too. But only if the freedom comes with safety."

"That goes without saying," Maya said. "But there has to be a way to have both."

"I hope you're right," Riley said. "But there are all kinds of prisons. Cade has been in one all his life and learned to deal with it." She forced a smile. "Which reminds me. He was supposed to join us for lunch." She took out her phone. "It's time I nagged him and got him back here . . . You can convince him to be tough with Bailey. I don't seem to be doing so well."

CHAPTER

7

Cade was full of the stories he'd gleaned from Alex Galdar and the other island officers when he sat down at the table several minutes later. He turned to face Maya after one of the stories concerning the hunt for poachers in the mountains. "But you'd probably heard that one. Galdar said you'd led them into the mountains where they'd caught up with the bastard. Do you often go hunting with them?"

"Not often. Only when necessary. It's one of my duties to maintain the environment of the island and mountains. Poaching is forbidden. When I receive reports, I have to follow up on them."

"I agree." He lifted his glass of wine to her. "I'm a great one for follow-ups. And Galdar and his men seem to have great respect for you. You must do it extremely well."

"Well enough." She turned to Bailey. "Why don't you run

into the kitchen and get that dessert I saw Tashi making? And tell her that she's to come out and have it with us."

"Okay." Bailey pushed back her chair. "But she told me no when I asked her before." She was running toward the kitchen door but stopped to look over her shoulder at Cade. "My mother does everything extremely well," she told him quietly. "Particularly in the mountains. She's even better than I am there. She would never let any animal suffer or die. Naturally all those soldiers think she's terrific."

He smiled at her. "I'm glad you set me straight. I thought she was being too modest."

Bailey smiled back at him. "She says bragging is stupid and ugly. But I think people should be honest with each other. I wouldn't want you to believe a lie. I want you to be my friend."

"And I think I'm already that, Bailey," he said gently. "Do you want me to go help you with that dessert?"

"Nah." She turned back toward the door. "Tashi would just give me a lecture about obeying my elders. Maybe next time." She disappeared into the kitchen.

Maya shook her head. "She wasn't really being rude. I'm afraid she can be a bit defensive. Do you want an apology?"

"I wouldn't think of it," Cade said. "I just want her in my corner when I have my next brawl."

Maya smiled. "That can be arranged." She looked at Riley. "I told you so."

Riley nodded. "Yes, you did." She glanced at Cade. "And you're not going to be any help at all."

Cade's brows lifted. "Am I in trouble?"

"No, I think Bailey was entirely in the right." She added, "And that also makes me right. What could be better than that?"

"I'm not certain." He suddenly met her eyes. "There has to be something. Perhaps we should discuss it."

She couldn't breathe. The air between them had changed from amusement to intense sexuality. It had happened in the space of a second, and she could feel it in the swelling of her breasts, the pounding of the pulse in her throat. She was being bombarded by memories of the two of them together that were as explicit as they were carnal. He had caught her off guard and she was responding as she always did to him. And she could tell he knew exactly what he was doing, damn him. But that didn't mean anyone else at the table had to know. If Maya hadn't noticed already. "Why bother?" She took a sip of her wine. "Bailey should have her victory."

"I wasn't thinking of robbing her. I was thinking in terms of sharing." His eyes were twinkling, and for a moment she thought he was going to continue. She knew that streak of mischief in him. But to her relief he smiled and turned to Maya. "You must be even better than your captain told me if Bailey has that amount of faith in you. How much time do you spend in the mountains?"

"However much is necessary." She shrugged. "The mountains have always been a problem because we can't always keep the shepherds and farmers in the foothills as well protected

IRIS JOHANSEN

as I'd like. Between the poachers and human traffickers, they keep the sentries busy." She changed the subject. "Besides the fact that Bailey loves the mountains and insists on spending a lot of time up there. I have to make sure that she's kept safe." Her lips twisted wryly. "Though she's probably sure she can take care of herself. She was being generous when she said I knew those mountains better than her. I know enough track- ing lore, but she knows every cave and path on the entire range. But that doesn't mean anything now. I have to stay with her. I can't let her out of my sight, and I won't be able to keep her off the mountain."

"You're saying you have to be her shadow?"

"Wouldn't you?" Her voice was suddenly shaking. "You saw what I saw in that tent."

"I can see we have a problem."

"Which we'll solve." Riley reached out and squeezed her hand. "Though it would be better if we could keep her here temporarily. Can't you persuade her?"

Maya shook her head. "Not unless you want me to lock her in the temple prison. But even then, she'd probably find a way out. She's been helping take care of some of the animals for the shepherds in the foothills and she won't leave them for long. Tashi has kept her here at the temple about as long as she'll tolerate. Maybe another day or two." Her lips thinned. "And once she's in the mountains, she'll be twice as vulnerable to attack from Nadim. He's probably waiting for his chance."

"Then we'll make certain he doesn't get it," Cade said. "I've

180

been working on it, and I believe I've got it covered. We were just caught unaware when the bastard hit us before the plane had even landed. It won't happen again. After I talked to Alex, I called Kirby and told him that we're splitting up the team. He's to bring half to the temple area together with weapons and equipment. Alex will meet them and lead them down to the barracks. But Kirby is going to take the rest of the team and head for the mountain and set up camp in the foothills." Cade smiled at Maya. "If you'll agree to call your mountain sentries and keep them from causing Kirby and his men grievous harm when they show up. I've assured them a warm welcome."

"Without even consulting me?" she asked coolly.

"I'm consulting you now. After talking to Alex Galdar and getting a feel for the situation your forces are experiencing, I thought it wouldn't hurt to get the wheels in motion. You can use a little more help from my team. I've done nothing that can't be undone. I wanted to be ready for any development. Isn't that what you'd do?"

She was silent. Then she said grudgingly, "Yes, but it's lucky that you decided to tell me. You might have received some surprises you weren't expecting."

"You never expect surprises. That's why they're called surprises. I hope we'll both be able to furnish each other with a few before this is over." His expression hardened. "My teams will be ready to act by dawn tomorrow. I thought I'd take a trip up to the mountain then and make sure everything is in order."

Her eyes were narrowed on his face. "All those questions you asked me . . . You already knew the answers, didn't you?"

"Not to all of them. You're still a mystery. Besides, I had to know how you felt. That can be more important than anything else."

"I'm glad you realize that." She glanced soberly at Riley. "He's very dangerous, you know."

"I've always known that, but I can handle him." She grimaced. "And that's exactly the reason you decided to manipulate us into coming to the island. Stop bitching, Maya."

"I just thought I'd warn you." Maya shrugged. "Every now and then I have a tiny niggle of guilt stab me. But since you assure me that you can take care of yourself . . ." She looked back at Cade. "So everything starts tomorrow?"

"With your permission. It appears to be an area that needs to be reinforced, for a number of reasons," he said mockingly. "Otherwise we'll have a discussion and you can let me know when you—" He broke off as Tashi appeared in the doorway with an enormous apple dish that smelled delicious and a distinctly disapproving expression. "Ahh, something more important seems to have appeared on our horizon to distract us." He got to his feet and was heading toward Tashi and Bailey. "Welcome." He took the dish from Tashi. "It can't be as wonderful as it smells. Come and sit down . . ."

Riley was in the shower two hours later when she heard the bedroom door in the other room open and close. She tensed and then called, "I don't recall inviting you, Cade. Go away."

"I thought you might say that, but I can't do it." She spotted his blurred figure only a few feet away outside the glass shower door. "I've decided it's against my principles not to try."

"Bullshit. It wasn't against your principals to try to embarrass me in front of Maya. You knew exactly what you were doing."

"I wasn't being that obvious . . . She might not have noticed."

"But you wanted her to."

"At that point, I didn't care one way or the other." His voice was suddenly weary. "I was just tired of worrying about Maya, and Bailey, and all the other people on this damn island who were keeping me away from you. And I was thinking that tomorrow it was going to start all over again up in those mountains. If it's as cold and snowy as I've heard, it will make it even more difficult." He added softly, "And I was remembering how long it had been since I was inside you. I wanted you to remember it, too."

His words were striking her like the pulsating rhythm of the shower against her body. She could make out his shadow outside the glass, so close, yet so far away . . . She could feel the heat of the water stroking her, and the muscles of her belly were clenching. "You made sure that I would," she said thickly. "Bad timing, Cade."

"Like I said, it had been too long. I was beginning to feel as if I was being shut out."

"Heaven forbid that ever happen. You're such a shy, introverted soul. Whatever would you do?"

"What I did," he said simply. "Just a gentle nudge to remind you that you're what's important to me and anything else has to get in line. I thought that might be all you'd need if you felt the same. Do you?"

"I might." She drew a deep breath. "When you're not being an asshole. Okay, anytime, all the time. And why the hell are you still outside this shower? Get your clothes off and get in here!"

He chuckled. "I was being as sensitive as I could." The shower door opened. "And I've had my clothes off since I came through that bedroom door." Then he was with her under the spray, lifting her, pushing her against the shower wall as he sank deep within her.

She gasped as her hands slid around his neck and held on tight. He kept her pinned as he moved harder and then harder still. His hands clenched on her buttocks as he lifted her into every thrust. "More...I need...more."

It was crazy. She couldn't breathe. Fire. Electricity.

So deep, yet it wasn't enough for him.

Or for her.

Her legs tightened around his hips as his teeth went to her nipples and pulled gently and then harder. "Good? Tell me you like it." His hands parted her thighs, and he was rubbing her as his teeth pulled and sucked her breasts. "Tell me."

She was so dizzy and full of him that she could barely speak. "I...like it."

He bit harder.

The combination of sensations was incredible!

She cried out. "Okay, I *love* it, dammit."

"Then let's have more." He lifted her, carrying her out of the shower to the bedroom. Then she was lying on her back on the bed as he pushed her legs up and used his hands on her. She moved back and forth, whimpering with need. But then he held her still as he sank slowly into her.

"I...want to...move," she gasped.

"No, you don't. Think...about it." He was going very slowly, each movement only a flex and yet each flex was an excruciating tease as he went deeper and deeper. "You like this, don't you?"

"Yes." Her entire body was on fire, yet the hunger was all the more intense. She gasped as he flexed the tiniest bit again. "But if you don't let me move, I think I'll have to do something terrible to you—"

He chuckled. "I'm appropriately terrified."

Then she screamed as Cade sank deep and began to stroke hard, deeper, harder. Lifting her to every thrust.

Deeper.

Harder.

She could feel the tears run down her cheeks.

Heat.

Sensation after sensation.

Close.

Terribly close, but not there.

But he wouldn't let her stop. No teasing now. He was taking her all the way . . .

And past it, way, way past it . . .

———

"We got the bed linens wet from the shower," Riley said as she nestled closer to Cade. "I think it was probably your fault. You didn't give me a chance to think about anything practical."

"I'll accept the blame." His lips brushed her cheek. "Though I do have to remind you that at one point I noticed how damp you were and personally dried every inch of you . . . inside and out. I remember that distinctly."

And so did Riley. She could still feel the rubbing of the toweling as he had slowly and sensuously massaged her. "Then perhaps I'd better accept part of the blame."

"How generous," he said dryly. "It was only a little damp. Are you uncomfortable? We could move down the hall to the room Maya assigned to me."

She shook her head. "I don't want to move. I may not ever want to move again. I was just a little worried about whether these linens are antiques or something. It's difficult knowing when some of the furniture seems to be centuries old and other pieces are fairly modern. I think the main theme is comfort and making guests feel at home."

"It works for me," Cade said. "We'll replace them if there's a problem." He bent down and teasingly licked her nipple. "Stop worrying."

"I'm not really worrying. I was just thinking about Maya." She turned over and looked down at him with a grin. "I'm just surprised that she assigned you a room of your own. She might have tried to throw us together. She may be very focused, but she does have a conscience. She didn't like it when she thought that bringing us to the island to help her was creating relationship problems. She mentioned it on the plane right before we landed. I think she's trying to strike a balance."

"She'd be too smart to be that heavy-handed," he said. "And she'd know neither of us would tolerate being managed. If she steps in, it would be subtle. I'd just as soon she stay out of it entirely." He made a face. "But that may not happen. She's too strong. We can but hope." He pulled her down and kissed her long, hard, until she was breathless. "At the moment, I like the way things are going just fine. I might have been a little too impatient, although we did have a good time. We're not in the Eve and Joe ballpark yet; however, we're talking and doing things together. We may have a bit further to go but we're on our way. Right?"

She smiled at those words that were half bold, dynamic Cade and half tinged with explanation and apology. It was so like this complicated man who couldn't help but try to shape the world to suit himself. Exasperating? Yes, but at this moment she was finding it endearing. She reached out and touched his lips. "I don't know how much progress you think we've made. I never thought we had that big a problem. You have to admit we didn't do much talking tonight. And I believe we've always had this part right," she said gently. "But I'm always open to practice and experimentation."

"I've noticed that about you." He grinned slyly. "It's a quality I admire and appreciate." He moved over her. "Particularly the experimentation..."

———

There was a knocking on Riley's door at five the next morning. It was immediately followed by Maya's voice. "Time to get up, Riley. Sorry. Breakfast is in twenty minutes and Bailey is ready to invade you if you don't show up on time."

"I'll be there." She shook her head to clear it of sleep and then jumped up and headed for the shower. Cade wasn't there, which was just as well given the threat of that invasion from Bailey. Sometime during the night he had told her he was going to leave early for the mountain, but it hadn't really registered. Not surprising. Cade himself was the only facet of the night that had been important. Her body was still throbbing and singing with the memory of those hours. She tried to block it out as she took a quick shower, dressed, and then headed for the door.

"Good morning." Bailey gave her a brilliant smile. "Isn't this wonderful? We're going to have such a good time." She was sitting propped up against the wall across from the bedroom door and scrambled to her feet when she saw Riley. "There are so many things I can show you. I wasn't sure that Mama was going to let you come up to the mountain, but I should have known she'd realize how special you are. I couldn't sleep after she told me last night. I had to get up and go outside and look up at the mountain and think about today." She took her hand and was pulling her toward the dining room. "Did you sleep?"

"Not very much. I had trouble, too." Bailey's enthusiasm was contagious, and Riley found herself grinning down at her. "Maybe not for the same reason. No one told me about all the things you're going to show me. Now I'm getting excited, too. I hear the mountain is your favorite place. Why?"

"Because it's *alive*. You'll see for yourself. But you'll do more. I can feel it." She pulled Riley into the dining room where Maya was setting the table. "I told you she wouldn't mind getting up, Mama. She was like me. She couldn't sleep, either."

"Maybe not quite like you," Maya said. Her lips were twitching as she glanced at Riley. "But I'll grant that you were probably both suffering from the same impatience and desire to break the rules. I'm glad that it worked out for both of you."

She gestured toward the kitchen. "Now go and help Tashi with the porridge. It may be the last decent meal we have for a while."

Bailey nodded. "You're right. I think I'll be busy when I get there..." She was running toward the kitchen.

"Sit down. Relax." Maya poured Riley a cup of coffee. "We have five or ten minutes. It was just easier to harness Bailey with activity before she exploded. She's really excited about you and Cade coming to the mountain."

Riley nodded. "She said there was so much to show me." She took a sip of her coffee. "How right was she?"

"You won't be disappointed," Maya said. "Neither will Cade. It's all coming together. That's the only reason I didn't object to this trip. It's been a fairly hellish time for you so far. I want you to see that I won't allow you to be cheated."

"And this journey will prove it?"

"It will be a generous down payment."

Riley studied her expression. "Are we back to the coffers of jewels again?"

"Perhaps. Talk to me after we reach the mountain." She looked her in the eye. "I'm not feeling guilty any longer, Riley. I've been watching you and Cade together and I believe the two of you are strong enough to get whatever you want from life. You may have a hell of a difficult time doing it, but that goes with the territory." Her lips twisted. "You're in far better shape than I am right now. I figure that if I give you what I promised, it will be enough to soothe any lingering remorse I might be feeling. If you don't feel the same, we'll renegotiate." She paused. "But there's one other thing about our arrangement I wanted to speak to you about before we leave today. You have to know how important it is to me." She drew a deep breath. "I'm going to ask that you protect Bailey if anything happens to me. You'll find her a problem, but she's worth every minute."

Riley stared at her, stunned. At first she couldn't believe that she'd heard correctly. "What the hell are you saying? You sound like you're making out a last will and testament. This isn't like you."

"How do you know?" Maya's tone was suddenly reckless. "I'm just being responsible, the way a good caretaker should. I'm going to do my very best to stay alive to take care of Bailey. But there's a good chance Nadim may cut my throat before this is over. I have to make provisions."

"And we're the provisions?"

"If you please. I've been studying you for years. When Cade appeared in your life, I could see that he might not only help me with the island, but also be a safety net for Bailey. You and Cade are the kind of parents she should have. You'll see that as soon as you watch her on the mountain."

"Bullshit. You're the only parent she should have. Anyone could see that. She adores you."

"Yes, but she would get over me in time. I have to do what's best for her."

"I'm not going to talk to you about this. It's totally idiotic."

Riley felt almost dazed. "And what about her own family? What about her father? Grandparents?"

Maya shrugged.

"Don't *do* that," Riley said. "Talk to me."

"I don't know who her father was," Maya said quietly. "Bailey isn't my child."

"What!"

"You heard me." She looked down at the depths of the coffee in her cup. "One of the shepherds found her wandering around half frozen in the barn of a farm in the upper valley of the mountain. Both of her parents had been killed by raiders who had attacked the farm and stolen all their livestock. Bailey couldn't have been more than two or three."

"It's a wonder she was still alive," Riley said.

"She shouldn't have been. The shepherd found her cuddled next to a young female deer in the far back of the shed. They must have shared warmth and managed to keep each other alive. No one knew whether one of the parents hid Bailey out there to save her or if she found her own way after she found herself abandoned."

"And you were never able to find any of Bailey's relatives?"

She shook her head. "The farmers and herders on the mountain came and went like nomads. They moved around the foothills a lot and there were storms that winter. The sheepherder who found Bailey didn't find anything at that farm but the doe who managed to keep her alive. By the time the shepherds contacted Jann Lu—who was still caretaker—and got her to the farm, there was no way to trace any possible relatives." She shrugged. "And as usual Jann Lu had her own ideas about how to handle the situation. She was excited about how Bailey had managed to survive and still seemed to have a close affinity for the deer who had saved her. She watched her for several days before she made up her mind. Jann Lu knew she didn't have long to live, and she hadn't officially made me caretaker yet. She was looking at what happened to Bailey as a sign that she had to move quickly and perhaps tie both duties together."

"Wait." Riley held up her finger. "I can see where this is going. This is where you're going to tell me Jann Lu decided to throw a sixteen-year-old kid into the job of caretaker right away because she needed to get everything settled?"

"It made perfect sense to her," Maya said. "She could see something special in Bailey. I could see it, too. I kind of edged away from all that talk about signs because I was afraid of the job itself. But Bailey was just as adorable then as she is now. You just wanted to reach out and help her be all she could be."

"What about all *you* could be?"

"I'd been trained for years. It was just up to me to take over a little sooner than expected. I could have refused."

"But you didn't." Riley shook her head. "Bailey refers to you as her mother..."

She smiled. "Every child needs a mother. It was easier for both of us. I never lied to her. When she was old enough to understand and could draw comparisons to the relationship with the animals that surrounded her, we had a long talk. She knows the love is there and that's all that's important."

"I can see how it would be." She added soberly, "But there's no way I'd let you give up that kid now. You're perfect together. We'll just find a way to get rid of Nadim and solve the entire problem."

Maya chuckled. "Whatever you say. Maybe I trained too long as caretaker. Tashi would agree that Jann Lu would find that solution entirely adequate."

———

After breakfast Maya arranged to have a helicopter fly them to the foothills of the mountains, and they arrived there shortly before noon. The area was a turmoil of activity between Maya's mountain sentries and the team that Kirby had brought in last night on Cade's orders.

Cade was talking to Kirby, but he broke off as the helicopter descended and ran to meet them. "You have a good setup," he told Maya. "I asked Kirby to do a little combining of materials, but I don't believe we'll need more than that." He swung Riley out of the aircraft to the ground and then turned to Bailey with a grin. "I like your mountain. I can see why you spend so much time up here."

"You haven't seen anything yet." She jumped to the ground. "And Mama says it's okay for me to show you stuff. Can we do that right away?" She looked at Kirby and the other team members moving weapons and bedrolls into the shelter. "I know all this is kind of important, but it's not exciting. And I really want to share them with you and Riley."

"Them?" Cade looked at Maya. "And do you want to share with us, too?"

"Why else would we be here?" Maya asked. "And I believe Bailey is right about not wasting time." She was looking to the east where clouds were gathering. "I didn't like the weather report last night."

"It's only supposed to be a light snowstorm. I think it will hold until we get the equipment stored and a temporary shelter in place." He tilted his head as he glanced at Bailey. "But that's not good enough, is it?"

She gravely shook her head. "No, I might need you. I don't know yet." She looked at Riley. "She said you could fix things. It might be time."

"Well, then we wouldn't want to waste a second, would we?" He turned to Maya. "Give me a couple minutes to talk to Kirby with final instructions. You wouldn't care to tell me where the hell we're going?"

"The upper valley." Maya was heading for a jeep parked on the side of the road. "No more than a couple minutes, Cade. I might have to pull some of the workers out of the area."

Cade looked over his shoulder at Riley. "Do you have any idea what's going on?"

She shook her head. "The only thing I've learned recently is that we can't count on anything being what it seems. How far away is this valley, Maya?"

"Only a few miles." Maya jumped into the driver's seat. "But it's rough country most of the way." She started the jeep. "And if we get caught in a storm, it could be deadly. The passes close down and we could end up trapped."

"Then why not wait until the storm passes?" Cade finished giving his instructions and ran back and jumped into the vehicle.

"Because that's not how we handle things," Maya said. "Now be quiet and let me concentrate on this road. I don't want to end up running off the mountain."

"It's going to be okay, Mama." Bailey was looking up at the darkening sky. "We'll have time. And I don't think the storm is going to last long."

"I'm glad to hear it," Maya said. "But that doesn't mean that it might not cause chaos while it's going on. I've already called the shepherds to alert them of the move, but it's going to be edgy."

"Chaim will get them down. They're used to him," Bailey said. "I can help." She was sitting forward on her seat, her eyes shining with excitement. "I already hear them. They must be right around the next bend." She glanced at Riley. "They're so beautiful. You're going to love them."

"Am I?" Riley was smiling. "I can see that you do. I can't wait to—" She broke off and they turned the corner and she saw the vast green valley spread out before them.

The valley, and the great herd of wild deer being driven down from the barren mountains and across that valley by leather-garbed shepherds!

"Holy smoke," she murmured, stunned. "How many are there?" She shook her head as she tried to estimate. "A couple hundred or more?"

"Probably," Maya said. "We don't do a count every year. The deer are watched very closely by the shepherds to be sure there are no injuries. But it's not as if we're raising them for sale."

Cade was cursing softly as he took binoculars out of this pocket and raised them to his eyes, focusing on the herd. "You'd cause a riot if you did." His gaze zeroed in on the animals as they drew closer. "I'll be damned." He lowered the binoculars and turned to Maya. "Are they all the same? Only one horn?"

"Most of them. There are a few mountain musk deer in the bunch with no horns at all, but the majority of the main herd have only one."

Riley could see Cade's intensity as he looked back at the herd. She knew how much this meant to him, but she had to be sure. "Unicorns? They're unicorns, Cade?"

"That's what they appear to be. We'll have to take a closer look at them and compare them with the tall tales and literature." He glanced back at Maya. "I thought that they were probably extinct, if they ever existed. I believed you were using them as a lure."

"I was," she said. "But that doesn't mean I'd lie to you. It was a question of not letting anyone know there was a possibility that they did exist. You were right, it could have caused me problems."

"Besides interfering with one of your prime functions on the island," Riley said as she stared at the sleek, graceful animals. Now that they were closer, she could see they were tan with touches of white and had the most beautiful crystal-brown eyes she'd ever seen... "You're doing your duty as caretaker. Isn't that right?"

Maya nodded. "What can I say? It's tradition. Silvana brought the first deer here when she came from Rome. Actually, the herds were much smaller then because she'd paid a visit to her home in the steppes and purchased fifty healthy specimens from the nomads in the Kazakhstan camps where she'd grown up. She wanted her old life back, and that included the animals of her childhood."

"Kazakhstan," Cade repeated. He gave a low whistle as he leaned forward. "The story is growing by leaps and bounds. Are we definitely talking about unicorns, Maya?"

"We might be." She grinned. "I told you I might include them in the deal if we ran across any. But Silvana never referred to them as unicorns. She only called them 'the herd.' She said there were quite a few one-horned animals in her village. She'd heard tales of unicorns herself, but she was a warrior. She paid no attention to them. When she was captured and sent to Rome, you can bet she never mentioned them to

Antonio. She wasn't going to let them take anything else from her." She braked the jeep. "Now Bailey and I have to go and help the shepherds get those deer to safety."

"What can we do to help?" Cade asked.

"Nothing at the moment. They're excited and might trample you," Maya said. "We're leading them down to a hollowed-out cave in the mountain where we can protect them and keep them warm if the storm is worse than we think. They're always safe there. Silvana thought of everything when she set up her kingdom." She smiled. "Just drive the jeep down the rest of the way to the cave and meet us there." She turned to Bailey. "Ready?"

"You can go help the shepherds." Bailey was already out of the jeep and heading up the hill. "I'll bring Riva. She might be frightened. I'll see you at the cave." She glanced at Riley. "I told you that they were wonderful. Aren't you glad you came?"

"I couldn't be happier," Riley said. "You're right, it's exciting. We'll see you at this cave and you can introduce us on a more personal level. Be careful."

Bailey looked at her in surprise. "I don't have to be careful. They'd never hurt me. They're very gentle. Sometimes when they're mating, they fight a little, but it doesn't last long." She waved as she increased her pace to catch up with Maya. "And they're smart, they'd realize you wouldn't hurt them, either..."

Cade was beside Riley and nudging her back into the jeep. "Come on, we've had our marching orders. Let's find this cave

Maya was talking about. Maybe we can help get the animals settled when the shepherds start herding them into the enclosure." He started the jeep. "And I have a couple calls to make before we get tied up as Maya's prime unicorn-sitters. I knew she might spring something like this on us, but I didn't think the chances were very good."

"But you're glad we came." Riley was studying his expression. "You lit up when you saw those horns. You're still excited."

"You're damn right I am." He was struggling to keep the jeep on the road as he negotiated the rough terrain. "It's not that often I find a wild species that we haven't managed to try to kill off over the centuries. I had hope that the *Saola* might be saved in Laos, but I might have had to spend a decade hunting them down."

"Laos?" She was holding tight to the seat belt as she was jarred against the doorjamb. "*Saola?* What are you talking about? The last I heard you were being called the Elephant King because of your work saving the elephants from poachers. Now you're hunting down deer?"

"Only very special deer. I'll explain the difference once I get those calls out of the way." They were approaching a huge opening in the cliff that was guarded by two sentries. "And that must be the cave Maya was talking about. We may have to call her and get permission to pass those guards. We don't want to cause any trouble when she's been cooperative about assigning us that unicorn headache to solve."

"Solve? Which you just told me that you're happy about. You're not being consistent."

"I couldn't be more consistent than when I agreed with Maya that her bringing us to see those deer might cause a riot," he said dryly as he got out of the jeep. "I can almost feel the vibrations. Let's find out what other mischief we can stir up."

———

They had less than an hour for Cade to make his calls and get in touch with Kirby at the base camp before the deer arrived at the cave, driven by Maya and the shepherds. It was snowing harder by the time Cade was finished, and the deer were restless and willing enough to get out of the cold and ice.

"You wanted to help?" Maya called to Cade and Riley. "Give us a hand. Food always distracts them. That's why we always keep the caves supplied. They expect it when we bring them down here."

"Not a bad idea," Cade said. "In this case, I'm glad that they're normal enough to be tempted like any other animal in jeopardy."

"Where's Bailey?" Riley asked. Then she saw the girl across the cave beside a female deer, gently stroking her neck. "Never mind. As long as she's safe. Tell us what to do, Maya."

She grinned and motioned. "Follow the leader." Cade and Riley joined Maya and together they managed to get the animals settled enough to be fed grass and grain by the shepherds and sentries. But it was only after a few hours that they felt relaxed enough to take a break and Maya told the shepherds to make their coffee and afternoon meal.

Riley hesitated, her gaze going to Bailey who was still with the doe. "Should I go get her?"

"You can try," Maya said. "But I don't think she'll be ready to come yet. She'll want to make certain that the doe has had enough to eat." She smiled. "Why don't you take Bailey a muffin and a cup of tea and see if you get lucky. At least she'd like to introduce you to Riva."

"She'd pay more attention to you. You're everything to her."

"That's why I don't have to compete," Maya said. "I want to make sure you know how special she is."

Riley shook her head. "I know that already." She shrugged. "You're completely weird, you know." She turned toward the fire. "I'll take her a snack. I do want to meet her unicorn friend."

"Of course you do." Maya smiled. "That's why you get along so well. You're both into unicorns and searching for lost queens and saving the world. I told you that you and Cade were perfect." She poured herself a cup of coffee. "And while you're busy with Bailey, I'll go and give Cade a minor third degree about what he's planning to do about the unicorns and decide whether I'll go along with it."

"You shouldn't have brought us here if you weren't willing to let him do what he wants," Riley said curtly. "You as much as made them a part of the deal. Whatever he decides, it will be right for the deer."

"Perhaps. But I'll have to decide. It's my job."

Riley shook her head. "I don't think so. You brought us into this nightmare. Now you have to let us do what we have to do." She grabbed a muffin and a cup of tea. "If you'll excuse me, I'll go chat with your daughter. As far as I can see, she's much more reasonable than you."

"I won't argue on that score," Maya said quietly. "Though I've always tried to keep the bad things from touching her. And I always will." She started to move toward Cade. "I believe Cade feels the same about you. He has the instincts of a caretaker. But you're not a child and it must annoy you." She'd almost reached Cade. "I'll talk to you later, Riley…"

———

"Hi, Bailey." Riley set the muffin and cup of tea on a boulder next to where Bailey was feeding the deer. "I brought you a bite to eat. But you seem to be busy. May I help? You did promise to introduce me to your friend here. Her name is Riva?"

Bailey nodded. "That's what I call her. I like the sound of it. It's like music." She reached down for a brush and began to gently stroke the animal's back. "I'll eat my muffin later. She got a little excited on the way down the mountain, and brushing makes her calmer. Though I guess she gets bored because she's going to have a baby. I wish I knew what she was thinking all the time. Sometimes I believe she's trying to tell me stuff, but I'm never sure."

"She looks like she's getting close to her time," Riley said. "I'm no expert, but I've spent a lot of time in native villages while I was growing up and been present at birthings. She looks like she's almost ready."

"I think so, too." She stopped brushing and turned to look at her. "I'm a little scared. I've been reading books and studying how to help her since I realized that was what was happening with her. But I don't know if I'll do it right."

"Then we'll find someone to help. Maya will probably know a vet she can call on."

Bailey was frowning. "You don't understand. The female deer are very fragile. The males are strong and have great endurance, but the death rate of the does is twice that of the males. We can't bring outside doctors because no one can know about the unicorns. Mama says that they seem to be very sensitive, and in the past when the caretakers have taken a chance and brought in outside medical help, they usually die within a week. That's why the shepherds usually help with birthings. Chaim is wonderful. But Riva won't let him near her. I'm the only one she'll let touch her." She moistened her lips. "But maybe she'd let you help." She quickly stepped aside. "Will you put your hand on her?"

Riley reached out and tentatively touched Riva's neck. The deer swung her head to stare at her. Those huge brown eyes were magnificent, Riley thought. They seemed to be full of curiosity and wisdom and a strange wonder. Then the deer slowly, caressingly rubbed her head back and forth under Riley's hand before she turned back to Bailey.

"She likes you," Bailey whispered. "I knew she would. Will you help me?"

"If I can, though my midwife experience is limited." She reached out and stroked the doe's neck again. "But I can see why you can't bear the thought of anything happening to her. She's...extraordinary." She smiled. "So why don't you sit down and have your tea and muffin and let me get to know her a little better? While I finish brushing her, you can tell me all about her..."

CHAPTER

8

Forty-five minutes later Riley was crossing the cave to where Cade was sitting on the floor beside the door opening gazing out at the falling snow. She plopped down beside him. "Maya said she was going to give you the third degree about your intentions regarding the unicorns. Did she do it?"

"She made the attempt, but I told her that I hadn't made any firm decisions yet." He shrugged. "And that it was her fault for not giving me definitive answers regarding them when I first asked her. She didn't like it, but she let me get away with it. Though I could see her mentally filing it away to come back around and attack later. She does like to be in control."

Her brows rose. "And you don't? Takes one to know one. As a matter of fact, she mentioned that you have the instincts of a caretaker." She tilted her chin. "But she could see how it might annoy me since I wasn't a child."

"Ouch." He met her eyes. "Did you have a nice chat about it?"

"No, I try never to talk about you to anyone else. I figure you get enough of that from everyone else who tries to analyze or get something from you." She made a face. "I remember I did tell her once that I could handle you."

"And so you can. As often and as intimately as you choose." He added, "And we're both working on ways to take other more challenging steps."

"That's why I'm sitting here. Maya was right, you do have the instincts of a caretaker. But I'm trying not to resent it. Even though it does piss me off that you seem too busy to give me explanations that would make me feel more like a partner and less like a child." She held up her hand as he started to speak. "So I thought I'd corner you and have you keep your promise about explaining more about what you know about those unicorns. Because one way or the other that's going to happen. You're the one who was having problems with me not confiding in you—that's how we ended up here. Remember?"

"How could I forget?" He added, "And I had no intention of keeping anything from you. I think I can chalk this up to Maya's not-so-helpful remark. We have been a little busy since we got here."

"Yes, we have." She paused. "And Maya wasn't trying to cause trouble. She was just being…Maya."

"Which can be trouble in itself." He waved his hand. "But we'll get this over quickly. Tell me what you already know about the unicorns, and I'll fill you in on anything extra. We should be able to whisk right through this. Besides your archaeologist background, you're also a scholar who cut her teeth on legends and ancient history."

"What do I know? Only that there's mega dispute about whether unicorns ever existed or if they're another myth. Or if they did exist but became extinct sometime near the Iron Age." She shrugged. "And I admit I was more interested in the people who shaped the world than the animals that inhabited it."

"Like your Helen of Troy?" He smiled. "I don't expect there to be any competition. Yet the *Iliad* mentioned unicorns."

"And the *Iliad* was mythology. But it was Ctesias of Cnidus who was responsible for creating the first legend about unicorns more than two thousand years ago. He told of a wild ass in India that was as large as a horse or maybe even larger. It had dark blue eyes and had a single horn on the forehead that was about a foot and a half long. He was a physician in the Persian court and had a great curiosity that led him to dive deep into research." Her lips twisted. "Even though many later experts didn't have sterling opinions about the quality of his work. Later Aristotle and Pliny both were more respected."

"Very good," he said. "I was right, you already know quite a bit about unicorns. What else?"

"That there have been legends and descriptions of unicorns from practically every country on the planet, and most of them sound like pure bullshit. Unicorn descriptions varied

209

from looking like Ctesias's ass to antelopes to a very weird but popular belief that a unicorn really looked like a rhinoceros."

"Not so weird," Cade said. "I agree that the rhino's appearance is less than appealing when you compare it with the sentimental unicorn fables. But you have to look at what was most important to the people who were searching for the unicorn through the centuries: the single horn gracing the rhino's snout. Because if you could claim that you'd caught a unicorn and taken its horn, then you could sell it for enormous profits. Since even the existence of the unicorn was in dispute, it was an easy enough con. Which was what happened in late medieval and Renaissance times. Horns of any sort were one of the most popular gifts among royal families. The great horn of Windsor owned by the British royal family was valued very highly. But a unicorn horn would have been considered a special prize."

Riley nodded. "Because their horns supposedly not only had magical medical properties but could also protect anyone from poison."

"Right," he said. "And had several other applications depending on who you consulted during which millennium. Everyone wanted to believe the magic. Even some world-famous Victorian explorers like Sir Henry Stanley and Harry Johnston who were studying Pygmies in the Congo mentioned stories that the Pygmies might have discovered an ass-like creature in Africa that could have been a unicorn. They wanted it to be true. So did the dreamers who came after them." He added bitterly, "And the poachers are always eager to accommodate anyone willing to pay the price. Anything to do with those horns fetched incredibly high fees through the centuries. Even when their authenticity was suspect, they still brought in a bundle of money. Particularly in the Chinese and Russian markets." He cast a glance back at the herd moving restlessly in the cave behind them. "You can imagine how the price would skyrocket if the poacher could show proof that the horn was genuine. Not to mention any other vital organs that he could sell at top price. It would be a bonanza for the son of a bitch."

"And you hate it," Riley said. "Who could blame you? It makes me sick."

"You're damn right. I hate poachers on principle. But this makes me want to go after Nadim and harvest a few of *his* organs." His gaze was still on the unicorns. "These creatures have fought to survive through the centuries, and this may be their last chance if Nadim finds a way to capture them." He smiled recklessly. "Which he won't. I won't let the bastard get hold of even one of them."

"But how do we do it? If they're so rare that almost everyone thinks they're extinct, it won't be easy to keep them alive much less tuck them safely away somewhere."

"Good question," he said wryly. "I'm working on it. And it may not be a matter of tucking them away but letting them strut their stuff. Nadim is proving to be an aggressive bastard. We'll have to study his next move."

"And hope it's not aimed at us?"

"He's a poacher. It's what he was doing in India." He added grimly, "If he's found out anything about why Maya is protecting this area, every weapon will be zeroed in on taking those deer out. She told me Bevan was his informant. I'd bet if he doesn't know now, he will soon."

"Are we sure that they're that rare? You mentioned something about Laos. Were they sighted there?"

He shook his head. "But there was an animal in the bovid family who has been seen there. The *Saola*. It didn't have the same physical characteristics as these unicorns. They have two horns and generally live in the forests instead of the mountains. The Lao people refer to them as 'the polite animal' because they move quietly through the forest and are very gentle. I was interested because the IUCN Species Survival Commission asked for my help out of fears that they would soon be declared extinct. The press has been referring to them as 'the Asian unicorns.' Not only were the poachers after them, but the local hunters and tribesmen were killing them. A trip to Laos was next on my list."

"The polite animal," Riley mused as her gaze wandered across the cave to where Bailey was still brushing Riva. "Those *Saola* might not be the same exact species as these deer, but they could be first cousins. One of the things Bailey mentioned about that unicorn she's taking such good care of was that she was very solitary. After she mated, she wanted nothing more to do with the sire and went off to be by herself. She's spent most of her time waiting for the birth and just wandering around on her own."

"That's not totally unusual," Cade said. "Just a little ruthless to discard the male. She got what she wanted and then sent him on his way. Sounds vaguely...familiar."

She gave him a disgusted look. "No, it doesn't. And I'll bet no one ever just sent you on your way, Cade."

He was grinning. "Just kidding. No, they were too busy standing in line for my grandfather's cash."

She frowned. "And that's nothing to joke about. Someone should have been there for you." She added with sudden ferocity, "I would have been there for you, Cade."

"I'm touched." He took her hand and lifted it to his lips. "But I got along just fine, Riley."

But he wouldn't have admitted it if he hadn't, she knew. Well, her own childhood hadn't been warm or wonderful, either. It was probably what she would have said to him, too. "Bailey was making excuses for him. She thinks they probably each have their own jobs to do, and they have some inner instinct that tells them how best to complete it. She said she's studied Riva and she wouldn't mate with any male who would go off and desert her. She has to be the one to be in control." She shrugged. "And she thinks the fawn is going to be born soon. The way that fawn is kicking inside her, he is ready. Perhaps even tonight." She got to her feet. "And I promised I'd stay with her in case she needs help."

"I thought you might." He stood up. "I'll come over a bit

later and add my support. I have a few more plans to make before I turn in for the night. Though I might go back to the base camp for a while."

She stiffened. "Why?"

"Maybe because we both have our own jobs to do, and I need to do mine." He kissed her cheek. "Like Bailey's Riva. But I promise I won't leave you in the dark for long."

"Likewise." She moved across the cave toward Bailey. "But I'll be much safer than you will be traipsing all over the mountain in a snowstorm."

"The snow is stopping. Bailey was right about it not lasting long."

"She might be clever, but I'd rather not have to depend on her skill as a meteorologist. Be careful, Cade..."

"Always..."

11:15 P.M.

"You know you don't have to stay with Bailey," Maya said as she came across the cave toward Riley. "I'll do it myself as soon as I finish my final rounds."

"It's no bother," Riley said. "She's good company and it's not as if I was holding her hand. She had all the shepherds and sentries drop by talking to her and checking to see if they could do anything for her before she curled up and went to sleep." She grinned. "She's very popular, isn't she?"

"They all feel as if she's one of them." Maya knelt down and brushed a kiss on Bailey's forehead. "Maybe she is. She seems to be able to reach out to everyone." She sat down on the other side of the fire Riley had built in the corner where Bailey had settled. "Except Cade. He's managed to resist her so far."

"Not really. He said that he'd drop by and talk to her this evening when he got back." She made a face. "Whenever that turns out to be. He called me when he reached the base camp, but I haven't heard from him since."

"And you've been worried about him," Maya said quietly. "I've noticed you've been restless for the last hour."

"You've been keeping an eye on me?" Riley asked. "I know Cade can take care of himself."

"But that doesn't mean you don't worry," Maya said. "He should be back within thirty minutes or so. I had Kirby call me when Cade left the camp."

Riley tried not to let her see the relief. "Why did you do that?"

"Cade's on my mountain, he's dealing with my people. He may think he's totally in control, but not while I'm still the caretaker. I brought you both here and it's my duty to watch over you." She lifted her shoulder in a half shrug. "And it doesn't hurt if I can make you feel a little better just by sticking my nose in what's happening out there, does it?"

Riley smiled faintly. "No, it doesn't hurt."

"Good. Then I'll be as discreet as possible, but not—" She broke off as her phone rang. She took it out of her pocket and her smile faded as she checked the caller ID. "Shit! Bevan."

Riley gasped but Maya shook her head. "It will be okay. The weasel is probably only still trying to talk me into a deal." She took a deep breath and answered. "Bevan, you son of a bitch. Why the hell are you calling me?"

"Because I thought we needed to touch base," Nadim answered sarcastically. "You do recognize my voice, don't you? You'll pardon me for using Bevan's phone to talk to you. Since I agree Bevan is usually a worthless piece of shit, I thought it only fair that if you managed to trace anyone's call, it should be his." His voice lowered to sleek malice. "And I couldn't resist the chance to talk to you. Bevan didn't agree with me that I should indulge myself, but ask me if I care. I deserve any pleasure I can get out of watching you writhe in pain. And they told me that you did suffer in that tent. Did you think of me then?"

"How could I help it?" she asked hoarsely. "There's no one else who is evil enough to torture a young girl and kill half a village just to bring it to my attention. There's a special place in hell for people like you. I'm searching for it now."

"But you won't find it before I send your girl, Bailey, to join that little toy of mine you're so bitter about. I thought I'd made it clear that she was next. I can't tell you how pleased I was when Bevan brought me the info about Bailey. A weapon at last. The scar on that wound where you stabbed me suddenly didn't throb nearly as bad. I immediately set about making plans."

"It won't do you any good," she said. "You've been trying to attack me for years and you haven't succeeded. And you're not the only one who has been making plans."

"Yes, thanks to Bevan I've heard you're trying to call in a few old friends to get in my way. Riley Smith...She was the reason that you were able to get me sent away from the island five years ago. I have a few special plans in mind for her."

"Stay away from her," Maya said sharply. "Or I'll find a way to make you regret it."

"Ah, another weapon for me?" She heard the sly satisfaction in his voice. "And I thought my main worry was going to be Cade Morgan. My men almost managed to take her down at Duncan's house in Atlanta. I believe I'll have to increase the bonus now."

Maya knew she had made a mistake. "Do what you like. She's nothing to me. But just know that you'll die if you try to get in my way."

"We'll see. But Bevan is proving to be a valuable ally, and I'm going to use him until he hands me your head on a platter. I'll be in touch..." He cut the connection.

Maya's knuckles turned white as her hand clenched the phone. She gazed at Riley. "As you heard, it wasn't Bevan. And it appears I've brought you right into the middle of—"

"Shut up." Riley was suddenly around the fire and kneeling

beside Maya, her eyes glittering fiercely. "You don't have to be some kind of Wonder Woman every minute of the day." She reached out and grasped Maya's hands. "I could see what that asshole was doing to you when he was talking about Bailey. Ignore it. We won't let him touch her. He's not going to get anything he wants. Do you hear me?"

"I hear you." She was trying to smile. "But I can't help wonder why you're being so protective when at least half of Nadim's poison was aimed at you."

"He's a dirtbag," Riley said. "And I've already tasted his poison and survived it. I'm sick and tired of having him think he can do terrible, ugly things and get away with it. You're one of the good guys, and I can't stand watching him try to tear you to pieces. I won't do it and you can't—"

"What's happening here?" Cade was striding across the cave toward them. His gaze was narrowed on Maya's face and then shifted to Bailey curled up asleep a few yards away. "Something wrong with the kid?"

"No." Maya released Riley's hands. "Except that she'll probably wake up if we keep talking. I'd rather not face her right now. She can be very perceptive." She got to her feet. "And I've got to finish doing my rounds."

Riley didn't move from where she was kneeling. "Maya."

Maya glanced at her. "What a nag you are." She pulled out her phone and tossed it to Cade. "I can handle this, but you might want to consider a change of procedure or even personnel since Riley appears to be upset about it." She strode across the cave in the direction of the opening. "You'll probably want to talk to me later."

———

OUTSIDE THE CAVE

AN HOUR AND FIFTEEN MINUTES LATER

"Are you hiding out?" Cade slid down the stone wall of the outside cave to where Maya was hunched to sit beside her. "It's a little cold tonight for moon gazing."

"And there's no moon," Maya said. "Though the sky's beginning to clear." She glanced at him. "And I wouldn't be hiding out from you, Cade. I just finished checking the exterior sentries and thought I'd rest a moment." She paused. "And I needed to clear my head after talking to Nadim. I kept remembering that hideous tent and the expression on Siena's face."

"Just like Riley," Cade said roughly. "You should have known hearing the bullshit that son of a bitch Nadim was spitting would affect her almost as much as it did you. There's no one more protective than Riley. Naturally, she would want to go after anyone who threatened Bailey... or you. She was disappointed in the way you'd tried to use us, but it didn't last long. She never intended to take either one of you under her wing, but it happened."

She was silent a moment. "You're telling me that you want to send her away from here?"

"No, I'm telling you that it's too late to do it," he said. "And that I'm furious about it. Not that I'm blaming you. You have your own battles to fight, and you've tried to keep her as safe as you could under the circumstances." His tone was suddenly ragged with exasperation. "It's just that it's going to be difficult as hell to keep her safe now. Because she's going to want to trail you and Bailey and make sure that Nadim doesn't cut your throat."

"Do you think I want her to do that? I was going to agree with you that we had to get her away from here. I wanted her to just fade into the background as far as he was concerned. The minute Nadim mentioned Riley, it scared me."

"Not as much as it did me," Cade said. "And I tracked you down out here to tell you that I'm going to fix it. There's no way now Riley is going to leave here before this is over. I'll have to work around it. We'll do everything we can to make sure that we bring that bastard down and keep Riley safe. In return I'll probably do some things you won't like, but you'll still smile and not argue with me. Do you understand?"

"I understand. But that doesn't mean I'll go along with it."

"You will because you'll stop and realize I'm only trying to patch together a way to get Riley home safely."

"If I agree, then I might go along with you." She added wearily, "I don't want anyone to die on this mountain."

"I won't guarantee I can keep that from happening." He got

to his feet and his voice was suddenly gentle. "But I'll make every effort to see that it's not anyone you care about. Now will you get inside the cave, so I won't have to come after you again?"

She didn't look at him. "In a few minutes."

"Have it your own way." He turned and headed for the cave entrance. He deliberately didn't glance over his shoulder as he moved across the cave to Riley's sleeping bag, which she'd set up near Bailey's.

She turned over as he sat down beside her. "Did you find her?"

"Yes, she was outside getting some air." He lay down and drew her close, his gaze still on the cave entrance. "And being monumentally stubborn."

"She has so much responsibility. She's just trying to keep everything from crashing around her. She was hurting, Cade."

"She wasn't the only one." His arms tightened around her. "I can't worry about her right now. I'll do that after I get a little sleep." He'd just seen Maya enter the cave, and he relaxed. "She can take care of herself."

Riley was silent for a moment. "Maybe," she whispered. "With a little help from her friends..."

He stiffened. Then he chuckled. "Why did I know you'd say that?" His lips brushed her ear. "Go to sleep. We'll talk about it tomorrow."

———

NADIM'S LAUNCH

AN HOUR LATER

"You're looking very cheerful." Bevan helped himself to a whiskey from Nadim's bar. "Which probably means you were able to shake up that bitch Maya a little. Did you use the kid?"

"Of course," Nadim said. "And she was practically petrified by the time I was through with her." He frowned. "But it wasn't enough. I wanted much more."

"You always do," Bevan said caustically. "And we always give it to you, don't we?" He took a long swallow of whiskey. "And no I haven't heard from Shadburn, my contact on the mountain, yet. I'm waiting for an answer from my last message now. The last time he texted me he said that he'd heard from one of the sentries that there might be some interesting prey to be had up in the foothills. But he was too damn vague. I think he wants more money. I told him to get his shit together and get me a report."

"You probably weren't strong enough. You have to make them cringe. Let me talk to him."

And then Bevan's contact would either disappear or be taken under Nadim's wing. "I don't want to bother you. I can handle him." Nadim was entirely too cocky now that he'd managed to frighten Maya. "I'm expecting a reply any minute. I'll get you your answer." His phone pinged, and he pressed ACCESS for the text. Then his eyes widened as he read it. Son of a bitch.

Nadim was going to love this. "I've got it." He gave his phone to Nadim. "She's got some kind of fancy herd up there in the hills. Shadburn said he caught sight of them running down from the valley. Must be more than a hundred of those deer up in those mountains."

"Deer?" Nadim picked up the phone and then stiffened as he saw the photos. "Shit! I think they might be related to some of those *Saola* deer from Laos I've heard rumors about. They're very rare. I could make a small fortune on just ten or twelve of them if I have the right buyer. Find out more for me from your contact. I need to know how many and how to get to them." He was flipping through the photos at top speed. "And I need to know now!"

———

"Tea." Bailey was kneeling beside Riley when she woke the next morning. She handed her the cup. "I'll get you a bowl of porridge. I'll be right back."

"Wait." This was very strange. She shook her head to clear it of sleep and raised herself on one elbow. "You don't have to do that, Bailey. Thank you, but I can take care of myself."

"I know." She smiled over her shoulder. "But Cade and I had a talk and he said that we should always take care of each other. You spent the night watching over Riva and me, and it's my turn now. I set a bucket filled with snow outside the cave so that you can wash up. It should be ready by the time you've finished eating your porridge."

"When did you have this talk with Cade? Where is he?"

But Bailey was gone.

Riley would have to wait until she came back with that porridge, she realized with exasperation. She glanced around the cave and didn't see either Maya or Cade. Only several shepherds tending the deer and the guards at the cave opening. She sat up and began to drink her tea.

But she'd only managed a few swallows before Bailey appeared with a bowl filled with porridge. She set the bowl on the ground beside Riley and then sat down beside her. "This porridge is sweeter than most, with brown sugar and cinnamon. Mama was right when she said that porridge we had yesterday would have to last us." She grinned. "Even though she probably didn't know that we'd have to be down here with the deer. Or maybe she did. Mama is very smart about all kinds of things."

"I've found that's true." Riley changed the subject. "When did you have that talk with Cade?"

"I woke up early because Riva was restless." She linked her arms around her knees. "I started brushing her again and he came over and sat down and started to ask me about Riva. It was...nice. Then he was telling me about unicorns. I knew a lot already, but he knew even more. He even showed me Riva's hooves and told me that some people would say that they were like the hooves found in burial grounds in Siberia where unicorn remains were supposedly found a long, long time ago." She frowned. "That was kind of interesting, but I didn't like to think about it. Burial grounds are sad, and Riva and the other deer are so *alive*."

"Yes, they are," Riley said gently. "And that's why we're all working to keep them that way. I'm sure that Cade told you that."

She nodded. "And he promised me that he'd do it. It made me feel good. We talked for a long time, and I think he can do more than fix things. He knows about stuff."

"Yes, he does."

"And he asked me to trust him and told me that he'd never let me down, but sometimes we had to help each other." She smiled. "I do trust him, but I think that had something to do with you. Did it?"

"It could, but that doesn't mean you can't trust him. It only means that he's very complicated and I'll have to talk to him. Do you know where he is?"

"He got a phone call and went outside the cave to take it. He said he had to talk to Mama, too." She tilted her head. "Things are going to happen, aren't they? You'd better eat your porridge."

She looked at her quizzically. "You think I'll need it?"

"Maybe." She got to her feet. "But he did say we have to take care of each other. I've done my part. Now I've got to go feed Riva."

Riley watched her go back to the deer. Then she took a few

bites of the porridge that was not at all appetizing, finished her tea, and was on her feet to go search for that blasted bucket of snow.

———

Riley had just finished brushing her teeth and washing her face when she saw Cade coming over the ridge. He was smiling and waved at her. She stood up and waited for him to come to her. "Where have you been?"

"Just for a walk. I had a few preparations to make." He was studying her expression. "You're looking very wary. Why?"

"You had a talk with Bailey. It made me a little uneasy. But then I thought you'd probably guess that. You spent a long time not only getting to know her better but preparing the way for something else." She paused. "And she knew it had something to do with me, so she spent a little time following your suggestions about taking care of each other. I received tea, porridge, and snow to wash my face."

"Well, I definitely approve of the snow. I always like it when you're glowing and look like you're fresh from your bath." He grinned. "Though I admit I like the shower concept better."

"So did I." She paused. "But stop trying to distract me. What are you up to, Cade? And what were you doing with Bailey?"

His smile faded. "Nothing that's not in her very best interest.

I had to prepare her for what's coming. We've come to the crossroads and it's time we pin Maya down and start moving."

"Give her a break. After Nadim's attack on her last night, she needs to recover."

He shook his head. "Nadim isn't going to wait. He'll find a way to go after what he wants. And now that he has Bevan in his pocket, it will make it twice as dangerous for us. Maya said herself that Bevan probably knew too much about the property." He paused. "And I could tell she was thinking about that when I talked to her last night. She knows as well as I do that time's run out for us."

"You seem to be sure about that," Riley said slowly. "Why?"

"Nadim is becoming a threat to Bailey. And Maya realized he's also coming after you if he has the chance. She can't allow that to happen." He smiled crookedly. "After all, Maya's the caretaker."

"And?"

"And she didn't ask one question when I called her from my walk and told her to meet me here in front of the cave entrance. I was glad when I saw you standing there glaring at me when I came over the ridge. It saved me from having to go after you."

"You mean I was actually to be included?" she asked caustically. "Should I be grateful?"

"No, I told you we'd talk this morning. I just thought I'd let Maya cool down, and let you have a good night's sleep, before we started any discussion." He stiffened as he caught sight of Maya coming out of the cave. "Because I'm not in the mood for diplomacy at the moment. So I hope neither of you expects it." He gestured to the boulder beside the entrance. "Sit down." He turned to Maya, who was approaching. "Good morning, did you have a good night? I thought we needed to clarify a few things before we go forward. Is that all right with you?"

"Would it make any difference?" Maya asked. "I can see that you're going to do it anyway."

"It would make a difference. I'd prefer honesty and reason to struggle." His gaze narrowed on her face. "But I believe you're ready for that now anyway."

"Try me." She smiled at Riley. "Stop worrying. One way or the other we'll get through this. I always knew when I brought Cade into it that it might bring problems."

"I just don't want you hurt. But I won't let you hurt Cade, either."

"Oh, dear. What a conundrum." Her gaze shifted to Cade. "Go ahead. Attack. Clarify."

"I will," Cade said. "You offered us two specific prizes to lure us to the island and these mountains. The first, of course, was the Silvana sarcophagus and the coffers of jewels that went along with it. You thought that would appeal to Riley after what she'd done with the Helen of Troy memorial."

"I knew it would," Maya said quietly.

"But you had to dangle something for me," he said. "The

unicorns. You couldn't promise me, but you said just enough to make it a beacon shining in the distance. I thought at the time how clever you were. Yet you managed to be appealing along with it." His lips tightened. "But it was still a promise and it's time to collect. We're here, we're ready to get rid of your enemies. However, we need to know we're not fighting for phantoms."

"Those deer in that cave aren't phantoms," she said. "I brought you here and I'll give them into your care if we can figure a way to get them off the mountain safely."

"That's one prize for me. And that's the only thing I wanted when I agreed to come here," he said. "But what about Riley? The Silvana sarcophagus. Do you know where it is?"

She didn't answer.

"She knows," Riley said suddenly. "She has to know. She's the caretaker. The caretaker knows everything, and the tradition passes from person to person. Any secret would be carried down from caretaker to caretaker."

Maya grimaced. "I might have a good idea. It's on the top of a mountain not too far from here. Very high, very cold. You're right, I've been told the complete history and the location. It's always been the duty of the caretakers to make complete records of any events of importance. But I've never actually been there. Also, you'll remember our deal called for a portion of the jewels to be distributed to the people of the island. I had to be careful for their sake."

Riley nodded. "I understand." She glanced at Cade. "Is that all you wanted from her? Are you satisfied?"

"No. Not until we crush Nadim and Bevan. But that will come soon enough." He added recklessly, "Because we're going to go after them right away, and the only way to do it may be to let them find us. We can't get those unicorns out of here until we have a plan in place. Much less an extremely fragile sarcophagus. I've already started to pull together a plan, but you might not be too pleased with it." He took out his phone and started dialing. "We'll have to see." He spoke into the phone. "Okay, I'm ready for you. Come ahead." He listened for a moment. "Are you finished? Stop complaining. You're supposed to be a stoic Superman. You'll ruin your image." He pressed DISCONNECT and turned back to Riley and Maya. "He wants a cup of tea. Will you tell someone to bring it?"

"No, who were you talking to?" Riley asked.

"Stoic Superman . . ." Maya repeated. She snapped her fingers. "Kagan!" She took a step forward. "He's coming here?"

"On his way. He arrived at base camp last night. I arranged to meet him when I went for that walk on the ridge this morning. I asked him to wait until I called him to follow me here." He grimaced. "But I won't tell him you recognized that description. He'd enjoy it too much. He always likes it when the joke's on me."

"You know, I think I might like him." Riley was smiling. "But why do we need him? Why is he here?"

"Because I sent out an SOS with Kirby after I saw the

situation here on the island. We have similar interests. He has no use for people who destroy the environment, either. When he's not climbing mountains, Kagan has helped me out a few times bagging poachers who got in my way. And he has several Sherpa friends he can call on to aid and abet him. He's a regular Pied Piper." He glanced at Maya. "Not that your sentries aren't adequate. But Kagan is an expert in the mountains."

"I'm aware of that," she said curtly. "But what I'm wondering is why you had him meet you for a walk instead of coming directly to the cave?"

"I had a few things to explain, and I didn't want confusion when he met the two of you. It would have gotten in the way. Kagan doesn't like confusion. He goes straight from A to Z. You'll recognize that when you get to know him." He smiled. "And he should be here any minute, so why don't you order that cup of tea he requested like the wonderful hostess I know you to be."

She stared him in the eye. "I'm supposed to trust you that Kagan is going to help us get this done? Why?"

"Because I'm willing to trust him," he said quietly. "And if you don't trust me by now, we're in pretty bad shape."

She stared at him an instant longer and then reached for her phone. "I'll have someone bring his tea. Though it's fairly arrogant of him to order you to do it."

"It amuses him to make me jump through hoops. It's a game. It amuses me, too. He won't be that way with you."

"No, he won't," she said with precision. "Not ever."

Riley was gazing curiously at Cade. "You like him a lot. I think he's a good friend. But you never mentioned him to me before we reached the island."

"We didn't have time. But we do now. Just another sign that this trip is going to be a learning experience for both of us." He nodded at the ridge. "And here he comes. Prepare yourself. Because I think those sentries have seen him, too."

She stiffened as she saw the sentries were running toward him. "Are they attacking?"

He shook his head. "Relax. Kagan has rock-star status in this part of the world. They probably want his autograph."

They didn't seem to be wanting anything but attention, but those tough sentries were eagerly chattering, and their attitude was close to idolizing. But Kagan was smiling and talking to them and totally attentive to what they were saying. Under six feet tall, he was an attractive, muscular man with tanned skin and close-cut dark hair, brown eyes, and a face more appealing than conventionally handsome. But that smile lit his face with warmth, and she was aware of the almost roguish magnetism he was emitting. "Rock star, indeed," she murmured.

But he'd broken free of the sentries and was striding directly toward her. "You have to be Riley," he said as he shook her hand. "I've seen your photo with Cade in magazines, and I always wondered why I've never met you. He clearly wanted to keep you to himself when anyone more interesting was around." His smile was slyly mischievous. "That was it, right?"

"Absolutely." She grinned. "I was just telling him I didn't know why I hadn't met you. He obviously felt inferior."

"Ouch." Cade sighed. "And I thought I'd hidden it so well." He turned to Maya. "Protect me?"

"Not a chance." She stared directly into Kagan's eyes. "I don't think Cade needs protection. I don't think you do, either. I'm Maya. I hear I'm about to owe you a great debt. Is that true or is Cade conning me?"

"I doubt if you can be conned," he said quietly. "But if I do anything spectacular, I'll make certain you know about it so that you can be properly grateful. I like people to owe me favors. You can never tell when you might need one, and I'm not shy about demanding it."

"Good. That makes me feel better." She took the cup of tea that one of the shepherds was handing her. "Thank you, Laros." She handed the cup to Kagan. "That was your first demand, I believe. I hope you enjoy it."

"I will. Though I really wanted to make Cade give it to me. He left me out in the snow to be bored, without entertainment or sustenance." He took a sip of tea. "Excellent." He took another sip and then handed the cup to Cade. "Okay, now I'm ready to meet Bailey. Where is she?"

Maya stiffened. "Bailey?"

"She's inside the cave with the deer," Cade said as he started toward the cave opening. "You might as well get acquainted with both of them at once."

Maya took a step forward. "Why do you want to meet Bailey?"

Kagan glanced back over his shoulder. "Because as far as I'm concerned, she may be the most important person I'll meet here today. Cade has already told me that she's going to be my prime responsibility. With the possible exception of you."

Cade grinned. "As I said. He goes straight from A to Z. You'll always know where you are with him." He disappeared into the cave, closely followed by Kagan.

Maya muttered a curse. "What's that supposed to mean?"

"I have no idea." Riley took her arm. "But it's going very fast, and it probably means that we'd better get in there and monitor his effect on Bailey. I don't know if she likes rock stars, but he might have hidden depths that appeal to her." She was frowning as they walked toward the cave. "But on the surface, I like the idea that he thinks she's that important."

"Not if he's considering using her as some kind of pawn," Maya said jerkily. "I won't have it."

"Does he have that reputation?"

Maya grimaced. "No, everybody loves the asshole. He saves whole towns from earthquakes, and he's the first to go after a climber if he tumbles into a glacier. But that doesn't mean that everybody can't be wrong."

Riley stopped a short distance from where Kagan was now stroking Riva while he talked to Bailey. "I don't think Bailey thinks they're wrong. Look at her face."

"I'm looking." Maya crossed her arms tightly across her chest. "It's the rock-star syndrome again. Completely charming. Only he's able to adapt it to appeal to a sensitive kid like Bailey."

"Bullshit." Riley studied Kagan's expression: gentleness, warmth, a reaching-out, humor. "You know better. He's genuine and she realizes it and is responding."

Maya nodded, her gaze on Kagan's face, interpreting every nuance. "No threat to her from him. He...likes her. She amuses him. But I still don't know why he was so determined to meet her."

"Because he was telling the truth," Cade said as he strolled toward them. "Not only is she personally in danger from Nadim, but since she won't leave the herd, anything that happens to them, happens to her. Kagan has to know her and be able to judge every instinct. He has to be closer than a father to keep her safe."

"A father?" She shook her head in disbelief. "Don't be ridiculous. She has me. I'll take care of her."

"I don't think you'll object to having Kagan keeping an eye on Bailey once you get used to the idea," Cade said. "It was what I was going to do before we escalated the plans. But when it seemed best to split up the moving of the unicorns and the retrieval of the sarcophagus, we had a problem. I knew I might need Riley to help with the transfer and preservation of Silvana since she had extensive experience with Helen. That's one of the principal reasons why Kagan is here. I had to have someone both to protect the unicorns and to make certain you and Bailey would be all right."

"While we went after the sarcophagus and the coffers," Riley said slowly. "But this is the first I've heard about this escalation or my part in it. Why is that?"

"Isn't it what you'd want?" Cade asked.

"Of course, it is," Maya said quickly. "It's what she's wanted since I tried to tempt her with all those legends about Silvana five years ago." She met his eyes. "And you've taken care to make certain everything here is safe. You've even brought in the rock star to play his magic guitar. How can I object? You're giving me everything I could possibly want."

"That was my intention." He smiled. "But if you do have an objection, tell me and I'll try to solve it. I want everyone secure and happy."

Maya glanced at Riley. "That's what I want, too." Her tone turned suddenly fierce. "You take care of her on that mountaintop, Cade." She turned away. "I have to get the herd back out to the valley as soon as the snow melts. But tonight I'll have time to go over Silvana's burial plans and site with both of you. They were as unusual as you'd expect from her." She glanced back over her shoulder at Cade. "And if you don't want problems from me, you'll make certain Kagan realizes I don't like interference in either my personal or my professional life. There's only one caretaker."

"That goes without saying," he said quietly. "He'll understand. You'll find he's not hard to come to terms with."

She cast a final glance at Bailey, who was laughing, her face luminous as she looked up at Kagan. "We'll see. Bailey doesn't appear to be having any trouble..."

CHAPTER

9

It was late that afternoon when Kagan caught up with Maya on the slopes leading to the valley as they were moving the herd. "What a busy, hardworking lady you are. I had trouble keeping up with you," he said as he strode down the hill to where she'd been talking to one of the shepherds. "Everything going the way you want it?"

She shook her head. "Too many rockslides for the light snow we had. I'm going to have to have the shepherds go over the area and make sure that's not going to cause slippage."

"Can I help?"

She shook her head. "I'm certain you have enough to do."

"And you don't want me to get in your way? If you change your mind, let me know. I have to go back to the base camp— I'm expecting several friends to arrive in a few hours, and I want to smooth the way with your sentries and Cade's men that Kirby brought in. We need the entire unit to be one sleek machine. But I thought I'd have a few words with you before I left." He smiled. "We didn't have much time to come to an understanding before you were off helping your crew with the deer."

"I believe we understand each other," Maya said. "And you don't have to do anything to smooth me into your sleek machine. I operate pretty well on my own."

"I can see you do and from what I've heard, you're a remarkable woman whom everyone respects, and you manage to run things around here with amazing efficiency." His smile vanished. "And I wouldn't think of getting in your way. I'm the one who needs to adjust to the situation. But to do that you have to know what to expect of me. Cade brought me here for a reason, and I came because I respect him and want to help." He made a face. "And because he amuses me, and I think I'll enjoy myself. It's not often that I get a chance to break new ground, and saving a herd of unicorns is certainly that. And then he threw in the possibility of finding that female fighter's sarcophagus somewhere in these mountains and that intrigued me. You might have heard I do very well in the mountains."

"I've heard you're some kind of genetic miracle as far as your ability to handle altitude," Maya said. "It interested me, but I don't see how it would help you to handle my problems."

"You can never tell." He was smiling again. "I have a lot of experience in all kinds of situations. I tend to get bored easily, so I either let a situation come to me or go looking for it."

She studied his face. "Like Everest or K2?"

"Perhaps." His smile didn't waver. "But I'm here because Cade asked me, not because I was looking for another K2." He chuckled. "Unless it erupts in front of me. My job is to protect this herd from poachers until Cade can transfer them to a place they'll be safe and happy." He shook his head ruefully. "It's going to be difficult to find a place better than this. It's also to protect your employees... and Bailey. Most of all Bailey." His voice softened. "I don't believe you'll object to me doing that."

She was silent a moment. "Not if you can prove you can do it better than me. I'd stand aside for the devil himself if he could keep her safe."

He laughed. "I'm not the devil. I'm actually a good enough guy that you can trust with Bailey. And I believe you have enough devils hovering around you right now."

She nodded wryly. "That couldn't be more true. But how can I be sure I can trust you with Bailey?"

He tilted his head. "Let's see...." Then his expression hardened. "Because she's my primary job. Cade made that clear. If I had a choice of saving you or Bailey, it would have to be Bailey." He met her eyes. "And I think that's the way you'd want it anyway."

He meant it. She felt a ripple of shock. "Yes, I would."

He nodded. "But I'd try to save you both if it didn't get in the way."

Maya suddenly started to laugh. "How generous of you to

include me. But I liked you more when you just came out with the raw statement."

"But it wasn't the entire truth. I think you appreciate the truth. So I wanted to be clear so that we understood each other." He smiled. "It's better now, isn't it?"

"As long as you didn't do anything stupid to try to save both of us."

"I wouldn't be stupid." He turned to leave. "I'll see you when I get back, Maya."

"Yes." She watched him go back up the hill and found her lips twitching. No, she couldn't see Kagan ever being stupid…

———

Riley found Maya at Bailey's tent in the valley when she came to find her that evening. As usual Bailey was no more than a few yards from Riva, but she came running to see Riley. "I'm glad you're here. Kagan told me that you were helping Cade, but I didn't like it that you weren't with us. I feel safer about Riva if you're near."

"And I'll always try to be close," Riley said. "But I might have to be gone for a little while. Though Maya is here, and we both know she can take care of nearly anything that comes along."

"I'll certainly try," Maya said dryly. "But I'm not sure that Riva would appreciate my efforts on her behalf. You'd better keep studying that animal anatomy textbook I gave you. We might need all the help we can get." She bent down and gave Bailey a hug. "Still, we'll muddle through and everything will turn out fine. I won't let anything happen to Riva. How is she doing?"

"You never muddle, Mama," Bailey said. "It's just that I don't know how close Riva is. She doesn't seem to have changed except to get bigger. According to my book about deer, she shouldn't be ready to have the baby for at least another few days." She frowned. "But she's not the usual deer, is she? Unicorns might be different."

"And they might not," Riley said. "We'll take care of her, and you have shepherds who have helped with birthing other deer. They might be able to help."

She shook her head. "I don't think so. Riva hasn't wanted to be touched by any of them." She suddenly brightened. "But she didn't seem to mind when Kagan was stroking her. I could tell Riva liked him. He said that when he was a little boy, he took care of his uncle's farm animals during the summer. He told me all I had to do was call him and he'd come if I had a problem. Is that okay, Mama?"

"Why not?" Maya kissed her cheek and then stood up. "He seems destined to solve all kinds of problems while he's here. No reason why you can't come first on the list."

"Not me," Bailey corrected. "Riva."

"One and the same for the moment," Maya said. "But remember I'm here, too. Always."

Bailey nodded gravely. "Always."

"That's right." She grinned. "But I've got to go with Riley to have a cup of coffee with Cade now. We've got a few things to talk about that have nothing to do with Riva. If you need any help with Riva, I'm leaving the usual sentry outside and you can call him. I'll be back in an hour or so. Try to sleep."

Bailey shook her head.

Maya sighed resignedly. "Okay. Keep Riva company and we'll talk about sleep when I come back." She grabbed her notebook and jerked her head to Riley. They left the tent and walked toward the bonfire in the middle of the circle of tents on the upper slope of the valley where Cade was waiting. "Sorry. You shouldn't have had to deal with Bailey's angst, too, Riley."

"Don't be ridiculous," Riley said. "I'd already told her that I'd help her with Riva. It's my fault for having to back out and making her worry. I just hope finding that coffin won't take too long and keep me from getting back to her."

"I can't assure you that I'll be able to produce on schedule." Maya's lips twisted. "It's not as if any of the caretakers visited the site frequently. That would have defeated the purpose of all the secrecy Silvana wanted when she arranged her burial. Our orders were to visit only to check periodically and maintain. I'm not even sure that the access to the mountain is still viable."

"Why wouldn't it be?"

"Because everything else around us is changing," Maya said. "And Silvana was clever, but she couldn't think of everything.

Jann Lu didn't, either. She just threw it to me and told me to do my duty. I've done what I could." She added bitterly, "Now you have to do whatever you can to make this right."

Riley stared at her, puzzled. "What are you trying to say, Maya?"

"That sometimes the best-laid plans don't work worth a damn." They had reached the bonfire, and she saw Cade get to his feet. "Hello, Cade, should we get this started?" Then she saw Kagan come forward out of the shadows. "I thought you might be here. Cade invited you?"

Kagan nodded. "I know mountains. He thought I might be useful. But I'm only here to consult. If you want me to leave now, I will."

Maya stared at him for a long moment. "What the hell? In the end it won't make a difference. Stay." Then she pulled out her notebook and sat down in front of the fire. "Give me a cup of coffee and I'll start filling you in about Zokara Mountain." She took a sip of the coffee Riley handed her and gave Kagan a sardonic glance. "And don't bother trying to remember the name of that mountain out of all the peaks you're familiar with. You won't know this one."

"I wouldn't waste my time. I prefer to have you tell me about it," he said quietly. "There are over three thousand four hundred named peaks in the Himalayas alone. Not to mention the other Asian ranges."

"Well, this particular mountain wasn't named before Silvana purchased and took possession of that strip of the mountains at the same time that she bought the island. She had plans for the foothills and mountains because she was always afraid that the island itself was too accessible. There was always the chance that Rome might find where she was and send soldiers after her." She shook her head. "But no one could say those mountains were accessible. She would have a place to run to and escape if it became necessary. There was no way she was going to let them drag her back to those arenas and butcher her. The mountains served as an escape hatch, and there were valleys in the foothills where she could nurture the herds she'd brought with her. It seemed a perfect way for her to have it all."

"Good for her," Riley said as she sat down beside Maya. "It obviously worked. Those unicorns appear to be healthy and flourishing. And she never had to use her escape hatch?"

"No, but she never got over the fear that it could happen. Over the years she nearly reached the status of queen, one revered and respected by everyone. Yet the more she worked at creating her perfect world for herself and the islanders, the more she looked over her shoulder. She began to worry about what would happen to her little kingdom and her islanders after she was no longer there to protect it. Would everything she'd worked for be taken away from the islanders if Rome discovered she was the one who had made it a success?" Maya shook her head. "Being Silvana, she couldn't bear that idea, so she began to look around for a way to take herself out of the equation. When she died, no one must be able to find her remains and steal either her treasure or the glory of her accomplishments. Which would also keep the islanders safe. And she had one more requirement: She disliked the idea of her body being cut into and her organs removed, which was the common practice at that time in both Rome and Egypt. As a warrior, she thought it would be like a final defeat in the arena, and she refused to be defeated even by death. So she set about searching for another way to get what she wanted. It took her a few years, but she found a mountain that was close to the island but high enough that there would be no chance of any grave robbers or pesky Roman soldiers being able to raid her tomb. She named it Zokara and started to work."

"High enough," Cade repeated. He looked at Kagan. "Are you going to ask her or should I?"

"I don't believe she's going to be shy about spelling it out," Kagan's gaze met Maya's. "Altitude?"

She nodded. "The sarcophagus area was over eight thousand meters. That put it into death zone territory as far as altitude was concerned. But you know that."

"Very well. High-altitude pulmonary edema. Most frequent cause of death." He added, "And cerebral edema is even more dangerous because it causes fluid on the brain."

"But it doesn't affect you?" she asked. "You're the genetic miracle man."

He smiled. "My ancestors have lived in these mountains for centuries, so my genes have adjusted and I require much less oxygen. But then most guides I know have a similar ability."

"Maybe not quite as extreme?"

"Perhaps not. I'm multiracial in my heritage. I have a thread of Irish. I have relatives on the Tibetan side, and my great-great-grandfather was born in the Changbai Mountains in Manchuria—and heaven only knows where his forebears came from. But I can almost guarantee it was deep mountain country."

"Well, unfortunately Silvana didn't know about altitude sickness when she was preparing her sarcophagus," Maya said. "She lost three workers while they were constructing the central burial tower and the smaller treasure area. She was horrified. She didn't know until it was too late that they were suffering any more than a little shortness of breath. They hadn't complained. Her workers wouldn't have wanted to refuse her if they could help it. They had a duty to her and wanted to do it. They might possibly have lived if they hadn't worked so hard and long to complete the tower room. She ordered the rest of the workers down from the mountain, but she still hadn't given up her plan to be placed on that mountaintop. Now it seemed even more important because her islanders had died there for her. But it had to be done right and with no harm to anyone but herself. She had to be the only one who ever visited that tower room. She knew a lot about poisons and drugs both from her experience on the steppes and Antonio's dealings with the court. So she went searching for answers that pleased her."

"And did she find them?" Riley asked.

"She found them," Maya said. "She found a drug that would

act almost like an instant fast freeze when she was placed in the sarcophagus. She called it a forever drug because it would freeze time forever for the person receiving it. When she knew her time had come, she had herself carried up to the tower room. She gave herself a strong sedative so that she wouldn't have to struggle for breath until she was in the tower room. Then all relatives and servants had orders to leave the room and lock it. They were told to leave the mountain and not return after they watched her take the final drug." Maya smiled faintly. "Her daughter said the drug worked instantly. It was incredible. She was beautiful. Silvana looked younger than she had in years, as if she had just fallen into a restful sleep."

"Nice..." Riley said. "Though a little too much like a fairy tale. Particularly the bit about the freeze-drying drug she was given."

"Maybe not," Kagan said. "It could be that Silvana was just a little in advance of her generation. Though there might have been drugs like that in her day. It was a prime era for magicians and priests to work their magic. Besides, not all drugs are concocted in a lab. She might have gathered them in a forest."

"You're reaching," Cade said.

"Am I?" Kagan smiled. "Remind me to tell you about Chile."

Maya shrugged. "When you're finished, I'd like to go on. I've told you what her daughter and the servants who witnessed her death related afterward. Do you want to hear the rest?"

"I definitely want to hear where that mountain is located," Cade said.

"I thought you would." Maya reached for her notebook and tore out the first page. "The coordinates of the waterfall entry and the passage that leads from there up to the tower room where Silvana died."

"Waterfall?" Cade echoed.

"Look at the directions and the coordinates on the page. The entry path leads behind a waterfall in the jungle near the temple. Once inside there's a trapdoor near the cliff edge that goes down about fifty feet and connects with another path that goes east for about four miles and then starts upward to curve around the mountain until you reach the tower room they carved into Zokara. After that, you're on your own."

"Any suggestions?"

"Watch for broken stones. You'll be warm for only about a fourth of the trip up the path, then you'll start feeling the cold. The darkness can be overwhelming, so be sure your lights and batteries don't fail you. It's always a good idea to have someone close to you in case you become disoriented and wander off the path."

"And how many of those mistakes did you make?" Cade asked.

"More than I care to admit," she said wryly. "So I'm not about to do it. But you'll probably be able to guess when I tell you I made that trip by myself. As caretaker, I thought I should handle such a delicate mission with discretion." She hesitated.

"One thing I did do right. I took the precaution to get four complete oxygen units that you'll find about halfway up to the tower. It might save your life. By that time the altitude may be taking you down."

"What a touching gift," Riley said with a grin. "You always know what to get a friend."

"Actually, I bought them for myself," Maya said. "Just in case I decided not to count on getting help. There was always that possibility. I was considering regular space suits, but I found they weigh about four hundred pounds and have terrible mobility issues. I figured a pressure suit like jet pilots wear would be better if I added an oxygen tank and a plastic helmet with lights. That would create mobility problems, too, but you wouldn't have to put it on until you reached the halfway point—the death zone for altitude sickness. If you moved fast enough after that, it should be safe."

"Not bad," Kagan murmured.

Maya's brows rose. "But not perfect?"

"Nothing is perfect until you're staring it in the face. The worst danger would be accidental depressurization that would make you go unconscious in seconds and then suffocate and freeze you to death immediately. The suits would have to be carefully crafted to avoid any cracks or any faulty suit joints."

"I made sure they were," Maya said coolly.

Kagan smiled. "Then, as you said, all you'd have to worry about is that you move very fast."

"But I won't be the one to wear those suits now," Maya

said. "After I climbed up to the midway point lugging them, I noticed I wasn't breathing so well and I decided that it wasn't smart to go any farther alone. I stopped and went back down to the waterfall and began to make plans to try again later if I could persuade someone to come with me."

"And you did," Riley said. "You won't have to worry about that any longer."

Maya smiled. "Maybe not. But you were always the easy one. And I say that with heartfelt thanks." She looked around at their faces. "Is there anything else you need to know from me before I go back to Bailey?"

"Only one thing," Riley said. "When we first came, you said something about how the best-laid plans sometimes don't work worth a damn. You never told me what you meant."

Maya hesitated and then said, "Exactly what I said. I was thinking about Silvana."

"And?"

"I was thinking how hard she worked during all her time here on the island. Then when she decided she had to find a way to die that wouldn't hurt the people she cared about, she went out of her way to do that, too."

"But it *was* worth a damn, Maya," Riley said gently. "Every-thing she did had value."

"Did it?" Maya asked. "I hope you're right. I've always been a cynic, but I had to be the one to question everything when I took charge of the island. I thought it was my duty."

"Why wouldn't you believe it?" Kagan's gaze was fixed intently on her face. "Tell me."

"I think there's probably a good chance you know already." Maya's lips twisted bitterly. "Didn't you tell me how well you knew the mountains?"

"Tell me anyway."

She shrugged. "Because Silvana couldn't know that things wouldn't stay the same. Even before I took over from Jann Lu, I'd noticed things were changing around us. An orchard that had flooded when it never had before. An earthquake near the temple area. A river that had changed the direction of its flow. So I had a few experts come here and take a more in-depth look and give me some answers."

"And what did they say?"

She met his eyes. "What do you think? It was due to the effects of global warming. There were other signs on the island I hadn't noticed, but they gave me a complete fifteen-page report describing every one of them. Along with recommendations about what to do when conditions get worse." She added bitterly, "As they most certainly would."

"Shit." Riley stared at her, stunned. "Why didn't you tell me?"

"Why? It wouldn't have solved the present problem and certainly not any future ones." Maya gestured dismissively. "All this wonder and beauty around us...There's unlikely to be any major immediate damage to the island unless there's a tsunami or major storm cycle. I may have time to scramble and get together some kind of long-range plan. The mountains are safer than the island for the time being. But they're also being affected. The south glacier that took two thousand years to form has almost melted in the last twenty-five years. The Himalayas are losing their glaciers at an extraordinary rate, and the ice melt threatens agriculture and water supply— and eventually means rising sea levels. It will also increase the likelihood of avalanches."

"And rockslides?" Kagan asked. "That was why you were worried that the unicorns were going to have to contend with that problem?"

"Yes. The rockslides will constantly get worse." She looked back at Cade. "That's why I couldn't leave them here even if there wasn't a threat from Nadim. It was safe when Silvana brought those unicorns here, but it's not safe now. So it's over to you, Cade."

"I'll accept it."

"But you can see why Silvana couldn't accept it, because she couldn't imagine that we'd destroy it." Maya smiled sadly. "We even have to disturb that burial place she worked so hard to create for herself. If we don't move that sarcophagus and get it out of there to somewhere safe, we run the risk of an avalanche doing so for us. Those experts said the area around Zokara Mountain would be particularly vulnerable to damage from avalanches."

"She'd probably prefer that to being taken back as prisoner

of those Roman soldiers," Riley said. "She went through quite a bit to avoid that happening." She suddenly smiled. "But she succeeded and that's one thing we won't have to worry about. Though I don't know how the hell we're going to keep her body preserved until we can get it to a lab that will tell us what we should be doing. I don't even know what we're going to find when we examine the body. It's all very well for Silvana to tell her servants and relatives that she was sure she'd found a drug that would keep her frozen forever in time—but how could she be sure? How could she know how long it would last? We're talking about nearly two thousand years. In that age a hundred years might seem forever." She frowned. "I think I should call Eve and ask a few questions…"

"More than a few," Cade murmured.

"One more thing," Maya said. She picked up a soft leather pouch and reached inside to produce an ornate gold and bejeweled key.

Cade's eyes widened. "Is that—?"

"It's the key to Silvana's tomb. The same one her followers used in the last moments of her life." Maya handed it to him as she got to her feet. "It's all in your hands now. The only thing I'm asking is that you make it soon. Nadim sounded both hungry and vicious when I talked to him last night. I can't stand the thought of him near Bailey." She turned and left the fire. "Good night."

Kagan caught up with her. "You're going through a bad time," he said quietly. "It will get better, but not for a while.

You love this island and the mountains, and it came as a shock when you found out how it was being destroyed by idiots who don't care. I grew up loving the mountains probably even more than you do, but I could see the destruction happening all around me from the time I was a small child. All that beauty...I couldn't understand it. Sometimes the pain was almost unbearable. It only helped when I decided I just had to find a way to do whatever I could to survive until I found the people smart and willing enough to help me start repairing what had been destroyed."

"I don't need a pep talk, Kagan," she said jerkily.

"No, because you're instinctively doing what I'm doing. You found Cade and your friend Riley, and they're people who reach out and bandage and then repair. I just thought you might like to know you're not alone." He smiled. "Good night, Maya. See you in the morning."

Before she could reply, he was gone.

———

"A forever-in-time drug," Eve repeated skeptically. "Not impossible, but not likely, Riley." She hesitated. "But it is intriguing...and even more so since your Silvana swore that she found one. I've begun to have faith in Silvana."

"So have I," Riley said. "But like you, I have to consider that it was another age, and it sounds more like magic than science. I thought that I'd check and see if you'd ever heard anything like that."

"No, but I'm a forensic sculptor and that's not my field of expertise. Had anyone else at that meeting heard about a drug like that?"

"Not really. Kagan made some vague reference to Chile."

"That's a long way from the Himalayas. Still, you might follow up. In the meantime I'll be glad to do some research and see what I come up with."

"Don't do it. I don't want to be a bother. I just thought you might know—"

"Hush. I wouldn't offer if I didn't want to do it. It's not as if I'm too busy right now. Joe is back from Scotland and I'm only doing my forensic work."

"Which is always substantial," Riley said with a smile. "I'm not going to back you into a corner, Eve."

"I wouldn't let you," Eve said. "You've just given me an interesting puzzle to solve and I'm going to do it. It's rather fascinating. I had to turn you down when you and Cade took off for the island, but there's no reason why I can't dip my toe in this little problem."

"I very carefully didn't invite you," Riley said. "I felt guilty enough. Keep your toes out of this, Eve."

"As soon as I finish checking it out." She changed the subject. "How are you and Cade getting along?"

"Ups and downs. As he recently said, we're learning a lot

about each other right now." She chuckled. "But we haven't been able to reach the stratosphere you and Joe seem to manage."

"It took us a long time, and we're still learning. For instance, Joe has been very quiet since he came back home. I don't know why yet." She looked up as Joe came back onto the porch. "But I think I'll find out. I'll call you back when I find out something about your forever drug." She pressed DISCONNECT.

"Riley has a problem?" Joe dropped down on the swing beside her. "You were on the phone a long time."

"You could say she has a problem. It's more like a challenge." She laid her head on his shoulder. "But she'll work through it. She always does."

"But it wouldn't hurt if you decided to throw a little help her way?"

"I've been thinking about it. But not unless I can work around any problems it might cause here. We're still working on the boathouse."

"The boathouse?" He looked down at her and started to laugh. "What the hell are you talking about? You're prioritizing your efforts of choosing paint and hiring carpenters over doing work that no one else can do half as well as you?"

She frowned. "It's not as if we're talking about the forensic work I do for law enforcement. This is something completely different."

He reached out and cupped her face in his two hands. "Yes,

it is," he said. "And I've been thinking long and hard about how different. Lately, you're trying to be everything to everyone. You're mother and best friend to our kids. You've created a home for all of us. You're doing your duty to give forensic services to half the police departments in the country. Now you're trying to rebuild our boathouse?" He brushed a kiss on her lips. "And one other thing I didn't mention, you're being my love and my life. Which I absolutely refuse to give up."

She gave a mock growl. "You'd better not."

"No problem. But we might have to do some schedule changing to accommodate something new I've noticed on the horizon."

"And what's that?"

"The fact that you're changing and growing as a person and professional." He saw her start to frown and he added quickly, "Oh, it's not as if you've ever stood still in that category. Maybe it's because life has been zooming and changing around us lately that you've been zooming and changing, too, just to keep up. You're not satisfied with yourself, and you've been trying new things, reaching out, seeing how far you could push the envelope." He added quietly, "And you've been pushing it one hell of a distance. For the past few years you've been amazing. You helped with the creation of that bullet cure that could be a universal lifesaver, you did the extraordinary work on Helen of Troy, and you jumped in when Riley said she might need your help with Palandan Island and saved her life.

You could have said no, but you didn't. Because you wanted to stretch the boundaries you'd drawn for yourself. You knew it was time you took another giant step forward."

"You sound as if I was negotiating a moon landing. I was just doing my job, Joe."

"No, you were innovating and planning and doing what you were meant to do to reach your potential." He gazed down into her eyes. "But you've been drawing back lately and letting other things get in the way. I want to keep you safe, but I'm not going to let you smother that growth. It's wonderful and should be nurtured. We'll just find a way to work around it. Okay?"

He was the one who was wonderful. She had to clear her throat. "Very much okay," she said huskily. "But there's no reason I can't do it all if I figure out—"

"There you go again." He laughed. "Did I leave out the word *together*? Insert it and we'll start from there."

"We always start from there." She cuddled closer to him.

"But I believe you've talked me into trying for another moon landing if they manage to get Silvana down from that mountain to a place where I can work on her. It can't be on that island with Nadim hovering like a vulture." She could feel the excitement begin at just the thought. "But there will be a lot of prep work to do. Maybe I'll let you dip your toes into Riley's problem, too."

"Please don't. It sounds very uncomfortable and terribly soggy."

"No, it's only research and you're always great at that."

"You realize praise will get you anywhere with me." He sighed. "Where should I begin?"

"I'll have to call Riley back, but I think you should begin with Chile..."

———

Two hours later Riley received the call from Eve.

"I know it's the middle of the night there," Eve said when Riley picked up. "That's too bad. It's your fault for stirring things up here. I have to get things settled or I won't be able to go back to sleep."

"What's wrong?" Riley sat up as she saw Cade throw aside his covers and get to his knees. "Is your security still okay at the Lake Cottage?"

"It's fine. I'm always stumbling over one of the guards when I go outside. But that's another thing. We're probably going to need more sentries."

"That doesn't make sense. Why would that be—"

"Because Joe says I need to make another moon landing and it might as well be getting Silvana off that island if we can do it. But we both know how difficult that might be, so we should try to do it as soon as possible."

"Agreed." Then she caught up with that first sentence. "Moon landing?"

"Never mind. You'd have to be here. But the important

thing is that you need to make both the extraction and her new storage arrangement happen right away. I can't help you with the extraction, but I'll arrange for the temporary lab in this area where I can examine and perhaps even work on her. Cade will have to arrange security and take care of furnishing the medical expertise we might need. He'll need more—"

"I'm here," Cade broke in. "I'll take care of it."

"Of course you are," Eve said. "Well, get to work. Riley, I'm worried about that drug we may have to deal with. We don't know what we're facing. We don't even know if it worked for a short time or long time. Or if we'll have to face the fact that without Egyptian or Roman embalming, we'll be left with nothing at all in that coffin. Did you talk to Kagan about Chile yet?"

"That was two hours ago."

"And I've been lying here thinking about that blank wall I'm facing. Why don't you go and find out if he can help me?"

"I'll be on my way as soon as I hang up." She paused. "Eve, you don't have to do this."

"It seems I do," Eve said. "It has something to do with growth and potential and innovation. Since it has nothing to do with you, don't argue with me. Just get me the information I need and go get Silvana on a plane in the best possible shape you can manage. I'll get back to you if I think of anything else."

"We're sure you will," Cade said. "It will be as you command."

But Eve had already hung up.

"She would have been a wonderful emperor." Cade was starting to dress. "Or maybe a caretaker. Well, we have our orders. We should be ready to go after Silvana as soon as we can. It's just as well since we'll have Joe, Eve, and security on the other end. I'll go to base camp and make arrangements for a troop to accompany us to that waterfall and tell Kirby to get a refrigeration unit put on the plane right away." He glanced at her. "I could stop at Kagan's tent on my way and tell him about Eve's call. That might have been just a casual remark he made about Chile. Kagan has been all over the world and he has hundreds of stories about every place he's been."

"Maybe one of those stories will tell us what we want to know," Riley said. "I promised Eve I'd go talk to him right away. I have to keep my word. I'll go get Maya and take her with me to see Kagan. She knows more than any of us about what Silvana did that day." She was throwing on her clothes. "Besides, Maya and Kagan have a right to know about any change of plans even if they're staying here with the herd and not directly involved in them."

"I wasn't trying to keep anything from them," Cade said. "It was only a question of priority."

"I know that." She was on her way out the door, but turned and gave him a quick, hard kiss. "But after tonight I suddenly realize how alone Maya must be feeling now. You've heard how I grew up in the jungles trailing after my father. I was alone then, too, but it didn't bother me. There was always something to see, somewhere to go. And one of the things I saw was Maya's island, and it was so beautiful with all those apple orchards and the towering mountains in the distance and the legends she told me. I laughed and told her it must be like living in Eden. But that was her *home* and her history in a way I could never know." She could feel her throat tighten painfully as she remembered Maya's expression tonight. "But Eden is going away and she doesn't know how she's going to stop it. I don't know how any of us are going to stop it. The only thing I'm sure about is that we're not going to leave Maya out of a single minute of anything we do that might make a difference to her. Got it?"

"Without a doubt," he said gently. "I knew that would be the direction you'd be going. Anything else?"

"And Kagan is part of the team now, too. I don't want anyone to be alone. We're all in this together. I don't want to leave anyone out." She called back over her shoulder, "I'll call you after we talk to Kagan."

"Before you drop in, I suggest you call him, too," Cade said as he turned away. "It might save you some time. If I remember correctly, he usually sleeps nude."

"I'm glad you gave me a call," Kagan said as he opened the flap to let Maya and Riley into his tent. "It gave me time to make coffee."

"Really?" Riley said. "Cade said it would give you time so that you wouldn't be totally naked."

"That, too." He grinned. "It was like Cade to try to lighten the situation when I was trying to be cool and debonair. He has a habit of doing that."

"Because you know each other so well," Maya said. "And I notice you've no problem handling anything he dishes out." She took the cup of coffee he handed her. "And if we show up in your tent in the middle of the night, we deserve whatever we get. Riley did explain that Eve Duncan has agreed to help with doing the follow-up on Silvana. She's so good that we can't afford to let her get away, but she's concerned about the preservation procedure."

He nodded. "I've heard of her." He shrugged. "And she has a right to be concerned. But there's a chance that the drug could work. It depends on how much faith you have in Silvana and her ability to dig out talent from everyone around her. She said she found someone who could give her what she needed. Do we believe her?"

"I want to believe her," Riley said. "But Eve sent me to you. It's such a bizarre drug that even Cade thought you were kidding when you were talking about possibilities. Were you?"

"I was just telling him he shouldn't reject anything without exploring it." He handed Riley her coffee.

"And where would he explore it?" Maya asked. "Chile?"

"It's not as if I've ever heard about this forever drug," Kagan said. "It just reminded me of a climb I took in the Andes several years ago. I ran across a village priest who wasn't much of a climber, but he was a hell of a good storyteller. He told me about some Incan children who had been sacrificed maybe seven hundred years ago to the Sun God. Tragic story but according to this priest, the children weren't sad at the time. They were treated royally during the year before the sacrifice, and they weren't afraid when the time came. The priests fed them coca beans and an exotic drink that was almost surely a potent drug or narcotic. The children went to sleep and that was the end of their story." He smiled. "Except that the priests wrapped them in fine wool and kept them in a special altar room in the temple in the mountains and in time forgot about them. They were discovered by university students on a field trip, who found the three children were perfectly preserved and looked exactly the way they had when they were sacrificed seven hundred years before."

"Interesting story," Maya said. "Is it going somewhere?"

"It did for me," he said. "I was curious. On the way back from the climb, I stopped at Santiago and did some research. It wasn't a fairy tale; the children were real, and the bodies were sent to a prestigious university in Nassau where they're displayed by the science department several times a year." He paused. "And the drug that was still found in their bodies was sent to a lab at Johns Hopkins, where it's still being examined and tested. No results yet, but there's always hope. They won't

266

give up." He took a sip of his coffee. "Because that doesn't happen when it's a forever drug."

"You think it might be the same drug that Silvana found?" Riley asked.

"I think it could be similar," he corrected. "It's a big world and there's no reason why not. We should be very careful with it."

"You're an optimist," Maya said.

"I try to be." He grinned. "And as I said, why not? Did I forget to mention that the place where those children were found was very high in the Andes? Extremely thin air, rather like Zokara Mountain." He added quietly, "No matter what the odds, you can never give up, Maya." He turned to Riley. "So you can tell Eve about those children and have Joe call Johns Hopkins and see if they've found out anything she might be able to use."

"She'll probably pull in Joe's ex-wife Diane to do research, too. It's just Diane's cup of tea. She practically reformed public health. Why not this? I'll *do* it," Riley said. "Joe is very good with applied pressure. Subtle, but effective." She put her coffee down. "And I agree with you. We can't give up."

"I haven't given up," Maya said. "I'm only a little tired tonight. I'll bounce back." She handed Kagan her cup. "And Silvana was sharper than any of us. If she said she found someone she could trust to give her that drug, I believe her."

"Good for you," he said softly.

She was trying to ignore the surge of warmth those words gave her as she moved to leave. "Don't be condescending. I'll see you in the morning, Kagan. Drop by and see Bailey. She said she missed you..."

"I like him," Riley said. They fell into step together as they headed for their separate tents on the hill. "I think you would, too, if you let yourself. You're not giving him much of a chance."

"I don't have to," Maya said. "Everyone is willing to give him all the chances he wants or needs. I recognize he's very intelligent and appealing, but I can't let him take over my duty here on the mountain. I have an obligation."

"No one is trying to interfere with your duty, Maya," Riley said quietly. "We all recognize that we couldn't do nearly as good a job. I hope you don't think I'd ever try to get in your way. I was hoping that we might be going after Silvana together."

"And I would have liked that very much. It would have been my honor." Then she shrugged. "But this isn't about me. I realized I couldn't do everything. When I made that deal to bring you and Cade to the island, I knew I might have to give up control. The important thing is to get the job done with all the efficiency and respect it calls for." She looked her in the eye. "I trust you and know you'll do that, Riley."

"Yes, I will."

Maya smiled. "And I'll stay here and tend to Bailey and

the herd and try to keep Kagan from having his way about every single detail." They had reached her tent, and she nodded at the guard on duty before she opened the flap. "But don't expect me to make it too easy for him, Riley. I do have to wring some satisfaction out of this situation!"

CHAPTER

10

Riley had just finished talking to Eve when Cade came back to their tent an hour later. He tossed a cardboard box down near the tent flap. "How did she take what you told her about Kagan's story about the Inca kids? Still in emperor mode?"

She shook her head. "She and Joe are going to check it out at top speed, but she knows that it's probably a long shot. She's just moving as fast as she can and hoping to help us out. No emperor, no caretaker, only our good friend."

"And that's more than enough." He tilted his head and asked curtly, "Are you okay?"

She was suddenly aware of the stormy recklessness threading his words. "Why shouldn't I be?" she asked warily. Then she made a face. "Except that I was a little emotional myself when I left here before. I'm sorry, I promise I won't do that again."

She deliberately avoided his eyes and shifted her gaze to the box beside the door. "What's that? Supplies to take with us?"

"You might say that. Actually, it's a few little items for you."

"What?" She started to get up.

"Don't get up." He moved toward the box. "I'll bring them to you. I want to make a presentation."

She frowned as she watched him open the box. "What on earth? This is weird. What the hell is it?"

He reached in the box and drew out a pack containing a camouflage uniform. "I thought you might need something appropriate to wear." He threw it down on the bed with barely restrained violence. Then he took out a pair of combat boots and put them beside the uniform. He pulled out an automatic pistol and put it on the bed. "That should do it. If there's anything else necessary, I'm sure I'll get around to furnishing it." His lips tightened. "After all, I wouldn't want you not to have all the proper equipment when I drag you up the mountain to that sarcophagus. If the altitude doesn't get you, Nadim or Bevan might be waiting in the wings to take you out."

She shook her head in bewilderment. "I don't know what the hell you're talking about with this charade. Why are you so angry with me?"

"I'm not angry with you." He knelt beside her and grasped her shoulders. "If anything, I'm angry at myself. I was just down at base camp, and I saw all this crap on the shelves, and it suddenly hit home to me what a complete idiot I've been since all this started. I shouldn't have brought you to the island at all, and now I'm going to drag you with me up that mountain as if you were Kirby or one of the paid mercenaries and you didn't matter." His hands tightened on her shoulders. "But you *do* matter. No one matters as much as you do to me. We should stop right here, and I should send you back to Eve and let you help her where you'll be safe and surrounded by Joe Quinn and Loring's men." He added through set teeth, "But you won't let me do that, will you?"

"Of course I won't." She shrugged off his grip. "Because it's all nonsense. I wouldn't leave you here. You're not going to walk away. You promised Maya, so you'll still be here until it's over. And you brought Kagan here. Are you going to send him back to one of his mountains and let those unicorns be butchered by Nadim? I don't think so. I told you that we're in this together now. Forget anything else, including all that protective bullshit. That really pisses me off."

"May I bring it to your attention that I'm considerably more experienced at taking care of myself than you are?"

"You mean all those medals and going after poachers and other assholes? Yes, you have experience. But then so do I. I grew up in the jungle." She touched the barrel of the automatic pistol he'd placed on the floor at her feet. "You'll remember I'm fairly good at shooting one of these. Though I'm better with a Luger." She looked him in the eye. "And I'll admit that you're an expert at all that other stuff, but I'm smart and learn very quickly, Cade. Instead of worrying and trying to put me in a box, why don't you take me with you whenever you have the opportunity and start teaching me what you think I should know? Because that's the only way you're going to be absolutely certain that I'll be safe." She added with emphatic softness, "If I do it myself."

He swore and shook his head. "That's supposed to make me not worry? I want you surrounded by an army."

"I believe it will be fine once you get over the first painful twinges. I'll be reasonable, but naturally it will have to be reciprocal." She smiled mischievously. "To blend in with your theory that we have to learn from each other. As a matter of fact, I think I'll wear the camo uniform, complete with combat boots, that you so kindly brought to remind me." She scooted over on the sleeping bag. "Now come and hold me. It's late and we only have a few more hours to sleep before we start looking for that waterfall. You said the arrangements have all been made?"

"Except for the plane. It's taken some time to get the right pressure equipment on board." He was already undressing. "But we'll still have time to get it done before we need it. It will take us almost half a day to climb up to the tower room and get the coffin. Another half day to get it down and packed on the helicopter to take to the airport where the Gulfstream is waiting." He grimaced. "Providing everything goes well. We don't know what we're going to find when we get to the tower room." He was naked and sliding under the blankets. "Kirby will be piloting both the helicopter and the Gulfstream." He paused. "I can't talk you into going with him to join Eve at the Lake Cottage?"

"We've just discussed that," Riley said as she pulled off her nightshirt and threw it aside. "You never give up, do you?"

"Not when it's something I really want." He moved over her. "I can compromise and I will, but don't expect me to surrender. Not when it's about you." He kissed her. "Because there's nothing I want or need more." He was gently stroking her hair back away from her face. "I love holding you. It's one of my favorite things." He kissed her again. "But I wonder if the holding could be later instead of sooner?"

"I don't see why not." She was having trouble breathing as he came into her. "Later would give us something to look forward to." She gasped at a sudden deep move. "What do you think?"

He laughed. "I believe that it's all good and it's not going to matter one damn bit..."

———

Nadim cursed. He and Bevan had been driving for over an hour down a jungle road that seemed to appear and disappear almost every few minutes. They were on the island of Pulau Tiga, at the head of a three-car caravan and chasing a lead he was increasingly convinced would take them absolutely nowhere. He turned toward Bevan, who was driving. "Are you sure this isn't a complete waste of time?"

"Positive. I trust my sources on this."

"Tell me more about this man we're seeing. This... Chodak."

"Tenzin Chodak."

"Couldn't we have brought him to meet us somewhere a bit more civilized? Given him five thousand dollars and a charter plane ticket?"

"He wouldn't have come."

"Okay, ten thousand."

"He makes a good living right where he is."

"Here?" Nadim waved his hands at the jungle around them. "Doing what? Is he a drug dealer?"

"No. He owns a small boat on the island's south side. The oil companies pay him well to take their experts to other islands in the area. They'll be drilling all around here in the next five years or so. They've been snapping up leases like crazy."

"How nice for them. How does that help us?"

"It doesn't. But before Chodak came here, he spent almost twenty years working as a Sherpa in the mountains on and around Silvana's tomb. He knows that area like few people in the world."

"That means nothing. My people have reached out to some of the Sherpas up there. No one will even speak of Silvana and her tomb. It's a sacred trust to them, and has been going back hundreds of years. They're nutty about it. Superstitious, even."

"That's where this man is different. He has no use for those traditions. He broke with his people for a reason."

"*What* reason?"

Bevan shrugged. "I don't know, exactly. But apparently, Chodak came here and never looked back. It's why my sources think he may be persuaded to give you the information you need."

They rounded a sharp curve, and the road abruptly ended against a cluster of trees. Bevan slammed the brakes.

"What now?" Nadim said.

"Now we walk." Bevan unfastened his seat belt. "But from what I understand, it's only a few yards from here."

"You'd better be right about this."

Nadim, Bevan, and the four men in the jeeps behind them climbed out of their vehicles and walked through the trees. After less than five minutes, they emerged to find themselves on the island's south shore, at the end of a long dock with a run-down bar and even more run-down café. Several boats were tied up to the dock, which apparently supplied the establishments with their only customers.

Bevan pointed to a coal-fired steamer that was probably almost a hundred years old. "That's his boat."

"You're joking."

"No. It's not particularly fast, but it's extremely well maintained. He gets more for his charters than anyone else in the area."

A voice came from behind them. "Yes, I do. But it's worth every dollar."

They turned to see a small dark-skinned man, about fifty,

with a large potbelly. He smiled. "Unfortunately, the only guns I allow on the boat are my own. You'll have to leave your artillery here on shore."

Nadim turned to see that his men, as usual, had made no attempt to hide their handguns and shoulder holsters. He turned back. "We don't want to hire your boat. Mr. Chodak, I presume?"

"Yes." Chodak eyed him warily. "And you are...?"

"Someone who wants to make you a wealthy man."

Chodak laughed. "I have a lot of money already."

"I'll give you more."

He shook his head. "If you're from an oil company, I won't tell you about the places I've taken my other customers. All my trips are strictly confidential."

"I'm more interested in a certain mountain range where you used to work."

Chodak's smiled faded. "That was a long time ago. I don't really talk about those days anymore."

"Perhaps I can persuade you. And that brings us back to my 'wealthy man' proposal."

Chodak shook his head. "I'm a busy man. Maybe another day." He pushed past the men, but Nadim grabbed his arm.

"You should see this first."

Nadim nodded to one of his men, who stepped forward with an alligator-skin satchel. The man opened it to show that it was filled with U.S. currency.

Chodak's eyes widened. "A lot of money to carry around in these parts. That explains the guns."

Nadim smiled. "It's a hundred thousand dollars. One productive conversation and it's all yours. If I find what I'm looking for, two of my associates here will be staying behind to give you a million dollars more within a week."

Chodak stared at him for a long moment. "This can only be about one thing."

"And what would that be?"

"Silvana," he whispered.

Nadim laughed. "You speak the name as if you expect her to come down from the mountain and strike you down."

"Not her. But trust me, there are others who would. In a heartbeat."

"No one within a thousand miles, I'd wager."

"They'd make the trip."

"Then perhaps we should take this conversation somewhere less . . . conspicuous."

Chodak considered this for a moment. "We can talk in my boat. Your men with the guns can wait outside."

Nadim nodded toward the four men, then he and Bevan followed Chodak into his boat. As Bevan had indicated, the boat's interior was beautifully appointed, with teak finishes and leather-upholstered furniture.

Chodak poured himself a drink from the main cabin's mirror-backed bar. "Would you gentlemen like anything?"

"Yes," Nadim replied. "The exact location of Silvana's final resting place."

Chodak smiled. "I can see you're not one to mince words."

"I don't like to waste time. Yours or mine."

"You've already spent a lot of time coming to see me." Chodak walked across the cabin with his drink. "Something must have given you the idea that I would be amenable to your offer."

Bevan shrugged. "We understand you left your previous employment under less-than-ideal circumstances."

"I was fired."

Nadim laughed. "The Sherpa union kicked you out?"

"Not in so many words. But the suppliers wouldn't sell to me, and I was cut out of any and all of the reciprocal aid agreements the Sherpas have up there. After that, it was impossible for me to get work."

"And what did you do to deserve such treatment?"

"I took chances that others wouldn't. I would take my clients up in conditions that were less than ideal. I was always totally honest with them, and I told them the risks. For some, their expedition was the trip of a lifetime. And if some spotty weather got in the way, the other Sherpas would tell them that they had to go home and try again someday. For some clients, that just wasn't possible. For them, it was worth the risk to hire me to take them up."

"And you were always successful?" Nadim said.

"Sadly, no." Chodak sat in a large leather chair. "That

adventurous spirit can come with a steep cost. I lost people every season."

"But you obviously always made it back," Nadim said.

"I was a better climber than them. But in my last season, I lost six clients in four different climbs. That was too much for my fellow Sherpas, and they closed ranks. Apparently, I was giving our mountain a bad reputation. But I'd saved enough money to come here and start a new life for myself."

"Well, I can help give you an even better life," Nadim said. "*If* you have the information I seek."

"Oh, I have it."

"You've been there?"

"I've been close enough. Many of the Sherpas working up there are descendants of Silvana's subjects. They still adore her. As do I, to be honest. She was an extraordinary leader."

"I agree." Nadim took the bag of cash and placed it on the bar. "I promise she'll always be treated with the greatest respect. Do we have a deal?"

"When would I get the rest of the money?"

"Within forty-eight hours. Once I confirm that you've given us Silvana's actual location, you'll get the rest. All cash. My men will be staying behind to give it to you."

Chodak thought for a moment, stood, and walked across the cabin to a tall bookshelf. He pulled down a hardcover book and flipped through the pages until he reached a detail map. He picked up a pencil, scribbled on the map, and handed the open book to Nadim. "It's there. You have my word."

Nadim studied the map and traced Chodak's markings with his finger. "Zokara Mountain...Through a waterfall?"

"It's there, I promise you. Follow these instructions."

Nadim nodded. "Good. We came to the right place."

"You did. Now please go. I have a charter coming in less than half an hour."

"A pleasure," Nadim said. "I'll be in touch."

He and Bevan left the boat and joined the four men on the dock. Bevan smiled. "You're not really going to give him another million, are you?"

"If this is the location of Silvana, of course I will." Nadim closed the book. "I suspect Mr. Chodak would be a good ally to cultivate. Just as I cultivated you, Bevan."

"And if he's lying to us?"

Nadim cast a glance at his armed escorts. "Then my men will have no choice but to kill him."

MAYA'S TENT
6:05 A.M.

Kagan moved quietly, his feet making no sound as he crossed the few yards from Maya and Bailey's tent to the trees in the back where her deer was sheltering. He was so silent that he thought Bailey might be asleep when she didn't raise her head from the stack of straw where she was lying close to Riva.

But when he knelt down beside her, she turned and looked at him, her eyes wide open. "Hello, Kagan," she whispered. "I think there's another storm coming. Not like the last one. Riva's afraid of this one."

"Is she?" He tucked her blanket over her shoulders before he squatted down beside her and crossed his legs. "Is that why you're sleeping beside her?"

She nodded. "Though I've been doing that for the last few nights because it's near her time. But this is different. I could *feel* her fear. She needed me."

"And perhaps you needed *her*?"

"Perhaps. Do you think I'm being foolish?"

"No, why else am I here? I told you that I took care of many animals when I was a boy on the farm. I had bonds with all of them, and I know what it is to feel them call you when they're in need. We're all actually one with each other if we permit it to happen." He smiled. "Perhaps you're able to hear the call more clearly than most, but it's only a matter of degree. Maybe I also heard *your* call and that's why I came out here to see you rather than say good morning to your mother first. But you're actually reversing the traditional legends, you know. According to unicorn myths, the unicorn stationed herself beside a pure, gentle maiden to protect her from assault. Instead, you're protecting your friend, Riva?"

"I've read all those stories," Bailey said. "Why should I pay attention to fairy tales when this is real life. Those animals need us. Riva needs *me*."

"I'm not suggesting anything different," he said gently. "I admire your interpretation. I'm just pointing out that we might have to strike new ground to write new legends. However, we'll deal with that later. Right at this moment since I'm here on this early-morning visit, I should also mind my manners and say good morning to you." He inclined his head politely. "Good morning, Bailey." Kagan's voice was velvet soft. "Good morning, Riva. We're not going to let anything happen to either one of you." He got to his feet. "I'll have a surprise for both of you a little later." He paused. "And you're right, there *will* be a storm. I can feel it, too. I won't tell you not to be afraid, but I promise we won't leave you alone to face it." He turned away. "Now I have to go say good morning to your mother. I hope you're hungry. Because that's part of the surprise. Why don't you take Riva for a little walk around the campsite? She'd probably like to stretch her muscles a little."

She chuckled as she sat up. "Did she tell you she would?"

"No, I wouldn't presume to interfere with your relationship. I just remembered we had a goat once and if we didn't exercise her frequently, she'd butt us in the behind whenever she got the chance."

She laughed out loud. "Riva wouldn't do that. She's very polite."

Kagan reached out and tucked Bailey's coat more tightly about her. "If you say so. Just be sure to watch your back." He headed for the tent. "And stay close so that I can give you that surprise..."

Maya opened the flap of the tent before he reached it. "I know I asked you to come and visit Bailey, but you're a little early."

"She didn't think so." He ducked into the tent. "She was worried about the storm for Riva's sake. You're up early, too. Were you concerned about her?"

She shrugged. "She told me about it. Naturally I wanted to keep an eye on her. Though there's no sign of a bad storm warning from the weather bureau."

"Oh, it's coming. And it will be as bad as she thinks it's going to be. We're going to have to take the herd back to that shelter again."

She raised her brows. "Are you so certain?"

"Certain enough. I can smell it in the air. I've always been able to do that since I was a kid." He grinned. "I didn't need a Riva to tell me like Bailey. Though it would have been convenient."

"And when is this supposed to happen?"

"Not right away. Probably not before the end of the day. But you'll know when it's heading toward us. Sorry, I can't be more precise for you. It's not exactly an exact science."

"Because you have to smell it?" she said caustically.

"And you don't believe me?"

"Of course I do," Maya said sourly. "I wish to hell I didn't. But I grew up in these mountains, and I've run into this kind of Sherpa mojo before. And since you're practically the king of that category, I wouldn't dare discard anything you say."

He nodded. "I suspected you wouldn't. It's a relief that you're that intelligent. But I don't believe the storm is going to get in the way of what Cade and Riley are going to be doing at Silvana's mountain. Cade's got it timed so that they should be down from the mountain with the sarcophagus before the end of the day." He checked his watch. "They got off right on time from base camp. They should be arriving at the waterfall with Kirby's unit in about an hour."

"I'm glad you're so confident," Maya said dryly. "And I hope your olfactory ability is as keen as you think it is."

"So do I," he said quietly. "Because Cade left me in charge and there are things I have to do before I can be sure that everything will go the way I want it to."

"What things?"

"I told you that my unit had arrived at base camp."

"I remember, you said you had to blend them with the rest of the military units on the base."

"Only now I might not have time to do that. Things are moving very fast. Sometimes my men have difficulty being accepted by other military units."

She frowned. "Why? Troublemakers?"

"No, quite the contrary. You might say they're specialists. They're the best mountain fighters in the world. They're all Sherpas born and bred. I recruited them all myself when I decided that I wanted to do something with my life besides climb mountains. I'd been doing some work with Cade for a year or two and I enjoyed it. Everything from hunting poachers to going after child traffickers." He smiled. "My Sherpas enjoyed it, too. Sometimes a little too much. Imagine Sherpas with the skill of ninjas."

"I don't know if I want to imagine that. All the Sherpas I've come across have been kind and super-efficient."

"And so are my men. You'll like them. They're known as the Ice Rangers. They just move very fast and seem to read each other's minds." He made a face. "That can be disconcerting to some. I came to tell you that you should notify the shepherds to be ready to go down to the caves when you give the word." He paused. "And to tell them that if one of my Sherpas gives an order, they're to obey him."

She shook her head. "The shepherds are all very smart and independent. They know what they're doing. Look, I have great respect for Sherpas. I've studied their work all my life. I know that without the Sherpas accompanying climbers on Everest, a good many would never have made it. They were the real heroes on those peaks. It used to make me furious when I heard about a climber denigrating one of the Sherpas on his team." She held up her hand. "That being said, I won't disrespect any of the shepherds who work for me. Though I'll speak to them and tell them that they should pay attention to anything your men suggest." She shook her head and added resignedly, "I'll even tell them that the suggestion comes from you. Since you seem to have zoomed to the top of their hit parade. Is that good enough?"

"It will have to be. Probably better than I hoped. It's just that I remember how difficult I found it as a boy trying to prove himself on the mountain." He smiled. "I taught these men well so that they wouldn't have to go through what I did. But I also taught them good manners and ways to get around any rudeness in others. They will recall that and persevere."

"I can't imagine you as that struggling young boy." She tilted her head. "My, how you've changed."

"You believe I'm overconfident? It's true that I wasn't generous with people who wouldn't listen. But I did learn to listen and that was a saving grace. I believe you learned similar lessons when you were growing up. I think we were probably a good deal alike."

She stared at him for a long moment and then nodded slowly. "Perhaps we had a few things in common."

He was grinning. "More than a few." He changed the subject. "But now that you've come to believe me about the storm, I need to go a step further and tell you that I might not be around to watch over Bailey as much as I intended today. I've had to make other arrangements."

"You came to see her. That's all I asked. I'll do the rest."

"But that's not what I promised. You're going to be busy and possibly distracted." He turned and opened the flap. "That's why I brought Tazka Kun with me." He lifted a silver whistle to his lips. "I asked him to stay outside and keep an eye on Bailey until I called." He blew a short blast into the whistle. "You'll like him."

"He's one of your ninjas?" she asked as she saw a man of

short stature and shoulder-length shining black hair come running across the path toward the tent. He was dressed in white pants, top, and boots, and there was a broad smile on his tanned, triangular face. "He doesn't look very dangerous."

"He can be, but Kun is also a wonderful cook and fisherman and he's great with children. None of these men are cut of the same cloth. I wouldn't want them to be." He gestured to the man as he approached. "Tazka Kun, this is Maya Fallon, I told you about. She would be delighted if you could take care of her little girl today. Did you talk to Bailey at all yet?"

He nodded. "She is ten, only a year older than my grandson. She told me about the unicorn. How he would love to see her. She said she would show me her books so that I could tell him about them."

"You'll be able to see them for yourself and take a photo. Then you can send a photo to your grandson."

"May I do that?" Kun asked Maya eagerly. "Bailey said that I could, but I didn't want to impose." His brilliant smile lit his face. "Would you have the kindness?"

That smile was completely endearing, Maya thought. "I think Bailey would love you to have a photo," Maya said gently. "She's very proud of Riva."

"Why don't you go and tell Bailey that her mother said it would be fine," Kagan said. "And then bring her back to the tent and cook these ladies breakfast while Bailey tells you all about Riva."

Kun looked at Maya. "Could I do that?"

"Absolutely."

His smile widened. "It will be a fine breakfast. I'm very good, you know."

"I've heard rumors," Maya said. "Why don't you go get my daughter?"

He laughed and the next moment he'd turned and was running down the path.

Maya turned to Kagan. "You pulled out all the stops, didn't you? What mother wouldn't fall for a babysitter like him? A fantastic cook and he's a grandfather, too? Are you sure he has ninja skills along with the rest?"

"Would I steer you wrong?" He smiled. "He'll be able to protect her. Other than that, I told you that none of my men are cut out of the same cloth. They're very human with all the usual faults and virtues. After breakfast I'd like you to send her and Riva back to the cave with Kun to protect her. There's no need for her to be exposed, and you might get busy." He turned to go. "If you need me, call. I've got to get back to the base. I'll let you know if I have any other info about the storm."

"Wait." She took a half step forward. "You've furnished me with a fantastic cook. Why don't you at least stay for breakfast?"

"Ah, is that a break in the armor?" He looked back over his shoulder with a puckish grin. "I believe it is. And if I didn't have a duty to Cade to keep the home fires burning while he was on his way to that mountain, I'd take you up on it."

"Don't build it up to something it's not," she said with a grin. "For Pete's sake, it's only an invitation to breakfast."

"But that could lead down wonderful and mysterious paths." His eyes were sparkling with mischief. "It's all how you look at it..."

———

NADIM'S BASE CAMP ON THE APPROACH TO THE WATERFALL

Nadim pulled up the flap and strode into his tent at his own base camp. His mobile headquarters was staffed with a dozen of his best and most reliable techs, who had spent much of the morning setting up an array of monitors and satellite uplink hardware. Several of the monitor stations were dedicated to video feeds from several high-resolution camera drones buzzing around the mountain.

Nadim leaned toward one of the monitors. "What's the story?"

One of his drone techs was clearly having problems with his control stick. "This isn't easy. The winds are getting rough out there."

Nadim nodded. "Tell me about it. I almost didn't make it in."

"Well, we've already lost four drones." The video feed

shook wildly, then flickered and cut out entirely. "Make that five. Those are our only eyes on that side of the mountain."

"We have backups. And Bevan and my assault team should be in place soon. Have they made contact?"

"Not yet." The tech pointed to another screen. "But that's them on the snowmobiles, isn't it?"

Nadim squinted at the screen. The video feed showed fourteen snowmobiles speeding across a narrow valley, heading toward the spot where they had pinpointed the location of the route to Silvana's tomb. He smiled. "Good."

He picked up his satellite phone and called Bevan. At first all he could hear was the howling wind; finally Bevan's voice crackled through. "Hello, Nadim. Drinking a hot whiskey at base camp while we're freezing our nuts off out here?"

"It's not exactly the Ritz-Carlton down here, asshole. But I have a visual on you and your team. It's a glorious sight. The helicopters and their cargo containers are warmed up ready to carry away Silvana and her riches. Providing that our information is correct about the location. I won't be pleased if it isn't."

"I have a good feeling about this. Everything on our map is checking out so far. Just be prepared to slip in and attack when they're distracted. Then we'll take over the action. We're outnumbered. We won't stand a chance without the element of surprise."

"I've been coordinating with the copter pilots. They're tracking a storm headed this way. The sooner we get off this mountain, the better."

"Don't worry. We'll all be down there drinking hot whiskeys before you know it."

———

TEMPLE WATERFALL

PALANDAN ISLAND

10:20 A.M.

The waterfall was over forty feet high and beautifully picturesque, Riley thought. It looked like an integral part of the jungle surrounding it, and the mountains they'd so recently left appeared distant and far away from this vantage point.

"Ready?" Cade asked as he came back from talking to Kirby. "The area appears as safe as the proverbial church. Maya's Captain Galdar has had his men out here since daybreak and no intruders of any kind. They'll remain on guard until we return whether or not we're successful. Kirby's gone behind the waterfall to locate that sliding false door Maya told us about. He and Donal Wilson will be going up ahead of us until we reach the midpoint where we'll have to put on the oxygen equipment. Then we'll take the lead until we get to the tower." He paused. "Or you could sit this one out."

She should have known Cade would make one last attempt. She shook her head and smiled. "And miss finding the great lady herself? Silvana is waiting for me. Even Maya realized that, or she wouldn't have called me at Cambry House that night."

His lips tightened. "This isn't going to be like the time we found Helen. That was a magic night for you. Maya said that breathing was starting to hurt by the time she got halfway up the mountain."

Only that wasn't how Maya had referred to that point, Riley remembered.

"But we'll have protective gear. We'll just move fast and get in and then out." She added quietly, "Maya would have loved to be here, but she's leaving it to me. I can't let her down. No suicide missions, but we're going to try our damnedest. Okay?"

He stared at her for a frustrated minute. Then he muttered, "What the hell. It's good you wore those combat boots. You're probably going to be stepping on a lot of spiders while we're still down in that cave."

"Spiders?" She gave a mock shiver. "Oh, well, last time it was snakes."

"You have to take what you get," Cade said. "They'll probably scamper away when the temperature goes down." He took her hand. "It's time for us to get inside. Let's go find Kirby."

———

INSIDE THE CAVE
HOURS LATER

"How are you doing?" Cade asked as he stepped closer so that his head flashlight shone on her face. "You look fine."

Darkness. Freezing cold. Crawling creatures in the walls and coming out of the cracked stones of the path.

"I *am* fine now that I'm rid of all those spiders," she said lightly. "I thought you were trying to intimidate me when you mentioned them. One of them looked as big as a tarantula." She pulled her jacket closer to her body. "And I'm a little cold, but it's what I expected. Now stop hovering and let's get going again. We should be near that halfway point, shouldn't we?" She carefully avoided calling that halfway point the death zone as Maya had. "That should be a plus."

"Kirby just texted me. He and Donal reached there a couple minutes ago and retrieved the jewel chests. The oxygen equipment and suits Maya left were where she said they'd be and seemed to be in good shape. Since they started ten minutes before we did, you can do the math."

"Yes, I can." She hid a sigh of relief as she started up the path again. "And it can't be soon enough. Let's get this party started."

"By all means." Cade fell into step with her but was careful not to touch or offer assistance. "Because it's clear you're very fine indeed, Riley."

———

"I still feel like someone from outer space in this bizarre outfit," Riley murmured. "It might not be as bulky as a space suit but it's definitely awkward." They moved toward the ornately carved door with gold hinges that gleamed in the bright light of the headsets they were wearing beneath their helmets. "I wonder what Silvana would think of us."

"I think she'd believe we're very intelligent to find a way to approach her august presence without risking our necks." He took out the bejewled key Maya had given him and inserted it in the lock. "Unless she mistakes us for enemies from Rome, and then we might be in deep trouble. I imagine she'd rise from that burial coffin and attack us with her bow and arrow."

"That's not funny. Be a little respectful."

"I couldn't be more respectful." He turned the key. "I have the deepest admiration for warriors, and she was amazingly intelligent along with it. Just the fact that she saved those unicorns would be enough for me. Of course, it would be even better if she had a sense of humor..." He swung open the door.

Ice. Ice everywhere.

Gleaming like glass on the blue tile floor. Icicles hung from the two chandeliers in the room. The case of weapons and shield against the far wall glittered with it. Across the small room a gold-trimmed coffin also shimmered with ice.

"How do we get to the coffin?" Riley asked.

"Very carefully," Cade said. "But the combat boots we're wearing may help." He took her arm and they carefully shuffled across the intervening space until they reached the coffin. "Not so bad," Cade looked for the closure on the lid of the coffin. "No lock." With utmost care he lifted the lid.

Riley stepped closer to help and held her breath as she looked down at Silvana.

More ice.

Her gown was gold cloth, but it was covered in a sheet of ice. Riley slowly raised her gaze to look at Silvana's face. It was not a youthful face but that of a woman in her seventies. But it was a smooth, unlined countenance that appeared much younger. And there was one other characteristic that shocked Riley.

No ice!

Though her head was covered in a golden headdress that was sheathed in ice, her face looked incredibly normal. The skin texture appeared soft and full and almost glowing with health and vibrancy.

Cade was swearing softly. "I'll be damned. Silvana may have just pulled it off."

"We don't know what she did yet," Riley said. "But I've got to tell Eve that she may have to deal with more complicated problems than she has any idea of." She started to smile. "Though I'll bet she'll welcome it."

"Well, I don't relish the prospect of being responsible for keeping Silvana in this same shape until we can hand her to Eve and whatever scientists she'll get to examine her." He was testing the weight of the coffin as he spoke. "Her gown and headdress are gold, but the coffin is only trimmed. That may give us a break as far as weight's concerned." He reached for his phone. "I've got to call Kirby and Donal up here to get the sarcophagus out of this tower and onto the Gulfstream ASAP."

"You didn't expect this?"

"I thought anything even resembling this would be a stretch. Did you?"

"No, but maybe I should have. Silvana was a remarkable woman."

Cade was talking on the phone now and walking toward the door. He probably expected her to follow him, but she didn't move. She wanted to stay here for a little longer.

Then Riley was alone with Silvana, looking down at all the ice and gold and the other more human miracle this unique woman had managed to create in the tower room.

"You got your way, didn't you?" Riley whispered. *"Congratulations. And I'm sorry that we can't leave you here with your victory, but it might turn into a disaster, and you deserve better than that. But I promise you that we'll take care to keep you safe and let everyone know what a wonderful warrior and splendid person you were. You'll be honored, and I believe you'll come to think we did well by you."*

"Riley." Cade was standing at the door. "Kirby and Donal will be here at any minute with the protective blanket to wrap the coffin. I need you to get out of here."

"I'm coming." She was looking at the small weapons case against the far wall. "Is there any way we can take that with us? I think she'd like that. It's probably not very heavy. Maya told me Amazons always preferred to fight with lightweight weapons."

"I'll bring it myself." He held out his hand. "If you'll get out of here. I want you to be a safe distance down that path before your oxygen runs out."

"What about you?" She was across the room and taking his hand. "You said the three of you would be taking the coffin."

"We'll be moving fast. That coffin shouldn't be that difficult for the three of us to remove. Silvana is as small as most women were during that period in spite of her warrior status." He gave her a gentle push. "After you pass the death zone, keep on going. When you get outside, your job is to make certain the helicopter is ready for instant transfer. I've called down to Galdar and told him to send up more men to help with the coffin and those jewel chests. We should be able to meet them at the halfway mark. I'll be right behind you."

"You'd better be." She was still looking over her shoulder. "Or I'll come back for you."

"Go!"

Then she was going down the path away from the tower room.

It was weird, but she realized somehow the fact he'd called that halfway point the death zone when she'd been avoiding referring to it in those terms had made her feel more optimistic. Maybe because it meant the nightmare was almost over and they'd done their duty and were leaving it behind...

———

But that small moment of reassurance vanished the instant she saw Alex Galdar's expression when she ran out from the cave beneath the waterfall. The captain was definitely not happy and was snapping orders to his men that were scattering them in all directions. The minute he saw her he grabbed her arm and jerked her back against the cliff. "Take cover. I don't know what the hell we're facing yet."

"What's wrong?"

"I just got a report from one of my officers patrolling the temple area that he'd spotted several combatant forces on the eastern border who seemed to be coming down from one of the mountain passes. Nadim must have an encampment near there. It's a sizable force, and there are large containers in the mix. They may be heading in this direction. We've got to be ready for them. I've already sent a unit to intercept."

"Nadim?"

"Probably. I don't know who the hell they are yet. But we've got to assume that's who it is. Even if they don't realize what's happening at the waterfall, they might know the temple is nearby and be heading there. Either way the caretaker would want you all protected."

"And there's something else that has to be protected." Her gaze flew to the helicopter. "Cade told me I had to be sure the copter was ready for a quick transfer. Is it?"

"Yes, fueled up and ready to go. But the situation has changed, I need to move the helicopter and bring it back later."

"No, you don't. All you need to do is make certain this particular site is safe until we can get that helicopter out of here and start those rotors. Cade and the others should be here any minute. Then you can do whatever you have to do to please Maya."

But his loyalty was totally with Maya, and he would probably keep arguing with Riley. She didn't have time for this. "Never mind, I'll take care of it." She broke away from him and ran for the helicopter. "You do your thing..."

She heard him call out, but then she was inside the cockpit of the helicopter and started the ignition.

The rotors began to whir!

"Out!" It was Cade outside the window, yelling at her.

She nodded as she saw the cargo door open, and the coffin being slid inside. She got to her feet as Kirby pushed past her and sat down in the pilot's seat. Then she was out of the helicopter and Cade was grabbing her arm and running with her toward the protection of the cliff where Galdar was still yelling orders at his men, only halting long enough to give her an extremely displeased stare.

She gave him an apologetic glance before muttering to Cade, "He wasn't listening to me."

"He had his hands full from what I gathered when I was running past him on the way to the helicopter," Cade said.

"Well, so did you, but he didn't realize exactly what was happening with those bastards. They weren't even near here yet, so he shouldn't have argued with me. We had to get Silvana to the Gulfstream." But the helicopter was taking off now, and she breathed a sigh of relief.

You're on your way, Silvana. It must seem very strange to you. Just try to look on it as a new adventure.

"I'd better go and check out what's happening," Cade said as he turned away. "It's a little too coincidental that Nadim's men suddenly appear here in this neighborhood at this particular time. Are they going after the temple?"

"That's what Galdar was worried about. But the temple is so difficult to access, that's surely doubtful. It has to be the sarcophagus itself."

"Not if Bevan has been able to pay his spies enough to make it worth their while. It could be either one. He has Nadim's rich pockets to tap," he said grimly as he turned and headed for the cliff overlooking the entire property. "But I believe I'll go take a look at where they spotted those soldiers. Though Galdar said his men had them on the run almost the minute they caught sight of his unit."

———

"We're too late!" Bevan's voice shouted over the radio. "It's gone. It's all gone."

Nadim gripped his phone harder as he surveyed the bank of monitors. "What are you talking about?"

"We met some resistance when we were still about ten miles from the tomb site."

"Resistance? What kind of resistance?"

"I don't know. Major numbers, it had to be Maya's people.

They were well armed. They had us pinned down for over twenty minutes. Then they disappeared. The next thing we knew, there was a large military-style helicopter at the tomb site. They had a whole team there emptying the contents into the copter."

"No!" Nadim reared back his fist as if he was about to hurl the phone but then gained control of himself at the last second. "Cade. It has to be Cade."

"Well, their helicopter just took off. You can probably see it on one of your drone video feeds."

Nadim moved from one monitor to another. Half of the screens were black due to the number of drones destroyed by the high winds, but two of the remaining feeds clearly showed the helicopter soaring away from the mountain with the treasure.

His treasure.

One way or another, he would make damn sure Cade would pay.

He suddenly became aware of laughter and excited chatter at the far end of the tent. Did his failure amuse them? He looked up. Several of the techs were gathered around a monitor, pointing and gasping.

He stepped toward the group. "What in the hell is going on?"

"You're not gonna believe it," a female tech said.

"Try me."

"One of our drone cameras spotted a group of animals on a plateau on the north side. Hundreds of them."

"And how could that possibly interest me?"

"I think you should look for yourself." She reached toward her console, zoomed in on the image, and motioned toward the monitor.

Nadim scowled. Fools. He was surrounded by fools. Their entire operation was falling apart and all they cared about was—

He froze. What in the holy hell?

He stepped closer to the screen, transfixed.

Unicorns.

My God. It couldn't be, but it was.

Unicorns!

It can't be. But deer of some sort.

Hundreds of them. Running and playing in the snow, prancing as if in a children's story.

Nadim raised the satellite phone back to his ear. "Bevan, are you still there?"

"Still here."

"We have a new objective."

"Are you serious?"

"Yes." Nadim stared at the amazing creatures on the screen. "My friend, we're going to leave these mountains with a prize far greater than we ever imagined. Stand by for coordinates and further instructions. I'll have a helicopter take me up there with a snowmobile to join you."

CHAPTER

11

Riley looked at the helicopter disappearing over the horizon as she hurried after Cade. "How long will it take them to get to the airstrip?"

"Less than twenty minutes," Cade said. "The cargo plane is warming up for them now. They'll load the sarcophagus and coffers and take off as soon as the copter gets there." Cade turned toward her with an uneasy expression as he looked down on the sporadic fighting to the east. "Galdar may be right, they do seem to be fleeing the area."

"Then what's wrong?"

"It's not like Nadim to give up so easily."

"That didn't feel easy to me. Considering that we almost had an army to intimidate them."

Cade crouched at the cliff's edge. "Did you see which

way his men were headed earlier when he first saw the attack coming?"

"No. I was busy with getting the helicopter ready for you." She looked at the mountain's north face and the valley just below. "They scattered, and then...nothing. I don't even see their snowmobiles now."

He picked up his thermal binoculars and trained them on the snow-covered expanse. "That's because they're not there. It's like they totally gave up on the sarcophagus. But it doesn't look like they're trying to get away, either. It's almost as if..." He froze. "Wait."

"What is it?"

"I just caught some thermal trails, probably from their vehicles." He lowered his binoculars. "Son of a bitch! I bet they're heading for the unicorns."

"No!"

"My thought exactly. But I'm afraid so." He gave a low curse. "They were ready for a switch. Those crates they have would be able to handle deer as well as a sarcophagus and treasure."

"Shit. How'd they find out about them?"

"Spies? Bevan? Or someone may have spotted them when they were trying to get the drop on Kagan's friends in the stronghold."

Riley bit down hard on her lower lip. "If they realized what we had up there, they'd know it was far more valuable than the sarcophagus. And Maya told me Bailey's up there in the cave.

We need to get there before Nadim's men do." Riley looked up as the wind and snow began to blow harder. "This storm isn't going to make things easier for any of us."

"I won't argue with that." Cade extended the antenna of his own radio. "You try to get hold of Bailey and Maya. I'll tell Kagan what's happening and see if he and his team can intercept Nadim's squad. Either way we've got to get up there and help."

INSIDE THE CAVE

"It's almost over, Riva. It has to be."

Bailey's voice was agonized as she moved away as the deer lurched forward, her legs trembling.

Oh, no. Something was wrong, she thought desperately. Really wrong. She'd seen live births before, and they were nothing like this.

Riva panted and wheezed, then let out a pained honking sound.

Poor thing, she was hurting and Bailey couldn't stop it . . .

Bailey's walkie-talkie beeped, and she heard Riley's voice. "Bailey, do you copy? I need you to pick up."

Bailey grabbed the radio from its resting place on a rock. "Riley, I'm here."

"Good. Bailey, listen to me." Her voice crackled through

the static. "If any of your gear is still outside the cave, I need you to bring it in and run to the back of the cavern. Just lie low. Maya is on her way to the cave. But there may be some bad people headed your way. Do you understand?"

"I can't. I'll take the stuff back, but I need to stay here with Riva. I don't think she'll move. She's too weak."

"What?"

"Something's wrong with her. She needs me."

"Bailey, she'll be okay. Right now I need you to hide. Now."

Riva trembled as she almost lost her footing. She made even louder honking sounds.

"I can't leave her," Bailey said. "The baby isn't coming out."

"Maya said you have Tazka Kun with you. Can't he help?"

"Riva won't let him touch her. All he can do is hover."

"Bailey, we're sending people who will help you and her. But you need to get somewhere safe."

"I won't leave her. I'll be right here. Hurry."

Bailey put down the radio and turned back toward Riva. The animal twisted and turned in a way that didn't seem at all natural and was barely even possible.

Whatever was wrong, it was killing her. Bailey couldn't let that happen.

Bailey pushed up the sleeves of her jacket and moved closer to the unicorn. "It's okay, we're together. We'll get through with this. Just trust me..."

———

"Unicorns." Nadim's voice was gleeful as he spoke into the radio as his squad of snowmobiles neared the plateau. "It was the truth." He stared at the clusters of horned animals moving out of the valley. "I can't believe it."

"I think they're some kind of deer, actually," Bevan responded on their encrypted channel. He was fifty yards behind.

"It doesn't matter. These creatures are where the legends began. Each one is priceless. And they're all ours."

"Then we need to regroup," Bevan said. "When we were spotted down on the island near the temple, we lost a lot of men before we pulled out and headed up here. We'll come back with reinforcements."

"No. The time is now, Bevan. Are the helicopters still down at the base station with the cargo containers?"

"Yes, but the pilots don't want to fly up here now. There's a storm coming in."

"Triple their fees. If any of them abandon us, tell them I'll hunt down and kill them and their families."

Overkill, as usual, Bevan thought. "Copy that. But if you don't mind, I'll just propose the fee increase first."

Nadim eased off the throttle as the squad neared the plateau. "Everything we planned for the sarcophagus will still work for us here. We'll load as many of the animals into the containers as possible and come back for the rest later. Then take off before the storm hits. This will be the biggest score in history. Just shut up and follow orders."

———

Kagan crouched behind the wall of the snow fort the rangers had quickly built earlier that morning when they'd seen Nadim on the attack. Blood was drizzled across the ice-packed ground. Fighters were still wrapping their wounds with bandages from their latest encounter with Nadim.

He stepped toward the team leader, Bantu. "I just heard from Cade. Nadim's men know about the deer. They're headed toward them as we speak." Kagan gestured toward the wounded and exhausted rangers. "Your team has been through a lot already, so I'd understand if you need to fall back. There would be no dishonor in that."

Before he could respond, several of the rangers pulled themselves to their feet and began assembling their gear. Bantu cocked his head toward them. He said quietly, "You know them better than that. Just as I know you would never retreat from this fight. You told me these people have nurtured and protected those animals for over a thousand years. That is honor in itself; we won't stop now."

Kagan smiled. "Thank you."

"Just tell us where we're needed."

Kagan lifted his radio and spoke. "Cade, we're going to have help. Lots of it. Nadim isn't giving up, but I think we might have a way of tripping him up. We weren't able to get nearly all the deer down to the cave to protect them, but that might not be all bad..."

———

"Bailey!"

Bailey paid no attention to her mother's shout. She was up to her right elbow inside Riva's birth canal struggling to find what was causing the animal such distress and didn't even hear Maya's call. She'd seen the village veterinarian help births along, but she really had only a vague idea how he'd done it. All the books she'd read might help, but she felt helpless at the moment.

How she wished he was here now.

"Bailey!"

The baby's legs were probably crossed and blocking its path out. She felt movement. The baby was alive! But she couldn't feel the legs.

"Bailey!"

She turned to see her mother standing in the cave entrance, holding her knapsack.

"Mama!"

Maya ran toward her and the still-wailing Riva. "What are you doing?"

"She needs help. Her baby won't come out."

"All hell is about to break loose out there, honey. We need to get you to the back of the cave. And you'll need to turn down the battery lantern."

"Not until we get the baby out."

"Bailey..."

The girl's hands closed around something. "I think I have it!"

Maya glanced back at the cave opening, where it sounded as if thousands of bees were buzzing their way. "Do you hear that? Those are snowmobiles. Nadim's squad. They want the deer. All of them. And if they find you, they'll hurt you just to punish me. I won't let them do it. Do you understand?"

"I'm not leaving her."

Maya hesitated and even took a step forward, looking as if she was about to yank Bailey away, but her expression suddenly softened. She knelt beside her. "Okay, Bailey. I'll give you a few more minutes. What can I do to help?"

"Go around to Riva's head. Stroke her head and neck and try to calm her down. She's moving around too much. She's making it hard for me to get hold of her baby."

"Kun, watch the cave entrance." Maya moved around to face the deer's head. She lightly rubbed the animal's head just under both ears until she quieted.

"It's working!" Bailey pulled on the baby's twisted legs as blood and the fetal membrane drenched her arms and the cave floor.

The buzzing outside was replaced by a low roar. Then another. And another after that.

"What is it?" Bailey yelled.

Maya stared at the opening. "Helicopters. At least three. Maybe even four. Hurry, Bailey. We don't have any more time."

———

Cade pocketed his satellite phone and turned to Riley. "Kagan and the Ice Rangers have a plan. But it involves all of us being off this side of the mountain in the next sixteen minutes."

"Sixteen minutes?" She wrinkled her brow. "That's pretty specific."

"But not usual for him. I've seen him plan their operations down to the second."

"What's the plan?"

"He didn't go into a lot of detail. Either he didn't want to take the time, or he was afraid Nadim was intercepting and listening in on our call. He said we'd be okay as long as we get ourselves to the other side of the ridge." He pointed to her phone. "Call Maya. Tell her that she and Bailey need to get the hell away from that cave."

Cade readied his and Riley's snowmobiles while she tried to call Maya. After a moment, she put down her phone. "No go. They may be getting too much interference from the storm."

"We'll pass that cave on the way over the ridge." He set a

timer on his wristwatch. "We'll have to pick them up on the way out."

She looked at Nadim's helicopters hovering in the distance. "Reinforcements. How in the hell will we get past those?"

"I have it on good authority those won't be a problem by the time we get there."

She smiled. "You have a lot of faith in Kagan and his friends."

"They've earned it. Those Ice Rangers are legendary, but from what I've seen, they're even more amazing than their reputation."

She walked toward her snowmobile and flipped up her thermal hood. "Then let's get a move on. We only have fifteen minutes and thirty seconds left."

———

Nadim looked up at the four helicopters rocking violently in the high winds and heavy snow. Large cargo containers swung on steel cables, further destabilizing the craft. One banked right and dipped low toward the ground, sending his men scattering before the helicopter righted itself and soared overhead.

"It's only going to get worse," Bevan said. "We need to start loading the deer into the containers, but the copters are scaring them."

"We can use that," Nadim said. "We'll load them one container at a time. The other helicopters will pull back and coordinate with our men on the ground to corral the unicorns and guide them where we need them."

Bevan nodded. "Okay. We can probably get one or two containers loaded before we need to pull out."

"No!" Nadim shouted. "We're taking them all."

Bevan looked up at the buffeting helicopters. "It's your show. I just don't want to be anywhere near those things if this storm gets any worse."

"Fortune rewards the brave, my friend. Each one of these creatures will be worth a fortune. Each one we leave will be the same as leaving millions behind."

"Then we better get going. I'll radio the lead copter and tell them to—"

A high-pitched wail sounded from a nearby mountain peak.

The two men glanced around them, trying to locate the source of the sound.

The wail came again, this time louder.

"What the hell was that?" Nadim said.

The wail sounded again.

"I think it's some kind of…horn," Bevan said uncertainly.

The deer were reacting to the sound, all looking up in the same direction. They began to call out in response.

Nadim's men stopped their vehicles and just watched as the animals' calls grew louder. Their sound was eerily beautiful, creating ethereal harmonies that cut through the roaring winds.

"Incredible," Bevan said. "It almost sounds…"

"...magical. More unicorn proof," Nadim finished for him. "We're going to be *very* rich men."

Then, almost in perfect synchronization, the deer moved toward the ridge. Slowly at first, but in a matter of seconds they were sprinting at breakneck speed.

"After them!" Nadim shouted into his radio. "Don't let them get away!"

Another wail sounded from the peak, and the deer responded with another beautiful call even as they picked up speed.

"Go!" Nadim screamed into his radio.

The fleet of snowmobiles and the helicopters took off in pursuit.

———

Cade lowered his binoculars as he and Riley slowed to a stop on the icy slope. "Amazing. I don't know how Kagan and those Ice Rangers did it, but Nadim's men and the helicopters are moving away."

"Good," Riley said. She tapped her Bluetooth headset. "Because I still can't reach Maya. We need to get them out of that cave."

"We're running out of time. Let's hit it."

Cade gunned his snowmobile's engine, and Riley hit her accelerator a moment later. They sped through the storm, which had already obscured Nadim's snowmobiles and helicopters to the point that Riley couldn't see them.

They jumped over an embankment and a strong gust of wind tore the clear shield from her face. Subfreezing winds tore into her face like hundreds of icy needles.

Shit. That *hurt*.

She flung her scarf over her nose and mouth but was surprised how little the fibers blocked the cutting wind.

Damn. And to think she'd once actually *liked* cold weather. Foolish woman.

Visibility was getting worse by the second and as the snow swirled around them, she lost all sense of direction. It was easy to see how mountain climbers could lose their way and freeze to death just a few hundred feet away from civilization. She looked down at her GPS screen. Thank goodness for modern technology.

They finally stopped at the coordinates where Maya had pinned her location a few minutes before. At first Riley thought there had been a mapping error, since there didn't appear to be any sign of a cave or nearby openings in the mountainside. But as they continued past, she caught sight of a shimmering glow.

She pointed toward the light. "There!"

As they rode closer, they saw there was indeed a cave opening, all but obscured by the blowing snow. Riley dismounted and ran toward it.

"Wait!" Cade pulled out his gun. "They may have been captured."

Riley stopped. He was right. She reached into her parka and produced the semiautomatic he'd given her. They nodded toward each other and moved into the cave, ducking under the long icicles that stabbed downward from the cave's ceiling.

They saw Maya's snowmobile, then rounded a corner to see a gun barrel leveled at them. It was Maya. She lowered her gun. "Sorry. Can't be too careful."

Now they could also see the herd of deer and a few of the shepherds trying to soothe them.

Riley and Cade lowered their weapons. "Our thoughts exactly," Cade said.

Riley rushed toward her. "Where's Bailey? Is she okay?"

Maya stepped aside to show her daughter kneeling on the floor of the cave, next to the deer and her newborn.

Bailey was luminous, beaming. "Look!"

"I see." Riley stepped closer. The fawn was nestled next to its mother, and both looked sleek and positively exquisite. The newborn had a slight bump where the horn would soon grow, but in most other respects its proportions were already similar to those of adult members of the herd.

Riley turned to gaze at Bailey in agreement. "You did this?"

She shook her head. "They did the hard work. I just helped out."

"The fawn's legs were tangled in the birth canal," Maya said. "Bailey saved both of their lives. I've never seen anything like it."

Riley knelt beside the deer. She whispered, "It's wonderful."

"Agreed," Cade said. "But I'm afraid we need to go."

"Go where?" Maya asked.

"Over the ridge. Away from this side of the mountain. We only have a few minutes left."

Maya still looked confused. "Left until what?"

"We're not sure," Riley said. "Kagan and those Ice Rangers have something planned for Nadim. All we know is that we need to get off this side of the mountain in the next ten minutes."

"Seven and a half," Cade said. "We have to go."

Bailey stood and motioned toward the deer. "I can't leave them!"

Maya gripped her arm. "We can't take them with us, Bailey. They're both too weak. They'll be safer here."

The girl crossed her arms. "Then I'll stay, too."

"That's not happening."

Cade stepped toward Bailey and leaned close. "Whatever is about to happen, these deer will be safer here than out there in that storm. They're far enough back that they'll be okay. This is the safest place for them on the mountain. They've existed here for hundreds and hundreds of years. And I promise you that we'll come back here to check on them. Right away. Trust me. But we're running out of time, and there's no way we're leaving you, Bailey."

Riley could see that the girl wasn't totally convinced, but Cade's tone let her know that he was prepared to forcibly remove her from the cave if necessary. Bailey knew this was a losing battle.

Bailey finally nodded as she made the decision. "I asked

Riva to trust me, and it worked out okay. I guess it's only fair I trust you to fix this for me. But I'm coming right back."

"Of course." Cade smiled and looked up at Maya. "This girl definitely takes after her mother."

"For better or worse." Maya took Bailey's hand and gestured to Tazka Kun. "Come on. We're not leaving you either. Let's go!"

———

"Where are they?" Nadim said.

His squad had followed the deer over the mountainside, but as they rounded the Angel's Hammer rock formation, the animals had vanished.

The wail from the nearby peak had stopped, and the animals' beautiful calls could no longer be heard.

"What the hell?" Bevan said. He scanned the area with his binoculars. "There were hundreds of them. They couldn't have just...disappeared."

"Maybe somebody should tell the unicorns that."

"Look!" Nadim pointed to a nearby cliff. "Something flickering."

"It's just the snow."

"No, you fool. It's something else. Do you see it?"

"Holy shit!"

A moment later, dozens of human figures took flight from the cliff and soared toward them!

Nadim's breath left him. What in the hell...?

They looked like angels descending from heaven above.

Not angels, he realized in frustration. More like demons. It was the Ice Rangers outfitted in their white uniforms and using winglike arm extensions to ride the air currents down toward them. If he hadn't seen it with his own eyes, he never would have believed it.

The first wave of rangers touched down on their skis. They darted across the icy plateau attacking his squad one man at a time, eliminating them with the most astonishing display of martial arts moves he'd ever seen. Most of the rangers attacked with a series of strategic blows, but some used lengths of razor wire pulled taut in front of his own snowmobile-riding assault team, effectively decapitating them. When his men finally started to pull out their guns to respond, the rangers ducked and swerved around them with almost superhuman speed. The snowmobiles were slow and positively clunky in comparison.

Within two minutes the rangers had eliminated half his squad without firing a single shot.

Nadim screamed into his radio. "Shoot them! Shoot them all!"

But the icy plateau was already strewn with the blood and corpses of his assault team, and the ones who remained were clearly hesitant to engage.

The second wave of Ice Rangers touched down in front of them. This group was on snowboards.

RAT-AT-AT-AT-AT-AT-AT!

Nadim looked up. Two of the helicopters had swooped low with gunmen leaning out and firing automatic weapons from the open side-panel doors.

"Yes! Yes!" he shouted.

But the rangers were clearly prepared for an aerial assault. An instant later over a dozen ice boulders flew through the air fired from massive catapults on the mountainside. Two of the boulders made contact with the low-flying helicopters; one struck a rear rotor, sending it spinning crazily until it finally struck the ground in a fiery explosion. The other boulder smashed through the second helicopter's front windshield, instantly pulverizing the cockpit and its occupants. The helicopter fell from the sky as if it had struck a stone wall.

The remaining two helicopters hovered in place for only a few seconds before peeling off and roaring away.

Nadim screamed into his radio. "Get back here. Now!"

The helicopters' only response was to speed away even faster.

He turned to Bevan. "Find a way to get them back here!"

"I can't do that, you idiot. They're only doing what we should be doing. Getting the hell away."

Nadim smiled with fierce satisfaction and pointed behind Bevan where his men were now firing at the rangers. "You spoke too soon."

"What do you mean?"

"See for yourself. We've got them on the run."

Bevan turned to see that the rangers were indeed retreating

on their skis and snowboards, dodging the squad's gunfire. "Where are they headed?"

Nadim trained his binoculars on the fleeing rangers. "It looks like there's a trail on the far side of this plateau. It may lead to another valley. That would answer the question of where our unicorns went."

"But we've lost our cargo containers."

"We'll send for more. Once we slaughter these rangers, there will be no one to stop us. But we have to strike now." Nadim spoke into his radio. "Kill everyone who gets between us and those unicorns. Go!"

Nadim, Bevan, and the surviving half of Nadim's squad tore through the wind and snow, chasing the rangers down the steep path. They finally emerged below the massive notch between mountains where, as Nadim suspected, there was another snow-covered plateau. Slightly more than halfway across, the rangers were clustered with hundreds of deer.

"Hold your fire," Nadim said into the radio. "We can't hurt the animals."

Bevan shook his head. "Those bastards know that. They're using the deer as shields."

Nadim wrinkled his brow. "Maybe."

"It's obvious, isn't it?"

"No. Those rangers are the shields here. They're risking their lives to protect them."

"So what's their play?"

A lone figure appeared on an icy ledge overlooking the

plateau. Nadim trained his binoculars on the man. "That's Kagan."

"The so-called super Sherpa?"

"Yes. He was working with Cade. What in the hell is he doing?"

Kagan was smiling at him. He reached into his parka and pulled out a small cylindrical device. He raised it over his head.

Nadim gasped. "I think he has a remote detonator."

"For what?"

"Oh my God." He lowered the binoculars, panicked. "Those unicorns aren't a shield . . . They're the bait."

Kagan pressed the detonator with his thumb, and a series of blasts rocked the mountain above them!

The rangers and the deer immediately ran from the plateau, flying across the icy slope toward the protective claw-shaped peaks of yet another valley.

"We have to turn around," Nadim said, panicked. "Now!"

"We're so close!" Bevan pointed. "Less than a mile. We can make it!"

"It's not close enough." Nadim's gaze was wide with sudden horror.

"What do you mean?"

The ground shook and a deafening rumble echoed across the mountainside.

Nadim spoke in a grim whisper. "Avalanche."

Both men looked up as the mountain's highest peaks appeared to crumble before their eyes. Bevan instantly gunned his snowmobile's engine, speeding toward the safe path taken by the rangers and the herd.

On the slope below, Nadim's squad scrambled, trying in vain to outrun the millions of tons of snow hurtling down the slopes. Nadim looked around. There had to be a way out, something he could do. But what?

His men were screaming now as the avalanche's first wave barreled toward them. He watched in horror as a boulder bounced toward Bevan and crushed him flat, staining the snow with his blood for a few seconds until being covered over by the mountain of snow immediately behind!

CHAPTER
12

F aster!" Cade shouted. "We need to get to the other side of that ridge!"

He, Riley, and Maya gunned their snowmobile engines as snow, ice, and boulders tumbled down the mountainside above them. Bailey squeezed Maya tight as their snowmobile slid across the icy slope.

"*This* was Kagan's plan?" Riley shouted.

"Pretty effective, you have to admit."

"Only if we survive!"

"Give it everything you have," Cade yelled. "We'll be safe on the other side of that ridge."

"Are you sure?"

"Kagan was sure. That's good enough for me!"

The ground shook beneath their vehicles and chunks of ice

dropped all around them. They leaped over the ridge and skidded to a stop on the snowy slope.

They sat on their snowmobiles and watched for several minutes as the avalanche with all its beautiful and destructive power reshaped the mountain.

Bailey rested her chin on Maya's shoulder. "Wow."

Cade's phone rang in his pocket. He pulled it out and answered it. "Hi, Kagan. Yeah, we're all fine. Maybe a little annoyed you couldn't let us in on your plan." He listened for a moment. "Okay, then I suppose it's worth it. We'll see you later."

Cade cut the connection. "Kagan, the herd, and the Ice Rangers are all okay."

"What about Nadim's men?"

"Buried under thousands of tons of snow and ice. Maybe someone will dig their bodies out in the spring…fifteen or twenty years from now."

"Can't say I'm sorry to hear that," Riley said.

"We need to go back to the cave," Bailey said. "Now. We need to make sure Riva and her baby are okay."

Maya turned and squeezed her tight. "We'll go back soon. I promise. But things may be too unstable out there."

"We have to go there *now*. They might need help."

Maya shot Riley a helpless glance. Clearly, she was afraid of what her daughter would find back in the cave.

"You promised," Bailey said.

Cade exchanged a glance with Riley before replying.

"You're right, Bailey. We promised. If it's okay with your mom, let's go see how mother and child are doing."

Maya nodded. "If you think it will be okay."

"The worst of the avalanche hit the next plateau. We should be all right."

The group headed back in the direction from which they had just come. Riley was shocked at how much the mountain's topography had changed in the space of just a few minutes. Nothing looked the same to her; were it not for their GPS devices, they'd have no hope of finding their way back to the cave.

"Take it slow," Cade said. "The ground will still be unsteady in places."

Riley pointed to a ridge lined with daggers of ice pointing upward like glittering swords. "I think we'll also want to avoid those."

"Ice spikes. You see them after every avalanche. They're as sharp as razor blades, and they'll be here until the first thaw. They can slice right through our coats and gloves."

Maya pulled alongside them. "And still you thought this was a safe place to bring my child?"

Bailey squeezed her tight. "I'll be careful, Mama. Are we almost there?"

Cade checked his GPS monitor screen. "It says it's just ahead."

They slowed to a stop, and Bailey jumped off Maya's snowmobile. She pointed to a triangular rock formation jutting out from the snow. "The cave was here! It's been buried. They'll suffocate!"

Cade quickly dismounted and flipped up the storage compartment lid on the back of his snowmobile. "There's a small shovel in every kit. Everyone pull one out and start digging!"

The entire group attacked the snowed-over tunnel, half digging, half chiseling until they managed to pierce an opening large enough for Bailey to climb through.

"I'm going in!" she yelled back at them. "There's no snow after this point."

Maya put a hand on her arm. "It's been a little while for them in there. You know how weak they were when we left them."

"I don't care. Cade said they'd be safe. I've got to keep them that way. I'll be okay."

"Be careful, Bailey. We'll be right behind you."

Bailey had already crawled through the opening.

A full minute passed, then another. Cade, Riley, and Maya worked frantically on widening the opening while leaning inside, waiting to get a glimpse of Bailey.

Then Bailey's brilliantly smiling face suddenly appeared at the opening. "They're fine! They're alive! Thank you. Thank you. Thank you."

"Don't thank us." Maya cupped her face in her hands and kissed her. "Hey, this is your rescue. We were glad to help, but it's all because of you, Bailey."

Cade stepped back from the widened hole. "We should all be able to get through now."

Maya shimmied inside the cave, followed by Cade and Kun. Riley backed away and pulled out her phone. "I'm going to call Eve and Kagan to let them know we're okay. I'll see you in a minute."

Riley stepped away from the rock formation, trying to give her satellite phone the best line of sight. Mobile communications had been spotty since they arrived, but maybe she could—

"Hello, Riley."

She stiffened in shock as she turned. It was Nadim. His face was bruised, and he was covered in blood. He was pointing a semiautomatic handgun.

She swallowed hard. "You survived."

"Sorry to disappoint you, but I still have a score to settle." He nodded back toward the opening. "I assume Maya is in there?"

"No. She's with the sarcophagus a hundred miles from here."

He smiled and stepped toward her. "You're an exceedingly bad liar. I believe she's in that cave with her beautiful young daughter." He wiped the blood dripping from his face. "When the avalanche started, I went back when my men went forward. I survived, and they're all dead. Some of us are survivors, some aren't. I've always been a survivor."

"You'll never make it off this mountain alive."

"I'm tempted to say, *Watch me*, but I'm afraid you won't be alive to see it. But whatever happens, I'll have the pleasure of making Maya watch her daughter die in front of her."

Maya's voice came from behind him. "Like hell you will."

He spun around just in time for Maya to strike him in the head with her shovel. "Never again, you son of a bitch!" She struck his hand twice, sending his gun flying.

He staggered toward her, and she swung with one mighty final blow. He screamed as he flew back off the embankment, onto a bed of ice spikes. They pierced his throat and torso, sending up geysers of blood as he gagged and drowned in his own bodily fluids.

Finally he was still.

Maya drew a deep breath as she looked down at him. She turned back into the cave. "When you reach Kagan, you might tell him he has more cleanup to do. I don't believe he'll mind."

"Somehow, neither do I," Riley said.

———

Kagan and his team weren't able to reach the cave until several hours later. By that time they'd totally cleared the cave entrance. The storm had almost abated and the shepherds were able to begin driving the rest of the herd into the cavern to protect them until they could clear the hills and valley.

Kagan stopped outside the cave to stare down at the twisted corpse of Nadim. "I'd like to keep him there, but I suppose we have to take him down to show that we aren't the same kind of savage as he was." He grimaced. "Too bad. It would certainly take anyone's attention off the unicorns until we find somewhere safer for them. Excellent job, Maya."

"Then kindly remove him before Bailey wanders out here and sees him," Maya said. "So far she's been too occupied with Riva and her baby to leave the cave. She's gone through enough trauma today."

Riley nodded. "And Cade has been on the phone most of the afternoon with the world at large in India and Tibet trying to smooth things over and keep them off our mountain. Your spectacular hijinks didn't exactly go unnoticed. Really, Kagan. Avalanches?"

"It got the job done, and I made sure we did no harm to the mountain that we can't repair."

"But it aroused a hell of a lot of curiosity in the outside world," Cade said as he came out of the cave. "And we don't need that. I'm going to have to come up with a distraction until we can get a handle on everything."

"Distraction?"

"Not your kind of distraction," Cade said. Then as something occurred to him, he suddenly grinned mischievously. "Or maybe we can do something in that vein after all. I hate to leave you totally out of the picture. At any rate, I can't do anything more on the phone. I've got to not only get back to the Lake Cottage, but also work on this bit of sleight of hand." He turned to Riley. "Are you ready to go?"

"No. I don't have any strings I have to pull," she said quietly. "I can help more here for the time being. I'll follow you later."

He frowned. "I think you should go with—"

"But I don't," she interrupted. "So that's the end of it." She gave him a quick kiss. "Go back and do what you do best. Now I've got to get back to Bailey. I'll talk to you later, Cade."

Cade watched her disappear into the cave "Yes, you will," he murmured. "No doubt about it, Riley . . ."

CHAPTER

13

LAKE COTTAGE

TWO DAYS LATER

I thought you'd be at that lab you set up in the city," Riley said as she entered the cottage. "You weren't able to get Diane here for Silvana's exam?"

"Of course I was. Did you think she'd miss coming here and becoming involved with the warrior queen? She's already at the lab herself and examining samples of the drug Silvana took to ensure preservation." Eve hung up the phone, crossing the room to embrace Riley. "We both know a brilliant scientist like her would never be able to resist the chance of developing a magic potion like that. But I wanted to see you when Cade turned up here without you. I was uneasy. I told her I'd join her later. How are you?"

"Good enough." Riley stepped back. "I wanted to stay with Maya and her daughter until I was certain that she didn't need me any longer, so I sent him on ahead. He had a lot of pesky diplomatic details to take care of about what happened in the mountains. And we'll both have work to do once we get together about the unicorns and the island itself."

"And you're ready to face it?" Eve asked.

"How could I not be?" she said quietly. "We all knew it was coming. We just didn't know it wouldn't give us a little more time to prepare. We're lucky with whatever time is left to find a way out. I'll stay committed to my career, but we all have another career to worry about now. What happened in the past is important, but saving the future will probably take precedence. Still, there are all kinds of brilliant people out there, a lot of them my very best friends. We'll get there as fast as we can." She smiled. "And now I want to see Cade. The goodbye we said in the mountains was brief, and I want everything understood before we go any further. Where is he?"

"He's out with Loring and Joe making certain the property is absolutely as secure as he left the lab yesterday." She grimaced. "But I know he must have seen the helicopter and I'm going to get out of here before he runs in. He's seen enough of me and Joe since he got here." She gave Riley's cheek a pat. "I'm off for the lab. I'll see you later when we come back for dinner." She was already going out the door but stopped for an instant to look back over her shoulder. "Did I tell you the decision you made about going to the island turned out to be damn smart? I'm glad I was part of it if I can claim a tiny bit."

"You can always claim a gigantic piece of any decision I

make," Riley said. "As any best friend should. None of this would have happened if you hadn't been there for me."

Eve grinned. "Not true. But I'm proud to be along for the ride. See you at dinner." The door slammed behind her.

But Riley heard Eve say something to Cade before she reached the bottom of the steps, and Riley was halfway to the door when Cade came in. Then she was in his arms and everything was right with the world.

"Hey," Cade said softly. "What a welcome. When you called, I thought you told me everything was going as good as it could be back at the mountain."

"It is." She forced herself to take a step back. "I'm just glad to see you." She tried to smile. "Because when the world is threatening to crash around us, you're the one I want to help me keep it in its proper place. I believe we've clarified that but I wanted to be sure. We have plans to make, and I wanted to touch base about a few things so that everything is clear. First, I love you and I'll always love you. That's a given. You'll always be the one I turn to first from now on. But you'll have to stand back and let me walk my own path if that's what I choose."

He leaned forward and brushed his lips across her cheek. "Is that a warning? We'll have a few problems, but I can accept the concept."

"You should, because it's almost what you wanted when this all started." She grimaced. "Except I believe you've learned a few things yourself during our time on the island."

"There's a possibility." He grinned. "Anything else?"

"Yes, I want you to promise me that from now on we're going to spend every spare moment enjoying and appreciating every single time we have together and not waste a minute. I want every day to be a celebration." She moistened her lips. "I'm a little scared and I believe that's the way to solve the problem."

"I think that's a wonderful solution," he said softly. "A celebration and a holiday. You've obviously been thinking about this."

"Yes, I have, and I had to get it all out." She drew a relieved breath. "Because it was important to get all this settled before we moved on to anything else." She kissed him and then took his hand. "Now we can go out on the porch and sit on the swing and hold each other. Then after a little while we can let the world in again and work on saving the planet. Okay?"

"Oh, yes." Cade was already leading her toward the porch. "What a fine plan. I'm sure that we'll be able to accomplish both with hard work and ingenuity."

"Optimist."

"Absolutely." He drew her closer. "And that's the way we'll get through this. But we might have to make adjustments. We'll have to talk about it later..."

EPILOGUE

BASE MOUNTAIN CAMP

PALANDAN ISLAND

TWO MONTHS LATER

C ade told me you were here," Kagan said as he strolled toward the truck where Maya was standing. "Complete with clipboard and shepherds and rather bewildered unicorns."

She whirled to face him. "Where else would I be? This is my job." Her gaze raked his face. "How are you? You don't look as if you could have been tottering at death's door like the media claimed."

"I never totter." He reached out and stroked one of the deer being loaded on the truck. "I have my reputation to uphold. Cade just circulated that story to gain sympathy for the island guard and bring attention to the fact that if the Himalayas can melt, what about Miami Beach or Paris? It struck a resounding chord."

"It was a good idea," she said. "The whole world adores you and almost went into a tailspin when he told everyone you

339

were badly wounded. They lit candles in every city that had a mountain. Very good distraction."

"But surely Riley told you that I was doing fine?"

"She might have mentioned it. I've been very busy here."

"Not too busy to tell Bailey that I was okay," he said softly. "Because I've been receiving all kinds of sketches of the deer, shepherds, and you from her while I was in the hospital 'recuperating.' Some of them were very amusing. Some of them were just touching; I was glad to know she cared. It's always good to realize that you matter." He chuckled. "Though we both know you've always had trouble expressing that where I'm concerned."

"As if you needed another fan," she scoffed. "It's better to keep you grounded." Then she smiled. "But if you'll be quiet for another five minutes, I'll get this shipment of deer off the mountain and on its way to the airport to go to the new haven in the Rocky Mountains that Cade's set up. Then I'll take you up to the tent to see Bailey and we'll have supper."

"You're only sending twenty at a time?"

"We decided that it would be better to get them used to a new place if they didn't have to compete with a huge herd. I send twenty plus a shepherd they know every couple weeks. So, when Cade found that haven in the Rockies we started to work." She tore the sheet off the clipboard, handed it to the driver, and waved him away.

Kagan watched him drive down the road. "It's going to take much longer to get them settled that way."

"But it will be safer, and we don't know how the unicorns will adapt to a new place." She smiled. "Though we have great hopes for them if they managed to survive not only Silvana's and her Amazons' world but a couple thousand years here in this valley."

He started up the hill toward the tent city. "But they had Silvana's caretakers to guard them."

"They still have a caretaker," Maya said. "I'll be here until the last one is transferred to safer ground. Then I'll go to the new haven and make certain all is well with them."

"And then?"

She met his eyes. "By then I hope that we've found a way to save the island and all the villagers who live here. Somebody out there must want to help them. Cade does, Riley does, you do. There have to be other people who can change minds and make it happen. In the meantime, I'll do my duty and be the best caretaker that Silvana could ever want."

"It might be the most difficult job a caretaker could ever undertake," Kagan said. "And you may not be qualified for it."

"I beg your pardon?"

He chuckled. "I'm not insulting you. But while I was in the hospital 'tottering,' I was thinking that you might need someone to lighten the load occasionally. Like Bailey did for me with those sketches. You have a tendency to be a little grim and serious, but I bet you can still go out and save the world if you find something to smile about occasionally."

"I'm not grim. I don't appreciate you saying that." She made a face. "But I admit I *am* serious. Still, I have Bailey to lighten any load."

"That's a big load for a kid." He smiled. "But it's no load at all for me. That's why I decided to spend half my time here on the island doing unicorn duty and filling in when things might not go splendidly. The other half I'll be with Cade and Riley trying to change those minds you mentioned."

"I don't need you here."

"I didn't expect you to admit to needing anyone at any time. But there were times when we were fighting to keep Bailey and Riva alive that it wasn't the question at all. We reached out to a point beyond and now we can't go back. Though heaven knows where it will lead us. You know it as well as I do." He reached out his hand to her. "And none of it really matters now. The question isn't if you need me here. It's do you *want* me here."

She looked down at his hand. It was a strong hand, and yet there had been so many times when it had been so gentle with Bailey and Riva and her. Just as his expression could be so fierce one minute and yet dissolve into laughter the next.

"I wouldn't think of obligating you in any—"

"Stop dithering," he interrupted. "Answer the question."

"I was getting to it." She looked him straight in the eyes and then she reached out and took his hand. "Like it or not, you're not getting away. You're damn right I want you here, Kagan!"

ABOUT THE AUTHOR

Iris Johansen is the #1 *New York Times* bestselling author of more than fifty consecutive bestsellers. Her series featuring forensic sculptor Eve Duncan has sold over twenty million copies and counting and was the subject of the acclaimed Lifetime movie *The Killing Game*. Along with her son, Roy, Iris has also co-authored the *New York Times* bestselling series featuring investigator Kendra Michaels. Johansen lives in Georgia and Florida.